THE
CURRENCY
OF
PAPER

Library of Congress Cataloging-in-Publication Data

Kovacs, Alex, 1982-
The currency of paper / Alex Kovacs. -- First edition.
pages cm
ISBN 978-1-56478-857-3 (pbk. : alk. paper)
1. Swindlers and swindling--Fiction. 2. Capitalism--Fiction. 3.
Satire. 4. London (England)--Fiction. I. Title.
PR6111.O68C87 2013
823'.92--dc23
2013007218

Partially funded by grants from Arts Council England and the
Illinois Arts Council, a state agency

www.dalkeyarchive.com

Cover: design and composition by Mikhail Iliatov

The photograph on page 80 is reproduced with the permission of
Edwin Smith/RIBA Library Photographs Collection.

Printed on permanent/durable acid-free paper

THE CURRENCY OF PAPER

ALEX KOVACS

DALKEY ARCHIVE PRESS
CHAMPAIGN / LONDON / DUBLIN

". . . labour is *external* to the worker, i.e., it does not belong to his essential being; that in his work, therefore, he does not affirm himself but denies himself, does not feel content but unhappy, does not develop freely his physical and mental energy but mortifies his body and ruins his mind. The worker therefore only feels himself outside his work, and in his work feels outside himself. He is at home when he is not working, and when he is working he is not at home. His labour is therefore not voluntary but coerced; it is *forced labour*. It is therefore not the satisfaction of a need; it is merely a *means* to satisfy needs external to it. Its alien character emerges clearly in the fact that as soon as no physical or other compulsion exists, labour is shunned like the plague. External labour, labour in which man alienates himself, is a labour of self-sacrifice, of mortification."

—*The Economic and Philosophic Manuscripts of 1844*, Karl Marx

CONTENTS

Observing the Progress of Time

(1950)

Maximilian Sacheverell Hollingsworth wondered if he could dictate the entire course of his life on a single day. After some deliberation, a process lasting the length of a Wednesday morning, he concluded that it was possible. Suddenly, with no prior warning, it seemed to him a matter of some urgency to plan all of the details of his adulthood whilst he was still a young man. Brimming with optimism, he hoped that it was simply necessary to decide what he most wanted to do and in which order. Immediately he set to work upon the drafting of a plan.

At noon he sat inside a public house in Bloomsbury. This was a place populated only by solitary male drinkers, isolated men wearing ruffled coats and smoking pipes emitting circles of smoke that hovered and drifted in an unfurling cloud above their heads. Grey sunlight dissolved into the dingy huddles of shadows thrown from the battered furnishings. In studied silence the barmaid washed empty glasses and placed them in long neat rows along the dark mahogany shelves. Maximilian sat at the left end of the bar, beside the thick length of rope that dangled from the mouth of the silent brass bell, drinking a succession of pints of bitter ale, his gaze directed out towards the street in the hope of discovering fresh inspirations. With the progress of his imbibing he felt the slowness of the afternoon unwinding down the length of his spine.

No matter that his plan had to exclude innumerable torments and banalities which he was destined to encounter, that it could not possibly survive for years on end without mutations and excisions, that in many of its details it was probably lacking in all pragmatism, all that was significant was the necessity of forming a definitive set of strategies, a declaration of intention based upon his genuine desires, distillations of urges that he had possessed since he was a child. In all the foolishness and idealism of youth, he forged a series of eternal vows.

Disappearing without leaving a single clue to his whereabouts, he would dedicate himself to the completion of numerous projects, living out a life crowded with impossible undertakings and miraculous pursuits, all incognito, with no one privy to his role until after his death. He would investigate arcane branches of knowledge, brand every neglected street and alleyway with his footsteps, consecrate secret temples to the gods of wisdom and delirium, serve as an unseen philanthropist to thousands of people.

Ordinary ambitions did not interest him. He possessed no desire to excel within a regular field, to build any sort of successful career. Instead he would perform acts of a kind that had barely been encountered before, challenging the boundaries of what it was possible to do within the span of a lifetime. His projects would perhaps fall within the category, broadly speaking, of "art," but would refuse to utilise the terms or follow the strictures of any artistic establishment or school. Primal experience, rather than formal aesthetic statements, would be his priority: experiencing it, guiding it, making a gift of it to others. All would be done in secret and no one else would be permitted to see his work for what it was until he had died. Only then would he reveal the extent of his labours to those who were prepared to listen.

Having broken all contact with his aristocratic family and their milieu, Maximilian found himself employed for forty hours each week at a printing works in Dagenham. His time there was dominated by a series of awful mindless repetitions, cycles of tedium that almost succeeded in destroying him. Already he had been there for nearly two years and he was finding it difficult to see quite how he would escape. Entering the workplace each morning was so dispiriting that it felt like he was being repeatedly punched in the face. Headaches would soon settle in for the duration of the day. Exhaustion clung to his limbs, became engrained, a part of the mechanics governing his body motions.

The little education that he had received was due to his own appetite for the reading of books. His attempts to build an intellect within the confines of his room became the great secret that he shielded from his colleagues. Passing his days at the printing works largely in silence, on the few occasions he was required to speak he would imitate a working-class accent with whichever monosyllables seemed necessary. He was a cipher to his colleagues; no one had any idea that when he returned home he was engaged in the furious processes of study. Towers of books, perennially in danger of collapsing, reached up towards his ceiling. Every night he would read for hours on end, often until he could no longer adequately focus his eyes upon the words that lay before him.

On that fateful Wednesday in Bloomsbury, time he had stolen for himself by feigning sickness, all of his energies were poured into the completion of his plan. In the space of three hours he weighed up the relative importance of each of his ambitions, estimating how long he would need to devote to them. He then placed them into a timetable that ran to exactly fifty years, with each individual year taken into account. Some of his schemes were grand enough to take up months or years at a time, whilst others were minor, relatively insignificant actions that might be performed in the space of a few minutes. As soon as the words had been declared upon the page, rendered elegantly in black ink with his fountain pen, it seemed certain to him that they spoke of the truth, that what they described would one day exist. Even before he had finished writing them, the plans began to possess a definitive hold on him, a mysterious authority that few other forces could lay claim to.

He imagined the span of his entire life. How would it feel to wake up each year and discover that he was older? To observe his features in the mirror as time gnawed them away? Recently, as a consequence of thoughts like these, he had found himself obsessed with the minutiae of the era into which he had been born. He noted its conventions of form, observable in newspapers and advertisements and bus tickets.

How long would it take for fashions to change? Which course would they take? Would he notice when they did?

In one sense, the idea of learning how the future would alter such details caused him great excitement. Every year ahead would possess its own peculiar character, for him individually as well as on a much wider scale. He hoped that he would prove to be capable of noticing the changes as time moved on. A part of him was frightened of remaining fixed to his current mental co-ordinates, of never evolving in tandem with the shifts of history that everyone else acknowledged. He was determined to never fall into any sort of complacency.

Looking up from the pages of his notebook, he registered the details of his surroundings for the first time in more than an hour. Many of the old men were still present, emptying their glasses of drink as slowly as they could manage. Despondently, the barmaid leafed through a newspaper. Maximilian smiled to himself. Whilst the rest of the world remained locked in perpetual stasis, he had shifted the course of his life. His plan was complete. Soon the bar would be closed for the duration of the afternoon.

Emerging back out on the street, he came upon a burst of pigeons, scattering in profusion as they broke into flight. Strolling across Bedford Square he peered into the well-polished windows, encountering scenes presided upon by men wearing suits, framed within black brickwork and cream-white arches, figures moving with the authority of learning and money, enclosed by definitive partitions of black railing, their offices looking out onto a giant oval-shaped park that could only be entered by key holders.

Visitors spilt out from the great doors of the British Museum, thronging the courtyard with footsteps and murmuring before walking away down Great Russell Street towards many separate destinies. A few streets away the beacon of Senate House appeared to him, the bulk of its body rising towards the skies with malevolent grandeur. Wandering amongst the university buildings, he gazed upon the rooms in which he imagined extraordinary conversations taking place, occasions that could leave indelible imprints upon those who had been present. Sensing the scale of the mass of rooms surrounding him, he considered the silences of the libraries, the academic offices holding bookcases and dishevelled piles of papers, the scientific laboratories and hospital wards and the residencies of eminent families. He wanted to be a part of this manic activity.

Nearby, a pullulating cloud of wood smoke emerged from the back garden of a house, drifting over the brick walls, winding itself into the grey air hanging over the stretches of lawns and pavements, seeping into Maximilian's nostrils, a scent which was destined to stay with him for the duration of his days.

A Short Essay Written by the Protagonist

(1951)

1. The conditions are now in place for capitalism to flourish once more. Inevitably it will do so, escalating further and further, until we finally face collapse.

2. The task now for anyone with any sensitivity and intellect should be to oppose this state of affairs in any way that they can.

3. The consequence of a society that places money at its centre is that forms of mental and physical slavery come to dominate human life.

4. Certain forms of expenditure are undoubtedly for the public good. Nevertheless, all that is moral in such cases is the intention that lies behind a given act of spending and the performance of that act. Sums of money cannot become moral in and of themselves.

5. Finally, money is impossible to define. It appears in such a vast range of contexts, being utilised for so many different reasons, that any objective explanation of its ultimate character becomes elusive to those who seek it.

6. The vast majority of ways in which money circulates have enormously destructive consequences. Human relationships inevitably suffer as a result, becoming insipid, superficial, mechanical reductions of what is possible. Tenderness is rarely achieved on the scale it could be because individuals are trapped within the structures of employment. In the current system most human beings have little knowledge of the full spectrum of the emotional and intellectual vocabulary that the species is capable of achieving.

7. Paradoxically, the only way for anyone to overcome the punishing effects of a world dominated by money is for them to acquire a large amount of money for themselves. Otherwise, different forms of poverty and slavery will ensue.

8. Money, considered from one perspective, can be seen as an enormous collection of numbers, somewhat arbitrarily selected by fate.

9. The usual ways in which money circulates are routinely accepted by society as the proper state of affairs. Given such an absence of reason, certain acts usually condemned as immoral have the potential to become moral if performed for the right reasons. Certain forms of larceny and fraud fall into this category.

10. Any free-thinking individual *must* do everything within their power to escape the obscene working conditions that prevail in the free-market system. This is equivalent to, and no less imperative than, for example, fleeing your country because it has descended into war.

11. Certain acts of labour are necessary and society must acknowledge those who perform them. That this acknowledgment must be financial in nature is an assumption whose basis in reality has not yet been demonstrated to any satisfactory extent.

12. When money is the sole objective of an action, a certain degree of idiocy is inevitable.

13. Money shows its true face in the context of mass production. There, it becomes clear that money necessarily poisons all that it touches.

14. Every advertisement could be replaced with a work of art.

15. The state requires that an individual be in possession of a certain amount of the currency that it has itself created and controlled the distribution of. The only *moral* argument for such an arrangement is that it would seem to encourage an individual to contribute a certain amount of his or her labour to society. However, one may nonetheless obtain money through means no less legal but in no way related to the performance of labour as it has been thus far defined. No limits have been placed upon these means, or those who exploit them.

16. If Members of Parliament wish to order millions of people to "participate in the national economy," then it is surely only fair that they should themselves contribute a certain number of hours of labour to the "necessary" factories, offices, and kitchens that they have forced into existence.

17. There is no good reason for governments not to introduce the concept of a "maximum wage" into law, with the parallel dictum of a "minimum wage" existing at a level not far underneath. The result would be societies of relative material equality in which both excessive wealth and poverty would have no place.

18. The horror of menial work as currently practised should not be underestimated. To spend forty hours a week or more engaged in unceasing cycles of senseless repetition, as do most human beings, is a destructive form of existence for anyone to have to endure.

19. In a more just and sane society it would be compulsory to partake in forms of whichever *necessary* menial work existed, distributing the quotas of such work fairly, whilst simultaneously providing the opportunity for educational and creative pursuits on a no less equal basis.

20. Throughout its history, money has been synonymous with anxiety,

intolerance, selfishness, anger, mistrust, and, of course, greed. That these states of mind are considered necessary consequences of the economic system in which we live is simply unacceptable. No system predicated upon such emotions can be considered salutary or, indeed, rational.

21. Money is the great patterning and organizing force in the world. It shapes the narratives within which most of us must live; it dictates the ways in which our bodies move and speak and think, thereby excluding an infinity of possible subjects and stances. We should attempt to challenge and overthrow these narratives.

I Promise to Pay the Bearer

(1952–1998)

Merely setting foot in the Dagenham printing works each morning was an activity that soon became loathsome to Maximilian. The proprietor of the business, one Mr. Bradley, was a corpulent white-haired man who was often engaged in the act of wiping sweat away from his forehead with a handkerchief. Most working days would see him sitting in his little office, fiddling around with figures in his notebook, or, simply, doing as little as he possibly could. Occasionally he would emerge from hiding in order to attend to his workers, frequently shouting abuse at them with a booming, guttural voice that challenged the roar and whir of the machinery by which they all were dominated.

In the evenings, Maximilian would shuffle back to his room, his clothes and hands covered with ink, his limbs aching from the day's boredoms and exertions, his mind exhausted and spent. When in this state, he was barely capable of any intellectual activity at all. Slumping on his bed, dejected, he would stare vacantly up at the ceiling, following the elaborate maze of cracks gradually forming there. Lighting a cigarette, he would watch the smoke rise and curl into spirals before him as he attempted to marshal energies he usually found he no longer possessed.

After spending a couple of months teaching himself how to pick locks, Maximilian began to break into the printing works in the middle of the night. He was working on a private project, a pursuit which kept him almost as busy as his "real" work: learning the art of counterfeiting. It was only through counterfeiting that he saw any likelihood of obtaining freedom. In all, he spent just over a year breaking into the works, entirely between the hours of two and four A.M. on weekday evenings only, hours when he was certain to encounter no one, but which were nevertheless wracked with paranoia and adrenaline. Returning to the building later in the morning, he would fight through waves of exhaustion, doing his best to pretend that he was alert and attentive.

Once he felt assured of his abilities as a counterfeiter, he began to produce an enormous quantity of currency that he initially kept inside a number of boxes hoarded underneath his bed. Once these had accumulated to the extent that he could afford to buy his own printing press, as well as property in which to operate it, he would turn his back on the premises of Mr. Bradley. However, it seemed to take a preternaturally long time for that point to be reached. His progress was exceedingly, unexpectedly slow and many months of boredom and toil ensued, until it seemed as if each working day was spent sleepwalking, and that there would never be any end to his ordeal.

It was during this period that Maximilian first found himself drifting into a state of complete solitude. Wary of his pastime being discovered, he no longer allowed anyone to enter his room. Feeling a general contempt for the direction that society was taking, he turned his back on the very few friends that he had, eventually refusing all meetings without exception. After only a few months of this, he could no longer even contemplate any other way of living.

Finally, in March 1953, he believed that he had printed enough banknotes to resign from Bradley and Co. That spring, Maximilian made a number of preparations for his future. Visiting a tailor in Marylebone, he bought himself his first suit of any genuine quality. Attired thus he began to scour properties all over the East End, paying particular attention to the factor of privacy. Settling upon a warehouse overlooking Hackney Marshes, he soon installed the equipment that he required and began his lifelong task of printing a relentless stream of illegitimate banknotes.

By paying great attention to every last detail of design, as well as keeping abreast of every change enacted upon UK currency, Maximilian produced replicas that were so exact, so perfect in every respect, that only the most attentive and experienced of cashiers noticed that a given slip of paper being passed between one hand and another was not in fact the authentic work of the Bank of England. No business ever found itself in trouble on account of Maximilian's actions. For forty-seven years he was entirely successful in using his notes without the slightest problem arising.

He took many elaborate precautions, of course, with the whole enterprise, not wanting to put the life that he was building for himself at risk. He would always wear a pair of leather gloves when handling the notes, and he was careful to wear only drab, plain clothes, always assuming an expression of bland contentment. His manner and appearance were so ordinary that it was almost impossible to remember him afterwards.

As a rule, he would never make a purchase in the same shop within a span of ten years. This required an enormous amount of travelling from one part of the city to another, an activity which he pursued doggedly on a regular basis for a number of decades, often passing through the hundreds of forgotten London suburbs, an itinerary that included Wanstead, Ilford, Barking, Bexley, Farnborough, Sidcup, Teddington, Hayes, Ruislip, Stanmore, Enfield, Wanstead . . .

He only printed notes of a low denomination because these aroused fewer suspicions. When spent they would generate a great deal of legitimate small change which he would discreetly collect in his briefcase and then take back to deposit in one of the many crates of money that were secreted in his warehouse at Hackney Marshes. If he wished to make a major purchase, he would always draw upon his pile of legitimate currency, most of which found its way over time into one of the many bank accounts that he kept, each bearing relatively paltry sums.

Maximilian often marvelled that the majority of people pay so little attention to the money that passes through their hands. Few people bother to hold a banknote up to the light and examine just what it is they're holding. This seemed more and more remarkable to him over time. How could so many manage to be blind to the forms that these slips of paper took?

Frequently, he found himself admiring the complexity of British banknote designs, particularly those which had arrived after the onset of decimalisation in 1971, an event which had necessitated several months of extremely hard work in order to produce suitable replicas. Only rarely did anyone consider that on the banknotes printed after this date the Queen mysteriously manages to maintain her youth; that on close scrutiny her eyes are revealed to be composed of a series of spirals, making her look like a victim of hypnosis; that detailed illustrations of various historical figures are made up of a complex series of colours, dots and lines; that the paper is thick and waxy, printed on a special cotton weave rarely encountered in any other context in British life; that each banknote has a separate number, a thin strip of silver, a watermark, a shining hologram; that on each side of each banknote a variety of different typefaces are employed— sometimes for the space of a single word alone; and that on each banknote is printed the phrase "I Promise to Pay the Bearer"—an entirely out-dated reference to the origins of paper money as simple promissory notes . . .

Maximilian often had cause to consider all of this. He came to the conclusion that to even notice such details was to challenge the moral authority of the banknote. Thoughts such as his might potentially move an individual towards the idea that their banknotes could exist in different forms, that, indeed, *they did not have to appear in the world at all*. Which is not a line of thinking that most citizens want to pursue for very long. Perhaps because it leads in short order to feelings of confusion and anger, to feelings of alienation, to a sense of separation from all of the many other people willing to accept the role of the banknote within their lives. Maximilian presumed that most people were anxious to protect themselves from the cognitive dissonance that might be caused by pursuing the many potential convolutions of thought hidden beneath the surface of the world.

Instead, he felt, everyone instinctively taught themselves to ask as few questions as possible, in the hope that this would bring as much lightness and prosperity as they were capable of attaining.

He never had any qualms about his career as a counterfeiter. Maximilian thought that it was absolutely necessary to challenge the moral authority of money. In his opinion such a system had to be held responsible for many instances of suffering, exclusion, degradation, ignorance, vanity, ugliness, violence, and poverty. In his own oblique way, by behaving as a criminal, he felt that he was staging a protest against this state of affairs.

Every time that he spent one of his own banknotes, he bought himself a newspaper. Over time he gathered these together on the second floor of his warehouse, arranging them in bundles and rows, carefully labelling them by month and year, keeping the tabloids separate from the broadsheets. The newspapers provided an index to his life. Sometimes he liked to walk from one end of the collection to the other, beginning in 1952 and ending in 1998. As he progressed, the colour of the paper gradually shifted from brown to yellow to white, with hundreds of barely discernible shades of each colour forming a spectrum of decay. The typefaces, layout and size of the words shifted with the whims of fashion. Photographs gradually took up more space, then became clearer, were eventually printed in colour. Society itself travelled from one era to another and then to another. Entire years and decades raced by in a matter of footsteps. His entire adult life was documented here and the memories that the newspapers provoked were different each time he ventured up to the second floor.

To enter the newspaper room he had to pass through a narrow trapdoor, his head peeping into the long cone of light thrown from the only window. Atoms of dust would rise in drifting circles, waver softly in the gaseous brown air, settle onto forgotten objects. He spent many hours there alone, idling. Hours when he would trace a finger over surfaces, following patterns and shapes found in the skin of the floors and walls. The smell of ancient paper mingled with the dust and rotting carpets. The room was lit by a single bare lightbulb precariously dangling from a thin length of wire. In odd moments of inspiration he had scrawled flurries of words in pencil on to the dirty beige walls. These were sometimes quotations from the news stories he had read, their dates and page numbers written at the bottom and circled. On other occasions he wrote hurried passages and fragments inspired by literary works.

His collection of newspapers became a resource that he would consult with regard to a multitude of purposes. If he wanted to generate ideas, objects, or phrases at random he would choose a particular date and then open the relevant newspaper to see what it contained. When, on a given evening, he wished to remember a certain year, he would go upstairs and linger in the attic. He found that it was the incidental details that most stimulated his interest and provoked the most potent memories. The choice of certain words, a particular font, the cut of a dress in a photograph, these could all bring back the look and feel of a particular year or period, evoking the often unconscious textures and attitudes he had absorbed, though not always aware of them at the time.

He never cut out any clippings from the papers; he found that he preferred the beauty of a complete and untarnished issue. He cherished the illusion of being able to open a newspaper "as if upon the day itself". This constituted one of his principal and favourite methods of time travel. When he concentrated, he was capable of convincing himself that he had actually taken up residence in a past year. It came down to nothing more than playing some music recorded in that year, looking over some old photographs, reading the relevant newspaper. And there it was, the year existed once more. If he then spent the rest of the day indoors and busied himself with a task that could conceivably have occurred in 1956, then for all intents and purposes he had successfully transported himself to 1956. Once more he would find himself living through its many pleasures and disappointments.

Surveying the many stacks of paper, Maximilian would often grin. It was a matter of some satisfaction to him that his activities in this one particular, not especially auspicious building had opened into a multitude of other events, stretching far beyond the boundaries of the present moment. From here he had begun to construct his own invisible world. All that he had known after a certain age had found its origins in this location.

Details of Some Principal Coordinates

(1953)

Parliament Hill, NW3

On five occasions that summer, Maximilian ventured here at night, bringing a deckchair with him, in which he would sit for some hours, gazing down upon the city spread-eagled below, forming a series of irreverent Morse code messages with a heavy torch.

17 Bisham Gardens, N6

Where through the front window Maximilian had once seen an enormously obese man, wearing a pink bowtie and white braces, being given a singing lesson by a teacher possessing a rather stern countenance, who was seemingly fond of jabbing his fingers into the air and making many excited remarks in Italian.

Putney Library, SW15

One of Maximilian's principal haunts at this time, where he would often leaf through a standard guide to astronomy of the period, a volume which he had not been able to locate at any other venue and which contained particularly beautiful illustrations of comets.

133 Amhurst Road, E8

Location of a public house which Maximilian always entered when following a route that he frequently walked that year (a walk that was planned to every last detail, which was circular, and which he only took on Saturday afternoons, the day and time for which it had been expressly intended).

Brompton Cemetery, SW10

The place in which Maximilian had decided he would most like to be buried. This was due to the cemetery's centrality, relative modesty, and the beauty it offered the visitor when approached at dusk in winter.

314 Grove Green Road, E11
A junk shop with window displays that Maximilian was often drawn to because of their absolute lack of order and decorum, indeed of any sense of composition whatsoever. Certain fascinating objects remained in perpetual window repertory, and of these Maximilian became particularly fixated upon a wooden figurine of a Japanese dancer, dressed in a navy-blue kimono, one foot lifted, frozen in air, its left hand clutching a pink chrysanthemum.

12 Caversham Road, NW5
Maximilian saw the head of one of the residents of this property briefly emerge from a window, an image perceived through a pair of binoculars after an extensive series of rovings through doorways, drainpipes, steeples, and chimneys.

The Oval, SE11
Maximilian enjoyed spending the entire day here during cricket matches, being ostentatiously preoccupied with anything other than sport. He would sunbathe, watch the animated faces of the many gathered spectators, eat packets of nuts, and read novels, but only rarely would he pay any attention to the vicissitudes of the cricketers parading in the foreground. As far as he was concerned, their presence was required to provide an ambience that would flavour his other, more pressing activities.

96 South Ealing Road, W5
A tailor's shop, home to a mannequin that Maximilian felt bore a startling facial resemblance to him. He liked to come and visit this individual, almost a perfected version of himself, physically speaking, and compare his own sartorial choices and general demeanour with that of his double.

6 Isabella Street, SE1
Final destination of a paper aeroplane bearing a handwritten message whose trajectory commenced within the immediate proximity of an adjacent address, and which, in the event, was encountered by no one other than Maximilian himself, who was engaged in a preliminary attempt at paper aeroplane making and throwing, and was in fact disappointed by the results of his efforts.

16 Blackhorse Lane, E17
Site of a café where Maximilian would occasionally dine, amongst clattering chairs, steam risings, stained mirrors, tables which each held a single occupant. He would gape at the void of his reflection, sitting through many dead idle hours.

8 Ballast Quay, SE10
Approximate source of an extended chain of considerations arising from the glimpsing of a turtle-shaped ocarina, which Maximilian had seen displayed in the front window of this property.

43 Roman Road, E2
Premises to which Maximilian would travel especially in order to communicate with a pair of blue-throated macaws, creatures with whom he felt he had begun to develop an affinity.

83 Blomfield Road, W2
Address to which Maximilian sent a mysterious chain of correspondence to an unseen recipient bearing the alias of "Jonah Plinkerton," an individual who claimed to have once been involved in the manufacturing of fondue-sets. After a prolonged dialogue about eighteenth-century fountain design, their letters eventually turned to detailed considerations of the representation of snails throughout the history of painting.

Camberwell Baths, SE5

On the 19th of November that year, a phial of green ink was opened in the swimming pool at this location, an act performed purely to facilitate aesthetic contemplation. Afterwards, a large compensatory cash donation was sent to the council anonymously, with an accompanying letter of apology and explanation, but the ideas and terminologies employed in the text were found lamentably impenetrable by the relevant authorities.

Growth Towards the Ceiling

(1954–1976)

One of Maximilian's first major acquisitions was an abandoned ware-house, located on the fringes of the city, in Edgware. At first he had not been entirely certain of the use to which he intended to put it, but a number of ideas occurred to him, and he enjoyed visiting the building regularly and dreaming of its potential.

Empty for many years now, the space had gradually fallen into a state of dereliction. It had once been a paint factory, but all of the machinery had long since been sold, and the only trace of its previous use at the time of purchase was a vague lingering odour of paint, somehow still embedded in certain pockets of air, from which it never seemed to leave, being clearly detectable for many years to come.

Maximilian enjoyed observing the forms of decay present in the property, and he spent many afternoons pacing back and forth through the space, often with no definite intentions in mind, some-times even sitting at a single fixed point for many hours at a time, so that he became intimately acquainted with the building's atmosphere and dimensions, its many interior vantage points, the uses it presented to him.

During the daylight hours, cold light would stream down into the expanses of the building through the enormous dirt-spattered slates of frosted glass that were fixed into its high, vaulted ceilings. Black weeds poked through the thick cracks that had formed in the walls, withering and drooping amongst a canvas of scratches and stains. Certain windows had been broken, leaving glass fangs protruding, as well as gouges that invited the entrance of cold drifts of air. Pipes emerged from the walls tentatively, decided on a definite course, curved for some distance in a new direction, and finally disappeared into other walls. Oily-feathered pigeons nested at the top of flaking iron columns, spraying down patterns of white shit that accrued and hardened over time. In one room the floors were coated with a thin layer of orange dust. Traces of the old factory workers were present in the form of short trails of footprints, mysterious tracks which faded away almost as soon as they commenced.

Finally Maximilian decided that he would dedicate these new premises to sculpture. To a single, giant sculpture, in fact. Commencing at floor-level, he would work on the project for many years, gradually building layer after layer, working his way up in a growing sprawl of forms, multiplying and sprouting strange protrusions, utilizing a vast array of different materials, until he had finally reached the ceiling. Each layer would be roughly the same height, representing the duration of a given year, with materials and objects discovered and purchased only during that period. Ladders would extend far into the air, reaching into the midst of the sculpture, leading towards a number of walking platforms that any potential visitors would be able to use. By the time that the sculpture was completed, the earliest parts would look worn and frayed, would be relics from the past already capable of provoking forgotten memories, vanished moments of life. It would not be long before the piece became an exercise in belaboured nostalgia.

Tending to be a slow worker, he spent many months away from the warehouse whenever he lost interest in the project, before returning to it with great energy. Once he had again become absorbed in the process, he would spend up to ten hours a day working on tiny details, attempting strange new juxtapositions, tinkering with small matters of form, attaching a miscellany of random objects to the central frame. In winter he could often see his breath appearing and dissolving in front of him as he worked. Shivering, he would rub his hands together or jump up and down on the spot until he felt certain of a vague modicum of warmth returning to his extremities. Despite the many difficulties involved, he came to feel a strange joy in the hard labour that such conditions required from him. Lost in the rhythms of his work, he would frequently return home late at night with weary limbs and a genuine sense of achievement, having forgotten all his other ambitions in the meantime.

He'd soon gathered together a vast collection of tools for this project. They were laid out on a large cotton sheet in a series of carefully ordered rows. Every imaginable object that he could potentially need lay there waiting for its moment of use. Saws, chisels, drills, mallets, brushes, clamps, ladders, boxes of nails, scaffolding poles, pairs of overalls, as well as hundreds of tins and bottles filled with every imaginable liquid, gel, powder. As time went on he became eager to add to his supplies at any given opportunity, purchasing any likely objects with the enthusiasm of a child collecting toys. There was a particular pleasure to be felt at reaching for the correct tool at a given moment out of instinct alone, and Maximilian often found himself grasping it in his hands before he had even decided what its precise purpose would be.

At first the sculpture seemed very small and insubstantial to him. For a number of years it had hardly gained any altitude whatever, seeming almost pathetic, a grand folly, waiting to collapse on him at any given moment. On many occasions he wondered if he was actually capable of achieving what he had set out to accomplish here, becoming frustrated by his lack of technical skill, and by the enormous lengths of time it took him to complete anything of even the slightest complexity. However, when he found himself assailed with doubts he would somehow still discover the strength necessary to continue his work, and finally, whenever he reasoned with himself, he could find no other purpose for continuing to live his life other than to proceed with his acts of creation. So he persevered.

Whilst he was working he would always leave a gramophone playing in a corner of the room. For many years he favoured selections of jazz whilst sculpting, a form of music new enough to him that it caused a riot of different sensations, even desires, to rear up inside, until, running out of space, they fought with each other in the pit of his stomach, as Maximilian followed the jagged rhythms with the movements of his hands, often stopping altogether and getting down from his ladder before a song had ended, so that he wouldn't have to face even a moment of silence. It was always of great importance to maintain the momentum that he had established. As the work progressed, he would look back at what he had completed from time to time and find that certain fragments of melody, nearly forgotten, would return to him with extraordinary force, along with other memories of the period when the music had first struck him.

After many years, he began to detect patterns in his thinking, objects and symbols that repeated. He eventually realized that he had a predilection for circles, spirals, vertical lines, particular shades of blue, and objects that were in some way related to the sky. He began to place his symbols more consciously and commenced composition of a voluminous series of notes, describing in great detail his own interpretations of the sculpture, recording where each separate component had been obtained, what he knew of its origins and why he felt he had chosen it. All of these notes were kept in a single heavy ledger bound in red leather. Adding to its pages on a regular basis, it soon became an obsession for Maximilian to give his entries as much detail as possible, so that if the piece should ever have an audience they would be able to have access to some of its possible meanings, as well as what the sculptor had felt to be his essential motivations. Despite this general attention to specifics, the piece never did acquire a name. Maximilian felt that a title might limit the scope of what it could potentially say.

Once he had reached the end of each day's work he would usually sit slumped against the wall at the far end of the warehouse, listening to a record, a bottle of water in his hand, staring at the sculpture and trying to gauge the progress he had made. When he was in one of his productive periods, he was eager each morning to return to the warehouse and look over how much he had managed to accumulate, to guess where the work would be leading him in the future. Once engaged with the work, he never allowed himself to stop until nightfall; then he would watch as the sculpture threw shadows across the floor at odd angles, a dark maze of contortions, alien shapes of irregular size, jarring lines liable to extend or break in any given direction.

Tall, snaking tubes writhed upwards, tangling with each other, stretching to infinity; a trellis of steel antennae threw dark scratchy webs across the vast concrete floors; the rotting husks of several cars were piled on top of each other, rust-brown and flaking; clay sculptures of white tortoises ascended for many metres before gradually diminishing into air; broken leather bus seats were pocked with holes that revealed the coils of horsehair within; aeroplane propellers were fixed to gargantuan machines of purely ornamental value, formed from random fragments of scrap metal; hundreds of glass pipes channelled a continuous stream of water from the warehouse's mains, collecting it into a series of porcelain receptacles arrayed across the floor; directionless staircases hurried towards the horizon with no sense of decorum; pairs of giant, tattered wings were attached to the grotesque forms of unknown creatures; straggling tubular foam tentacles grasped for invisible treasures; orifices gaped at random intervals, inspiring hopes of never emergent eggs; a leather aviator's helmet was placed upon the head of a naked mannequin wearing a blonde wig, its lips red with lipstick; looping pathways led towards pinnacles of spiky protrusions; paraphernalia associated with a variety of airlines had been strewn across the entirety of the piece, hanging precariously from one or another pole or hook; numbers were inscribed in blue chalk on a wooden doorway that was dangling from a length of rope; small birds of many varieties, carefully worked upon by taxidermists, were mounted on a series of plinths; antique telephones bore intimations of forgotten conversations; price tags were attached to wisps of air; monocles, ear trumpets, and gloves made fleeting appearances; toothbrushes once belonging to sailors were glued to a variety of surfaces; reels of celluloid stored in a series of canisters could be taken down and projected; crinkly bunches of blue cellophane gleamed with fluorescent light; kites bearing proverbs and inscriptions flew upwards, caught in their flight by the debris surrounding them; a broken piano was covered in plastic spiders; typewriters held sheets of paper that were almost blank; it felt, in brief, as if very little of interest had been omitted.

When he examined the sculpture Maximilian would often discover patterns created entirely by chance, by the whims of his mind, finding meanings that he felt he had not previously understood, hidden forms that lay within forms, entities he had not realised the existence of. Faces could be discovered in the fissures and gouges: soft masses of hair, weird hypnotic eyes, cruel jutting mouths. On one forehead he could detect a single tiny, bulbous wart. If he stared even more intently, he could see sweeping black jagged mountain ranges like rows of dislocated giant's teeth, and swarming galaxies burning and sparkling in vivid hues and colours.

Many of the objects were attached to the whole only precariously, swinging on hooks, balanced on top of one another, hanging in place by the grace of thin lengths of blue string. A number of the sculpture's components would creak and rattle as billows of wind drifted through the broken windows and the enormous openings that stood like solemn sentinels at either end of the building.

In one sense, Maximilian felt that the piece could never really be completed. As long as he was alive, it would always be possible for him to return to the warehouse, to add further layers, to let its forms expand outwards. There was enough space in the warehouse for the sculpture to grow to at least five times its current size. But he sensed he had to reach some point of termination in order to feel that his efforts had led somewhere in particular.

After finally reaching the ceiling in 1973, it seemed clear that he should soon declare the project finished, but some manic inner urge kept him working for another three years, until one morning in August, 1976, he finally became bored whilst nailing some planks of wood together. Stopping his work for a moment, he turned around and looked out at the world outside, seeing the morning sunlight drift and scatter through the rustling leaves of a beech tree in the back garden of a house that bordered his property. Descending from his ladder, he carefully placed his hammer and nails with the other tools on the dirty cotton sheet that lay on the floor, and then walked all the way to Hyde Park, where in the late afternoon he hired a rowing boat and paddled himself in long languid circles around the Serpentine, smiling benevolently at families as they passed him in pedalos, dimly aware of the distant roaring of the city as prickly droplets of sweat broke out across his forehead and under his armpits, allowing himself to bathe within the generous enveloping heat that had fallen upon everyone without warning that day, all the while gradually becoming aware that such occasions can never be repeated, because they occur almost as rarely as events which are not possible at all. And after that, he never returned to the paint factory again.

Aspirations to a Complete Inventory

(1955)

Amongst other things, Maximilian experienced the following that year:

3 badminton tournaments attended with mild curiosity;

5 buttons lost from shirts;

9 rides undertaken on Ferris wheels;

12 vivid colour photographs observed in the throes of fever;

17 circles drawn around particular dates on a wall calendar purchased for a discounted sum in early February;

23 ships in bottles;

78 potentially supernatural occurrences causing shivering motions to pass through his limbs and bones;

116 dreams featuring a peacock feather placed upon a red velvet chaise longue;

211 mathematical sums completed with relative accuracy;

328 park benches sat upon briefly whilst experiencing states of serious contemplation;

692 creases formed within the leather stretched across a pair of black boots;

937 moments of slight regret;

1,023 bus journeys to a variety of locations;

2,341 numbers heard called out in desolate bingo halls;

3,297 separate occasions on which he considered growing a beard, but thought better of it;

4,684 instances of wriggling his toes with pleasure;

23,497 minutes spent gazing listlessly at walls holding no particular interest for anyone;

46,319 steps belonging to staircases ascended;

81,682 flurries of steam emerging from his bathtub;

278,341 moments of finding things more or less unendurable;

356,986 blades of grass trodden upon with firm feet;

541,095 vertical lines observed forming deliberate patterns;

672,984 glances thrown at the face of his wristwatch in order to obtain knowledge of the positions of its hands relative to the circumference of the dial;

985,431 approximations of entities discerned on overcast Mondays;

1,762,298 repetitions of events that he found familiar, warming and comfortable;

3,173,902 doubts that his life had yet obtained a meaningful purpose or direction;

4,876,325 streams of bubbles encountered in mid-ascent through tall glasses filled with liquid intended for his refreshment, and for which purpose were being held in his right hand;

5,287,781 things impossible to analyse with absolute precision.

Writings in the Mode of Realism

(1956–1989)

During the course of his life Maximilian completed only one book. This came to be the project that he laboured on more intensively than any other, as he obsessively undertook library researches for each subject that he wrote about. From early on in the life of its composition he decided to call it simply *The Book of Essays*. Once finished it would be exactly one thousand pages long and would contain precisely one hundred essays, each consisting of exactly ten pages. They were essays about mirrors, pencils, magnets, centipedes, electricity, poker, banjos, silk, eels, make-up, cigars, ears, phenomenology, spaghetti, gin, astrology, string, cacti, karate, ophthalmology, semaphore, cinnamon, tattoos, hoaxes, planetariums, bones, surfing, earrings, ventriloquism, martyrs, whistling, curtains, justice, trombones, gunpowder, hats, swamps, Andorra, vases, adolescence, railways, nylon, shelves, bowling, doubt, glaciers, jumping, triangles, chance, steam, brass, sandals, go-karts, denial, superstition, gas, basements, advertising, truth, trout, bubbles, shadows, typography, lightbulbs, melancholia, plastic, acrobats, assonance, dots, houses, clay, benevolence, canoes, buttons, locusts, bells, apples, synthesizers, backgammon, saliva, bureaucracy, algae, aspirins, cuneiform, paint, magicians, noses, ponds, helicopters, melodrama, yachts, arrows, unicycles, radars, classification, singing, lampshades, serenity, riddles, and essays.

The style of the essays varied greatly. On occasion he would reveal little-known facts about the subject under discussion, assembling concise, truncated histories occasionally spanning several millennia in the course of a paragraph or two. Other attempts at the form would see him forming philosophical interpretations of the "meaning" of a given subject, rather than its material circumstances, employing examples from his own biography and mingling them with arguments that frequently involved a series of wild speculations and abstractions in an attempt to bring common assumptions into doubt. Equally, an essay might focus on a single instance of an object's manifestation in the world, building a tower of anecdotal surmises from nothing more than the way in which a vase was placed upon a table, or the manner in which a wall had been daubed with its particular shade of paint. Indeed, a few of his essays mentioned their "subjects" only in passing, hiding them within sentences focused on other matters, so that the often ambivalent relationships existing between one thing and another were opened up to potential scrutiny and wonderment. Any possible interpretation of a subject could be included, if only in a brief aside, existing as a stray fact standing at a moderate distance from the central narrative. In the end, Maximilian used so many different approaches to writing that his repertoire began to feel inexhaustible.

He soon became lost in trails of facts, in pages of library volumes teeming with unknown stories of individuals who had managed to instate themselves at the fringes of significance. Etymologies, distant years, Greek myths, quotations attributed to celebrated figures— there was no end to such trivia. A single bibliography could lead to hundreds if not thousands of new texts, which could in turn lead to thousands more. Maximilian would read through these books in perfect happiness for some months, gradually acquiring a mass of material before he was finally ready to commit himself to paper and declare his thoughts on a subject for posterity.

Once such a point had been reached he would seat himself with straight-backed solemnity, at the centre of the British Museum Reading Room, staring at the blank sheets lying before him, attempting to gather his forces and invoke the muses, until he felt that the optimum moment had arrived for unleashing a torrent of words. He would then generally spend the next ten hours writing, barely stopping to rest. After working in this manner for a few days he would scrutinize every word he had written and then destroy nearly all of them. Twenty or even thirty drafts of each essay seemed necessary in order to reach the pitch of perfection that he believed was required; but once a point of termination had been attained, there was no turning back. Every year he wrote three new essays. All of the completed works were stored inside a rectangular rosewood box that he kept at the foot of his bed. Once in the box, he would never again return to the subject of a particular essay, neither in thought nor on paper.

Each essay was a feat that did not have to take place, that might never have come into being were it not for the chance conglomeration of a strange series of events and persons. He always chose his subjects at the beginning of the year, at first relying on one of a number of different methods of selection by chance. It pleased him, at first, for his subjects to be chosen in this way, so that each essay would stand as evidence of the whims of fate dictated to him in a given period. Some years saw him opening obscure manuals at random simply in order to seize upon a particular noun. Other years saw him utilizing a pack of playing cards and a series of dice rolls. On one occasion he asked a bemused pedestrian to name the first three household objects that came to mind. A coincidence, a moment's flippant thought, could mushroom into hundreds of hours of diligent writing and research, until Maximilian possessed so great an overabundance of knowledge on certain subjects that it came close to being entirely useless. After a few years he was to learn that these aleatoric methods of selecting subjects were not enough to engage him, that he would need to discover suitably inspiring subjects in order to find the will to continue his efforts, as the energy and devotion that were needed to complete an entire essay were always considerable.

With the first essay he wrote, on mirrors, he found himself plunged into a proliferating universe of reflections and doublings, soon realising that he was studying a subject that involved every last single entity that was visible, including the infinity of things only barely perceptible to the human eye. He learnt of many facts; that "catoptromancy" was the name given to acts of divining performed by staring into a mirror; that Pythagoras was a devotee of this art, said to possess a mirror that he held up to the moon before reading the future in it; that the Aztecs had performed human sacrifices to a god named Tezcatlipoca, who had a mirror in place of a right foot and wore a mask containing eyes of reflective pyrite; that the ancient Chinese believed mirrors could be used as a charm to ward off evil spirits; that Louis XIV had owned 563 mirrors; that Asian elephants are capable of recognizing their own features in mirrors but that African elephants are not; that in 1781 the planet Uranus had been discovered by Sir William Herschel after he had built a telescope containing a parabolic mirror measuring six and a half inches in diameter. Ignoring all mention of psychology, his essay gravitated instead toward mysticism, exploring the fantastical realms supposedly contained within the frenzy of reflection. He concluded his essay with a number of bold statements about the "transcendental leaps of perception" possible for the individual who truly apprehends and understands the meaning of mirrors.

Naturally, he next turned his attentions towards the subject of pencils. He focused on the fragile and ephemeral nature of the object, expressing his anger at the common assertion that graphite should be considered inferior to ink because it is usually used to leave mere temporary traces and footnotes rather than indelible markings and incisions. Subsequently, he argued, pencils had been overlooked and taken for granted by society, which only rarely gave them the credit they undoubtedly deserved. He was at pains to point out how complicated the act of making a pencil was, citing the fact that a single modern pencil goes through about one hundred and twenty-five separate manufacturing processes before being put onto the market. Discussing the early history of the pencil, he told his prospective readers that for hundreds of years there had only been a single mine in all of Europe where graphite of a suitable quality for making pencils could be found. This was at the Borrowdale estate, in Cumberland, a resource that had been so precious it was frequently subject to thievery and was for many years protected at all times by a steward armed with two blunderbusses.

In the autumn he undertook a sustained consideration of magnets. Firstly, he discussed the origins of the word "magnet," its probable emergence from Greco-Roman antiquity, specifically from a town in what was then known as "Asia Minor," named "Magnesia ad Sipylum," standing adjacent to Mount Sipylus, the source of the ores which were used to create the first magnets, objects that originally bore the name *magnetes*, later evolving into *magnitis*. Next, he discussed individuals of the Victorian period who had claimed to live within bodies that possessed magnetic properties, so that they could make spoons, irons, and kettles stick to their outstretched limbs. Additionally, he outlined the theories of Philippus Aureolus Theophrastus Bombastus von Hohenheim, later known as Paracelsus (although both names were pseudonyms) a man who was a physician, botanist, alchemist, and astrologer who wandered relentlessly throughout Europe in the early sixteenth century. He had proposed the theory that magnets possessed magical healing properties, believing that magnetic forces could "draw out" diseases from the body. Maximilian's essay was founded on a great deal of conjecture.

In writing the essays, he wished to be continuously uncovering new layers of reality so that he might always have new ways in which to experience his everyday life. Each topic he took up hid a multitude of stories, and in the course of his research he would discover some of them, rooting them out from the murk of obscurity before depositing them into the deeper obscurity of his unknown manuscript, where they were destined to reside, neglected, for many years to come. Working on the essays fed his limitless curiosity for facts, and for encyclopaedic classifications of the world.

He believed that it was sufficient to produce a single book during the course of a lifetime. If anyone managed to write a single work of any lasting interest they would have succeeded in embellishing their existence with a little meaning, even if the work were to remain relatively obscure. In some ways he supposed that it might be preferable for every author to be restricted to the writing of a single book, as this would perhaps focus each author's mind upon the importance of the task being undertaken. Surely far fewer minor works would be written under such conditions, and there might be far greater variety, with less insistence upon the dictates of genre. Perhaps every book would then become interesting simply because it was a document of how a given individual had chosen to express his or her lifetime within lines of print. Maximilian thought that if this had been instated as one of the cardinal rules of literature many centuries previously, then perhaps the entire course of the development of civilisation might have been different. Egotism, competition, and hierarchy might have been replaced with a sense of sharing and equality, at least within the confines of the literary realm.

He learnt so many things. He learnt that the first go-kart was invented by Art Ingels, in California, in 1956; that the tallest species of cactus is *Pachycereus pringlei*, which has been known to grow up to 19.2 metres tall; that the oldest known canoe is from the village of Pesse in the Netherlands and was constructed at some point between 8200 and 7600 BC; that the word "telephone" is derived from the Greek *tele* (far) and *phone* (voice); that in 1874 the daily newspaper the *New York Herald* had published a front-page article claiming that animals had escaped from their cages in the Central Park Zoo; that the source of cinnamon (Ceylon) had been kept secret by spice traders in the Mediterranean for centuries in order to protect their monopoly on the substance; that radars were first patented in France, in 1934, by Émile Girardeau, receiving French patent no. 788795; that there are approximately eight hundred different species of eel; that since 1979 the World Backgammon Championship has taken place every year in the Monte Carlo Grand Hotel in Monaco; that the first plants on earth evolved from shallow freshwater algae in the region of four hundred million years ago.

General Advertisement to the Locality

(1957)

Maximilian stuck the following notice to the centre of an unlocked door that led from the street into a property that he owned in Islington:

PREPARATORY NOTES TOWARDS A GENERAL UNDERSTANDING OF THE SITUATION WHICH YOU FIND YOURSELF IN

initially it is probably worth remarking that you may well have been followed today. it frequently happens to people who end up reading this notice. if it didn't happen today, then most likely it did the day before, or perhaps it will happen tomorrow. the sole inhabitant of this household delights in following others through the streets and observing their habits and rituals. he studies mannerisms, listens to conversations, observes the goods and services which individuals choose to purchase.

all newcomers are advised that any cheering messages, cryptic intimations, secret bulletins and genuine grievances may be placed in the letterbox below. you can live secure in the knowledge that they will be received kindly and attended to with heartfelt thought and ceremony. written communications are treated with utmost respect in the place before which you are currently standing.

it is true to say that if you stare at a thing hard enough, paying very careful attention to what lies before you, that thing (anything) can become transformed into another entity altogether. a similar thing occurs when you repeat a word to yourself aloud enough times. the concrete meaning of the word blurs and eventually disappears. the sound becomes mere babble, a series of rhythmical noises. somehow this sound has taken possession of a thing we have mutually agreed is knowable, tangible and commonly understood. this moment of your reading of these words on this door might be the time to commence an experiment related to this phenomenon.

after reading this notice, perhaps fifty times, you may find that many of your ideas about what a door is will have shifted inalterably. this might be an experience that you would find rewarding.

A CONCISE EXPLORATION OF WHAT HAPPENS WHEN YOU WALK THROUGH A DOOR

we open doors and walk through them. we move from one place to another. when we open a door we expect to find certain things there. for most people it is a rare thing to walk through unknown doors. perhaps, when we do walk through a door for the first time, it should be regarded as a privilege. in doing so, in taking these steps, we have obtained access to another room, another fragment of the world.

rooms are often very similar to each other, but it is impossible for rooms to be identical to one another. at the very least they can never occupy the same positions in space. when walking through doors we should attend to the differences we can see in the space beyond them, however small these differences may be. we should always try to enjoy things that are unfamiliar to us. life should contain, amongst other things, a long series of adventures in which our ideas about ourselves and the nature of the world evolve continuously. this can begin to happen whenever we open a door, if we walk through a door in possession of the knowledge that we are walking through a door. we will only discover ourselves in our encountering the unknown. every door we arrive at offers this possibility.

doors are usually viewed from the outside. in this role, as an object-to-be-viewed-from-the-outside, for a moment or so, they are neutral objects, hiding nothing remarkable. consequently, doors frequently find themselves engaged in the act of looking as ordinary and respectable as possible. but let us not forget that doors are more significant entities than is commonly accepted.

AN OUTLINE OF WHAT YOU MIGHT EXPECT TO FIND ON THE OTHER SIDE OF THIS PARTICULAR DOOR

unusual things lie behind this door. amongst them are articles which possess the ability to shock, jolt, quicken, abstract. you may wish to encounter them. in particular, those of you who enjoy collecting cigarette cards will find a great deal to enjoy.

at least accept that in choosing to NOT open this door you are enacting a protest against curiosity. you will remain forever bereft of this particular form of knowledge.

nevertheless, it may be worth remembering that almost every door we encounter in our lives will remain closed to us. there are reasons for this, although it is not always clear what they are. but we should be mindful nonetheless that there are a great many consequences arising from this fact.

A CERTAIN FEELING OF CAUTION IT MIGHT BE WISE TO ADOPT BEFORE PROCEEDING ANY FURTHER

it would be wise for readers of this notice to consider the many possibilities present when one is still at the stage of anticipation. it is not always better to rush ahead, to be in a hurry to begin.

if you decided to walk away from this notice and only return once your anticipation had peaked, when it became impossible to stand the tension any longer, perhaps your enjoyment would also be increased. using this technique it would then become possible to imagine what lies beyond this notice and so invent your own room, which in your imagination may well seem a more perfect room than the one which you might actually encounter. this perfection can linger as long as you will allow it to and need never be shattered. to walk through the door now will only result in the disappointment of it being different from the ideal room that you will have fashioned in your mind.

still, a confrontation with the actual, tangible truth is surely preferable to fanciful flights of the imagination. perhaps you should simply discover what lies beyond the door and accept it for what it is.

THE ACCURACY OF PREDICTIONS BASED ON ACTS OF INTUITION

it might be possible for you to guess what lies beyond this door. or perhaps 'deduce' is the more appropriate term. you would be working from nothing more than various clues left in this notice. you would have become a sort of detective. not that there is anything deliberately hidden in these words. there is certainly no elaborate system of hints for you to follow in order to guess what lies beyond the door. i am only suggesting that it may be, in theory, possible for you to anticipate with some degree of accuracy what you will find on the other side.

if you do successfully manage to intuit what lies beyond the door i hope you will be made happy by finding your suspicions verified. considering the vast unlikelihood of this happening, i hope you might, in that instance, venture to take it as a particularly positive omen.

it is difficult to gauge precisely from where our intuition arises. perhaps what we refer to as intuition is in part an entirely rational process involving the ordering of facts of which we are already in possession. using these facts we grasp at the most likely possibilities through processes that are concealed from our conscious minds, employing a series of no-less-analytical and precise methodologies and forms of reasoning that we have however long since interiorised and forgotten.

this couldn't of course account for those things that are wholly unknown to us but of which we still manage somehow to grasp the truth. even if it is only a truth perceived vaguely, opaquely, seemingly untrustworthy. somehow, within this fog, we nonetheless arrive, sometimes, at the facts.

A COMPARISON OF THIS DOOR WITH EVERY OTHER DOOR IN THE WORLD

perhaps every door in the world has its own piece of writing, of a more or less similar length to the one you are now reading, scrawled in invisible letters across its surface. each such notice is doubtless different from every other, just as no two snowflakes are the same and no two people, etc. each notice presumably corresponds to the people who live behind each door, or the people who have lived there in times past, to the things that have been done there and the words which have been spoken inside.

perhaps, in each case, the words are waiting to be written, already existing, tentatively, in an indefinite future. these words are waiting to be caught and pulled from the air and brought to rest upon a series of notices like the one you are now reading.

in many cases this writing should probably remain invisible. imagine if words suddenly appeared upon the surface of every door in the world. the weight of the world would increase to an enormous extent!

so many subsequent actions would be affected. the continual

temptation to "read" every doorway might cause an epidemic of indecision and doubt. it would take some time for humanity to adjust and feel comfortable in such an environment.

gauging the relative importance of each notice would be a difficult enterprise. going about from day to day, completing one's chores and necessities, as one did previously, might suddenly seem an insurmountable task.

it feels almost immoral to go about encouraging such forms of behaviour.

feel content in the knowledge that writing will only appear on doors as and when it will. this will happen from time to time. that is the way of these things.

Possible Uses for Pockets

(1958–1959)

For a relatively short period of time, Maximilian became addicted to a strange practice for which he never coined a name. He wondered if, in fact, he was the first human being to engage in this activity, whatever it happened to be.

Riding underground trains during the afternoon rush hour periods, he would, for short durations of time, become the *opposite* of a pickpocket. With enormous care he would slip tiny objects into the pockets and bags of unsuspecting commuters. Sometimes these were merely slips of paper bearing quotations or messages that he had screwed up into tiny balls, often liable to be mistaken for pieces of litter. On other occasions he deposited small enamel lockets that opened to reveal picture puzzles cut out from the backs of matchboxes, or pieces of card upon which he had written lurid predictions of the distant future, or else discs the size of a fingernail emblazoned with barely perceptible swirling patterns and shiny-bright colours.

He would prepare these objects late at night, drawing the shadows and the hush of evening close around him before retiring to bed. Seated in an armchair, drowsy with the pull of dreams and oncoming sleep, he would find himself in a very particular mood, one in which his imagination felt free to wander far afield and grasp hold of new ideas. In some cases he would spend weeks preparing a single object, chipping away at its edges, licking it gently with a tiny paintbrush, holding it up to scrutiny through the lens of a magnifying glass. Whenever he had produced something that he felt especially proud of, he was very careful to reserve it for the "right" person, the individual for whom it would be most suitable, and who would, in turn, most deserve it.

Any object would do, so long as it was interesting enough, and then small enough not to be detected. This came to include examples of many tiny knick-knacks, odds and ends discovered in junk shops, in forgotten old shoeboxes, or lying discarded in heaps upon suburban street corners. It never ceased to bemuse Maximilian, the range of objects that he could find belonging to no one.

On the first occasions of his depositing these objects with strangers, he'd experienced exquisite feelings of fear. Nervous energy was generated by his constant thoughts of discovery. Specific scenes would play themselves over and over again in his mind. He could already hear the piercing shriek of a hysterical woman feeling him brush up against her. Suspicious eyes would fall upon him, to be followed by the indignity of being led away by policemen, who would proceed to interrogate him inside a small room without windows, where perhaps his counterfeiting activities would also be discovered. Nevertheless, nothing ever happened. Perhaps commuters were too preoccupied with thoughts of how they would spend their evenings to notice the subtle movements of his fingers.

For a brief period of time he attained a certain level of confidence and no longer worried about the possibility of being caught. However, it was an act that required a great degree of care and had to be performed at a tempo which would render his movements almost invisible, so that it seemed as if he had only given rise to a vague moment of shuffling or writhing that was indistinguishable from the many other anonymous movements of the crowd. He felt it was akin to a theatrical performance, one that had to be hidden from view, but which had originally needed as much practice and effort as that required by a stage actor. At first he would spend hours staring at himself in a tall mirror, mimicking his actions many times, until he became conscious of every last movement that he made, and was capable of manipulating his body into all manner of postures and poses.

Before depositing an object, it was of paramount importance that he first observe the crowd and decide which individuals were suitable candidates. He could always tell which commuter might be too sensitive or anxious for him to work on with impunity. There were always those passengers whose distraction or exhaustion or anomie left them seemingly oblivious to the fact that there was anyone else surrounding them at all. After rapidly assessing each candidate's particulars, and ruling out the obvious dangers, Maximilian would select his targets on the basis of their appearance: the way their faces spoke to him, attracting or repelling him, suggesting particular professions or ways of living. For the most part, he chose whoever appeared to be most empty, inert, and lacking in feeling. He found that he could not help but want to jolt such people into some more "genuine" state of being, even if only for a moment or two.

He was never caught, though there were a few close calls. Certain individuals could always sense when their personal space had been trespassed, no matter what their faces communicated. A vague twitch, dimly felt, at the top of a thigh, was more than enough to arouse suspicions. Then one of the throng of commuters might suddenly come to life, startled for reasons that he or she couldn't quite articulate, moving their heads to and fro to survey their fellow passengers and find someone to blame for their peculiar feelings of unrest. Undoubtedly it helped that Maximilian was only 5' 2" tall. At that size he was more easily dismissed by taller people, who tend to discount shorter people when it comes to assessing threats. Maximilian often thought that the ideal agent for this particular project would be a child or a dwarf.

The best moment to act was when a train pulled into a station. Amidst the confusion of jostling limbs attempting to evade each other, it was reasonably straightforward to slip one of his objects into a pocket or a bag. Whenever he noticed a particularly large or loose pair of trousers with pockets that were easy to access, or a bag gaping open at one corner, he found it very difficult to resist the temptation to quietly drop one of his mementoes into the space provided.

After he had disembarked, Maximilian could not help but continue to meditate upon his "victims." He would imagine their journeys home, the tiredness in the muscles of their feet, the look and feel of the properties to which they would return; the fact that in a few cases his actions might cause a quiet moment of rupture or revelation in the steady continuity of existence that most people were accustomed to inhabiting. He hoped that his creations would instigate worthwhile confusions: perhaps his recipients would ask "How did that get there?" "Who gave this to me?" "What *is* that?" . . . He saw their faces making their way out of crowded trains, ascending the escalators, passing through the station doors, and walking into the familiar and comforting tedium of the street, where the same newspaper vendor and flower seller sat metres apart, day after day, barely exchanging a word or a glance in the other's direction. He imagined their walk across the rain-slicked streets, the same route every day, passing landmarks reassuring in their banality. The public house, the fish and chip shop, the bookies, the newsagent, the shops that were closed but didn't bother to shutter their window displays. Journeying across the slabs of paving stone, a walk that added to the silent residue of other old, exhausted footsteps. And beyond each High Street the endless rows of identical houses with their creaking waist-high gates leading onto well-tended lawns and beds of flowers, before the advent at last of the long-awaited atmosphere of comfort circulating just beyond the front door, the reassurance that had settled over so many years into the odours in the kitchen, the grains in the wallpaper, the sounds of the children.

Maximilian wanted to interrupt this all-too-logical flow of events. Intruding—in a mild-mannered way, of course—he hoped to disrupt the sense of inevitability that pervaded such a scene. He imagined the few amongst the millions of men in black hats and suits who would rummage in their pockets and look for their keys, in the process discovering the unfamiliar outlines of an object that they would proceed to hold up to the diminishing light still trickling from the sky: an object that would reveal itself as a strange intruder, perhaps causing a faint wrinkle to impress itself upon their brows.

Most of his recipients would merely shrug their shoulders, he knew, whatever the nature of his gift, however extraordinary its qualities; then again, many would never even find them, or perhaps would assume that the objects were in fact their own possessions. But even if this were the case, Maximilian delighted in the fact that he had discovered another way to quietly alter the prevailing formations of social reality. To shift matter from one location to another, causing tiny disruptions in the accepted patterns of the city: this was his modest aim.

After a day spent in his habitual solitude, Maximilian sometimes found it a perverse sort of thrill to join the stream of humanity from 4:30 to 6:00 P.M., to steep himself in the tension generated by this manic convergence of workers joined together each day in order to ensure their collective survival. Even without distributing any of his objects, he felt as if he were engaged in silent communion with the populace simply by having placed his body amongst them, a location in which he could listen and observe. Surveying their faces for signs of familiarity became his own sort of comforting ritual. He liked to be part of the crowd, keeping his secrets to himself, lurking at the periphery, undetected. It soon reached the point where these expeditions were the high point of his day. He would wait the length of an afternoon in eager anticipation, unoccupied, anticipating the moment when all the offices would close and empty of their workers.

He chose to end this particular phase of his life's work when his eagerness began to be disrupted by bouts of paranoia. Nothing had actually changed, indeed he had met with nothing but success, but the early panic he had found the confidence to ignore now began to eat away at his own comfort, and he started to feel genuinely at risk whenever he boarded a train. Many times he would tell himself that this was absurd, especially considering the far greater dangers posed by his counterfeiting activities, but to no avail. His rush-hour activity had something of the sense of a physical violation about it, however minor. It was to this that he attributed his growing anxiety. And so he turned to other pursuits.

Occurrences of an Afternoon of Leisure

(1959)

(a series of thoughts, observations, queries, possibilities, and events encountered on the twenty-ninth of october)

12.00 P.M.
Maximilian sat in his armchair at home, legs crossed, pipe smoking, pondering.

12.01
He considered the many kinds of chairs in the world and their vastly different arrangements. This led to thoughts regarding the extent to which the style of chair sat in, and its precise spatial attributes, might determine the nature of the thoughts produced when seated in those particular conditions.

12.16
Flicking through a full-colour magazine feature on life in the Riviera, he found that these gaudy images appealed to him far more than the accompanying text, and it was to these that he directed his full attention, after reaching the middle of the second paragraph.

12.18
A soft, almost intangible belch escaped from within.

12.24
Imagining the commencement of a new life in a crofter's cottage, three miles away from the nearest human being.

12.27
Lying on his belly, he bent both legs and raised them into the air,

holding on to his feet with both arms outstretched behind. He kept this position for a full two minutes, a rough approximation of the yoga posture *Dhanurasana*.

12.34
Closing his front door behind him he began to whistle a cheerful tune entirely of his own invention as he commenced an unhurried stroll towards the West End.

12.37
Observations of a shadow thrown from a bench in the shape of a rhomboid.

12.41
Encounter with a film poster blazoned with gigantic red letters, a screaming woman wearing a yellow dress, rushing waters, aeroplanes, tanks, ranks of buildings tumbling into rubble or being consumed by fire.

12.44
He bent down to tie up his left shoelace (in order to match the strength of the knot with that of his right shoe).

12.53
He wondered if it was possible to re-establish naïveté after a certain level of self-consciousness had already been attained, or would this always then be a false naïveté, an impossible attempt at reversing what had been indelibly fixed?

1.17
Officious air of typists eating sandwiches during their lunch hour.

1.22
Screwing up a waxy ball of paper, Maximilian aimed it at the mouth

of a rubbish bin and launched it into the air.

1.24
The irritating way in which toothpicks become soft and useless almost immediately upon contact with the teeth.

1.26
Impertinent faces of the riders of horses featured in equestrian statues. The lack of imagination in all public sculpture.

1.32
A cold glass of pineapple juice placed to his lips.

1.41
Concerns about his shaving technique after detecting hairs sprouting from the skin covering his lower jaw.

1.52
Halting momentarily, he considered the commotion at a building site, a frenzy of hammer blows. An enjoyable sense of witnessing minor yet historical changes in one's environment.

1.58
An old man, with prominent boils and flaring eyes, seen pacing up and down the street and muttering quite audibly to himself about partridges.

2.04
Maximilian turned right off of Tottenham Court Road and onto Oxford Street.

2.06
Aeroplane glimpsed in the sky. Aviation daydream interlude.

2.08
A little girl beaming and holding a green balloon attached to a length of string.

2.15
Italian Gents Hairdressers—a giant comb and pair of scissors, crossed over each other, filling the entire window. Barbers within producing monologues about mortality and horseraces. Swirling red-and-white striped pole jutting out from shop sign.

2.17
Obnoxious displays of the accoutrements required for contemporary existence. Nothing more inspirational or remarkable on offer than that.

2.18
Everywhere the constant streaming of bodies, all neatly buttoned up, choking out each inner fire.

2.23
Shopping expeditions being undertaken for who-knows-what nefarious purposes.

2.27
Overcast skies casting a pallid gloom on all lying underneath them. At least rain would be decisive.

2.34
The possibility of inventing entirely new ways of spending afternoons. To become a seer of the leisure classes.

2.41
Considerations of what the maximum possible human achievement within the space of a five minute interval could be.

2.46
Passing resolve to risk involvement of paprika in tonight's dinner.

2.58
Maximilian's gaze fell upon an eighteenth-century paper fan depicting a couple seated in a garden beside an overflowing basket of fruit, a dog attendant at their feet, a gushing river in the foreground.

3.06
The way in which most objects seem improved when placed upon a boat.

3.19
A broken glass bottle seen in the gutter amidst dead leaves, scraps of newspaper.

3.21
Sudden apprehension of the face of a young woman staring at him from a fifth-floor window. Curious eyes, not hostile.

3.29
It struck Maximilian that experts on the subject of seaweed presumably reside somewhere in London. Where do they live? What do the rooms of their houses look like? Are they eaten up with melancholy?

3.45
Pigeons and their definitive place within the hierarchy.

3.48
He turned from Sackville Street onto Piccadilly.

3.51
He recalled that a number of buildings in London had beehives installed on their roofs.

4.03
Struck by the ambition to destroy a car completely, to annihilate its forms until no longer recognisable.

4.09
The garish, unreal effect of artificial lighting upon those objects which it illuminates.

4.18
The fascination of what lies behind each closed door, each shuttered window.

4.25
Memories of when he was a child and would climb trees and stay on top of them for entire afternoons, hiding from enemies, spying on mercenaries, equipped with his comic-book collection and some apples in a burlap sack.

4.32
He passed a young woman wearing a red angora wool sweater and white slacks.

4.38
Nasturtiums. Phosphorescent, encased in a rounded glass vase.

4.46
To live within his body with an aspiration to absolute knowledge of sensory awareness.

4.59
Idea: to visit ten museums during the course of an afternoon, each of them for no more than ten minutes.

Beyond the Turquoise Door

(1960–1998)

Early that year, Maximilian became the owner of a bungalow in Hackney. He would live there for quite some time. It only had six rooms, but he felt that this was more than enough for him. He had vowed to keep only a minimum of clothes, bedding, cooking utensils, foodstuffs, toiletries, towels, and cleaning implements. He also allowed himself a modest collection of books and records, neither of which could exceed more than one hundred items at any time. Furniture was limited to a mattress laid out along the floor and a single threadbare armchair, in which he would sit reading or musing for many hours each evening. Other than this, he kept the rooms entirely empty.

He had developed a series of moral arguments with regard to the expenditure of his counterfeit fortune. To pay exorbitant sums for housing, furnishings, food, holidays, or any other such luxuries would constitute, in his opinion, an abuse of the privileged situation he had created for himself. Although he did purchase many commodities above and beyond his strict needs, none of these, in his view, were indulgences, and he kept them, in any case, far removed from his Spartan living quarters.

Goods took on a different character and status as soon as they became part of a work of art, of course; never once did Maximilian purchase something merely to enjoy the act of possession. All of his accumulated belongings served an active, useful purpose. To his mind, these were not extravagances but *necessities*. His intention had always been to make his art public only following his death, but once this happened, all the materials he had purchased in the name of art would achieve apotheosis, becoming items with a real social value, no longer mere possessions. And this would be the case, Maximilian decided, whether the public appreciated his work or not. (He couldn't imagine that the vast majority of people could ever think well of what he had accomplished.) Naturally, then, he preferred to keep all his art materials far from the bungalow, storing them in one of his other properties, so that there could be no confusion between those things he bought in order to use—be they opulent or utilitarian—and those he bought in order, simply, to live.

Returning to his bare rooms each evening (one of which was always kept entirely empty) became an important daily ritual. The bungalow had a tranquil, calming influence on him. In truth, it was an entirely unremarkable building in which nothing very interesting ever happened, but this was precisely its charm. It provided Maximilian with a place in which every last detail was entirely predictable, a place to which he could retreat from the often chaotic states of mind to which he subjected himself, elsewhere in the city. Whenever his imagination strayed into difficult territories or he became overwhelmed by the scale of his projects, he would simply stay at home for a while, drifting through a series of empty days in which nothing much happened, during which time he might lie down or stare at the wall for many hours, until he had reached the point where he felt he could continue with his endeavours.

He never spoke to his neighbours. To avoid arousing their suspicions, naturally, but also out of inclination. His curtains were always drawn. Never once did he answer his front door. Whenever he departed from the bungalow he would immediately get into his car and drive away, not returning until dark. Of course, there was no way to avoid those liminal periods of entering and exiting during which it was possible for anyone on the street to see and hail him, despite his restricting his movements to those hours during which his neighbours were at work. Yet, Maximilian had no trouble adhering to his rule of total solitude: no one bothered to make his acquaintance. London was large enough to sustain an almost entirely anonymous existence for years on end, he found. Everyone on his street came to know him by sight, but they never asked his name.

In more than thirty years, Maximilian only had to suffer through two different occasions on which his neighbours attempted to speak to him. In 1961, Mick Prior, of Number 48, remarked that the weather was particularly nice, an observation to which Maximilian responded with his customary silence, keeping his eyes firmly focused upon the stretch of pavement lying immediately in front of his feet as he made his escape, never giving his interlocutor the slightest satisfaction as to whether this remark had indeed been overheard. In 1974, Nigel Wilkinson, of Number 56, saw Maximilian getting out of his car, and took it upon himself to mutter a "hello," only to be greeted by eyes darting towards and then away from his own with equal rapidity. After that, there was to be no more verbal contact with any of Maximilian's neighbours. Either they didn't notice him at all, or they were perturbed enough by his manner to think better of it.

Which is not to say that a number of people didn't wonder who he was, what he did, why he did it and so on. But these persons were never to uncover a single definitive fact about him beyond those that were already obvious, such as the numbers of his address or the placement of his nose relative to his eyes. Rumours circulated, but were no more than speculative fictions. Everyone was far too busy pursuing their own life to be bothered with Maximilian's wraithlike form traipsing through the neighbourhood at odd hours.

It was only during those lost moments of life, those pale and lethargic hours when people find themselves attempting to kill flies with glowing cigarette ends, or idly leafing through the pages of magazines, that Maximilian's neighbours pondered again the mystery of who he might be, sometimes even turning their heads to stare at the exterior of his bungalow, as if doing so might enable them to tear away the outward layers of his domain and reveal whatever lay within. But such speculations were short-lived.

In the period following his first moving into the bungalow, almost every single weekday came to follow the same pattern for Maximilian. He would wake up at 5 A.M. and consume a breakfast consisting solely of soybeans, perform his ablutions, and then leave the bungalow to pursue one or another of his projects. Lunch and dinner would usually be eaten in restaurants, but always in modest or lowly establishments, and then late in the evening Maximilian would return home and practice *zazen* for an hour inside his one entirely empty room, sitting cross-legged on the floor and staring at a blank white wall for an hour whilst attending closely to both his posture and breathing. Afterwards, he would read for a while, and then go to sleep. Nothing other than a terrible emergency could break this routine. He would feel lost, even nauseated, at the prospect of making do without it—consumed by an overriding sense of displacement and confusion.

Saturdays would see him dealing with all purely utilitarian chores and administrative activities. Cleaning, shopping, and exercising took most of the day. Afterwards, once evening had descended, he would avoid all revellers and go for long walks along the city's back streets, solemn undertakings that might last until dawn, during which time Maximilian would contemplate the previous week's labours, considering how they might be improved, made more efficient, more productive. Staring into the shadows and illuminated windows he came upon, he would seek solutions to his various predicaments.

Sundays were reserved for reading. He experimented with many different reading venues and positions: cafés, trains, bathtubs, rooftops, and cemeteries; sitting, standing, leaning, suspended in a hammock, balanced against a wall on his head, but finally he came to the conclusion that he was happiest at home, lying on his back on the floor. Maximilian would stare at page after page for ten hours at a stretch, finding that this method allowed him to finish a three-hundred-page book in a single day. Consequently, three-hundred-page books tended to become his favourites, and he found himself accumulating quite a few.

From time to time, Maximilian wondered whether there was something wrong, even perverse, perhaps hypocritical about his reliance on routine. Yes, he did like to control every element of his domestic life, for every last detail to be planned, for every inch of his living quarters to be entirely under his control; and certainly many people would have criticised his lifestyle as being unhealthy, a subject worthy of mockery. But these doubts never lasted very long. Maximilian was content. This was how he wanted to live. The hypocrites were the ones who believed they were any different. (Not, of course, that he had ever actually conversed with any such people, nor been subject to their criticisms.) Most people's lives were ordered to precisely the same degree. The difference was that he *chose* to order his life, quite consciously, and in a form that might be termed "idiosyncratic," not at all on the model of "ordinary" life and its concerns.

He never really asked himself why he had such a great need for solitude, feeling that there was no other way in which he could comfortably live. Social niceties would steal precious hours away from his work, leaving his creations neglected. A single sentence addressed to Maximilian—even those routinely fired in his direction by shop assistants—could throw him off balance and upset the rhythm of his work for the rest of the day. When he thought about the way in which most people lived, he could not help but recoil. The quotidian world sprawling about him in all directions was enormously depressing, if not terrifying. For him it was a place in which the imagination had been destroyed in favour of empty ritual; his rituals, by contrast, being heavy with purpose. He could not bear to open his mouth there, in that larger world. On some days even to walk down a perfectly ordinary street, populated with shops and traffic and pedestrians, would be enough to topple him into despair. After weeks of forgetting that the quotidian existed, he would come across a certain face or street corner and this would return him forcefully to the lives of others. So often he could separate himself from these lives, holding them at arm's length, but when he could not continue to do so, however transient his lapse, it often felt as though the ugliness of everyone else's realities had fallen upon him in some horrible, tumbling profusion, and he would retreat into himself once more.

Concerning the Utmost Privacy

(1961)

. . . wind shrieking into the bare branches behind the black railings
. . . the odour of creased green leather seats . . . families remaining
entirely silent for the duration of their eating . . . low windows
blocked by substantial iron bars . . . twisted leering shadows of doorways . . . short figures peering through keyholes with sly and malevolent glances . . . tiny rooms infused with dampness and the smell of
yesterday's fires . . . cold pale morning light seeping inwards . . .
cracked and discarded fragments of porcelain buried amidst the bris-
tling roots . . . thorns scratching the interior shapes of bones . . .
lighting the gas stove with the tip of a greasy match . . . flakes of silt
rising from the bottom of the canal . . . the needs of the body treated
as a matter of simple common sense . . . nights as dark as the inside
of a needle . . . an air of lacklustre apathy and indifference . . . the
clanking and droning of machinery . . . the low steady drone of
empty conversations . . . insipid voices that always sound as if they
were reciting rows of statistics . . . thin ice formed across the surface
of pavements . . . cats slinking amongst the dark masses of vegetation
. . . paranoid intimations of gestures possibly threatening . . . incho-
ate mumbling and blurting of curses . . . men in suits walking through
the gardens of the crematorium . . . dead hair falling onto the floors
of barbershops . . . a rusted nail jutting out from a plank in the scrap-
yard . . . any concrete enterprise becoming too dismal to contemplate
. . . the talkative young married invoice clerk at £9 10s a week less
stoppages . . . the decent fellow who is dull and righteous . . . the
landlady with her just-got-out-of-bed voice . . . the priest who
preaches about expressions of charity . . . the pretty young woman
swinging her shopping basket . . . the little boy obsessed with punishments and driven by a desire to escape . . . the spinster woman who
gives fierce scowls of disapproval . . . the pensioner who writes out

occasional invoices for the local builder . . . the respectable woman
on a night out at the theatre . . . the beggar with no teeth asking
pedestrians for cigarettes . . . the deadly and contagious lack of energy
. . . a single faded notice board displaced by building subsidence . . .
an unknown figure entering through a narrow doorway . . . parcels
of greaseproof paper secured with elastic bands . . . salt-coated lips
being moistened underneath the glare of strip lighting . . . red plastic
carnations displayed in a brown glass vase in the window of an under-
taker's . . . soapy plates stacked up beside the sink basin . . . silence
settling over the rectangle of red-brick administration buildings . . .
clanking steps of black leather shoes upon the polished floors of corridors . . . hands flicking through large steel filing cabinets . . . class-
rooms brimming with the confusions and hatreds of puberty . . .
blank and inert faces passing each other in the streets . . . blurred
dashes of grey and brown . . . leaves shivering against the white sky
. . . the rough and bleary smell of a garage . . . curtains taken down
from the windows . . . drone of organ music ringing from the interior
of a church . . . lunatic eyes staring upwards from the floor of the
slaughterhouse . . . blood seeping into a transparent glass tube . . .
diesel fumes drifting across an expanse of tarmac . . . dark pools of
water gathered in the gutters . . . the tang of oil and dust hanging in
the dark air . . . the silent labyrinth of empty Sunday streets . . . layers
of old posters peeling away from a brick wall . . . towering grey monuments . . . stark emblems of power . . . hints of evil lurking within
the folds of certain faces . . . the military precision of working through
the daily routine . . . the clamminess of the insides of coat pockets . . .
hot steam issuing from an aluminium spout . . . the need to appear
established and resilient . . . newsprint smeared black across bare fingers . . . the odour of gas leaking onto the stairwell of the boarding
house . . . sour curdled milk left in the jug placed upon the tea tray
. . . pricking a finger on the pin of a cheap broach . . . tension spreading through the stomach muscles . . . lone stragglers lurching through
the night streets . . . patches of lichen spreading over stone walls . . .

a tide of men and women flooding every day towards the labour exchange . . . streets that have been fashioned and moulded and regulated by money . . . the same products in the same shops purchased by the same people . . . the din of arguing voices in suburban living rooms . . . a pool of brown sauce beside a heap of fried eggs . . . rain streaming and plashing from tall umbrellas . . . running a finger idly down the arm of a chair . . . a soft issuing of poisonous yellow smoke . . . tourniquet and compress applied over the femoral artery . . . standing still and immobile and ugly . . . car headlights twisting and turning through smog . . . a mannequin stripped bare in the department store window . . . words that receive only the most perfunctory nod of the head . . . backs stooped downwards towards the floor . . . chiming cash registers pushed open by tired fingers . . . a tongue sliding across the edge of an envelope . . . carving slices of cold meat for white dinner plates . . . scratched-out faces in a black-and-white photograph . . . moths fluttering around a broken clock-face . . . shoulders bowed by some unknown burden . . . dregs gathered at the bottom of a white cup . . . glint of coins hidden underneath the floorboards . . . resentments that breed for years and become resident in minor details . . . gazing morosely through an open window . . . tossing back and forth underneath cold coarse linen sheets . . . drifting imperceptibly from one location to another . . . a passive acceptance of the amusements of the day . . . an obscure anxiety descending . . . bodies slumped forward over narrow desks . . . squalid habitations secretly returned to day after day . . . penis and testicles drooping and greying . . . pulling out weeds from underneath the flowerbeds . . . once again going complacently through the motions . . . white tablets dissolving inside a glass of water . . . wet prickles of skin rubbed against the rough surface of a thin towel . . . examining dirty fingernails in a pool of light . . . a single sheet of blotting paper on top of a neat stack of documents . . . appalling absences and silences and dreams . . . secret feelings of shame lingering within false expressions . . . forms of teasing that vaguely conceal searing

71

criticisms . . . the heavy and stifling air of nearly empty libraries . . . a wastepaper basket filled with crumpled balls of paper . . . grubby and disordered bedrooms . . . a glass door clouded with fingerprints . . . clouds of black dust hovering in circles . . . commuter trains shunting back and forth in the fog . . . acid-yellow glare of light thrown from a shop window . . . a lone figure diminishing into a blot at the end of an alleyway . . . radio voices echoing against the ceiling of a room . . . the cold dirty water of the municipal swimming pool . . . decaying teeth examined in morning mirrors . . . a shrunken bar of soap left on the side of the bathtub . . . scraping of chairs and table legs against the floor of the refectory . . . attempting to remove a stain from a pair of trousers . . . silent mouths amidst the throng of twitching faces . . . paint peeling away from iron railings . . . buttons fallen from heavy black coats . . . rubbing a dirty cloth over the surface of a trolley . . . stubby fingers grasping the ends of a pipe . . . neglected plants withering on the windowsill . . . dirt spattered across a pair of worn-out leather boots . . . blisters and bruises eased into the warmth of a bathtub . . . bitter flavours gathered in the back of a mouth . . . the constricting and malevolent influence of a society that is in essence corrupt . . . the ever-present likelihood of widespread annihilation . . . the planning and building of identical rows of houses . . . the anodyne pronouncements of advertising rhetoric . . . continuous attempts to impose a false objectivity . . . hoping for a knighthood and a seat on a major board . . . decisions taken from an industrial-relations point of view . . . obeying all commands of seniority . . . opinions that are absolutely final and decisive . . . the progress of a briefcase from one location to another . . . all the usual pastimes and distractions to hide behind . . . drinking glasses of port in upholstered armchairs . . . mink coats and cocktail parties . . . the talk of the town that amounts to so very little . . . falling into a permanent state of degradation . . . the fashioning of a fastidious brutality . . . the achievement of efficiency at any price . . .

The Faded Glamour of Certain Stairwells

(1962–1988)

One day he began to film the city.

At first this was entirely for the pleasure of the act itself. The instinctive, childlike desire to record, to take pictures. However, soon, and not without a sense of inevitability, his filming led Maximilian towards the creation of an epic work, a project that would last for more than a quarter of a century.

Drifting around the spaces of London, he would film dead alleyways, abandoned buildings, battered shop façades, crowds of faces. From these beginnings he gradually began to develop a structure and, eventually, a narrative of sorts.

Soon he became fascinated by the medium and began to attend many weekday film matinées, often sharing the cinema with only five or six other people, languishing amongst the voices of actors echoing against the walls, his feet sinking into the thick carpets, exotic vistas flickering before him. He lost himself on these occasions, forgot about everything else that mattered to him, drifting through the avenues of time.

Prior to his purchasing a camera, he had never been an advocate of the cinema, believing it inferior to both literature and the theatre. He had thought it was a medium founded entirely on the principles of commerce, propagating illusions and fantasies entirely for the purpose of profit. Later, in the 1960s, it seemed to him that the medium was entering a new phase of its history; many directors were learning to express themselves in highly innovative and startling ways, and it did not take long for him to begin to think of the cinema as the most exciting art form of the moment.

Within a few days of commencing his own filming he began to understand the extraordinary range and power of the medium, the many creative possibilities it presented to him, its frightening and intoxicating relationship to memory, to the movements and spirals of time, the subject shared by all films.

Encountering his destiny in the shadows thrown from empty shop windows at dawn, in the eyes of children and the movements of cats, within the improbable conjunctions of places and objects that he forced together in acts of appropriation, it seemed remarkable that it had taken him so long to discover the extraordinary convulsive beauty of images in motion. Their capacity as media for the recording of emotions had passed him by for so long; now he found himself succumbing to cinema as if it were an opiate, from which a complete withdrawal would be forevermore impossible.

Always a voyeur of sorts, in discovering the cinema Maximilian had also discovered the finest available means of glutting his appetite for the knowledge of other lives, and so he took to filming people round the clock, but always from a position of strict secrecy, concealing his camera in his car, or inside a shopping trolley laden with goods, or behind a windowpane in a darkened hotel room. Ultimately he saw that he could only guess at what lay behind the faces he filmed, as his camera drifted through the crowded streets, where so many people passed by, oblivious to his activities, disappearing within the measure of an instant.

Eventually he found himself becoming haunted by the faces of the elderly in particular, the fabric of creases and lines that they lived within, the deep indentations drawn into their foreheads, the many thin rings circling their eyes; sometimes he felt certain that he could detect evidence of psychic wounds there, terrible fears and discomforts—things, in other words, that he felt he could do nothing whatsoever about; a state of affairs which sometimes pained him immensely.

For his first ten years of filming, Maximilian couldn't decide whether he preferred black-and-white or colour film. In his view, the former tended to capture a more precise image, striking the retina with a direct vividness, reducing an object to its most essential qualities, revealing its naked inner face. Black-and-white also produced a sort of dream-world in which all ordinary reality was transformed into a realm of light and shade, within which almost anything could become beautiful, could come to resemble drifts of silver smoke floating across an expanse of glittering water.

Colour, however, expanded the dimensions of lived reality, amplifying its elements, whilst also providing a mirror, producing images that corresponded with a false exactitude to the world as observed. In the end, he found colour to be the more exciting of the two mediums because it presented a greater number of possibilities for arrangement and manipulation. There was simply more that could be created with colour; it held an enormous number of potential combinations of tone and form, an endless palette of gradations of light.

Alternating between the two mediums, Maximilian explored the potential of both, returning to the same locations to capture them on whatever latest type of film had been made available, whether it was Super 8, 16mm, 35mm, or even video, before editing the results together meticulously, cutting between one or another image of the same place, rendered in different forms of resolution that provided highly distinct records of particular times in particular places. Whenever new types of film came onto the market, it always seemed to Maximilian that cinema itself had changed, as if it now contained more, as if another subtle and important shift had taken place, ensuring that the future would now be witnessed in a slightly different way.

A part of him wanted to capture every last street corner and doorway, until his film project became a map of every potentiality available in the city, an encyclopaedia of forgotten locations and neglected vantages. For a long time he was even foolish enough to consider this as a genuinely workable plan. But the longer he spent filming, the more evident it became that completing a portrait of the entire city was far beyond his means. When first encountered, film had deceived him, he decided; given him the illusion that it was within his power to grasp the totality of a place, a situation, a person. Filming was an

Alex Kovacs

activity that came close to enacting this fantasy of possession, a fact which urged him onwards with this project for many years.

Once completed, his film ran for 429 minutes. At three junctures he placed spaces for short intervals, in case there would ever be any public. He knew that even the most dedicated of audiences would find the experience of watching his film to be a test of their patience. Anyone wishing to see his work would have to sacrifice an entire day of their lives. Despite possessing knowledge of this fact, Maximilian did not worry a great deal about whether the length would be received well. In the end he had simply made the film that he believed in making.

In its final form, the film had no opening credits, commencing instead with the words "Film No. 4," before launching into a barrage of names, words which all appeared across the spaces of the screen in large white capital letters, accompanied by long black-and-white tracking shots of buildings and empty streets, against the distant sound of a theremin swelling and pulsing in the background, all of which was then followed by an ellipsis of black leader.

What follows is confusing, incoherent, obscure. Telephones ring in anonymous rooms at night without being answered. A persistent layer of grey cloud glares down from above. Rain swilling along the streets seeps into gutters, gathers leaves and small objects, forms opaque mirrors. A thronging tide of pale, tired bodies presses onwards across the wet and indistinct pavements with hands that have reached out to hold the vivid objects of shop window displays. Long corridors of abandoned institutional buildings are shown in a state of deterioration, with sheets of pale wallpaper peeling away from their walls, prongs of dirty light falling through their shattered ceilings. Close-ups of the artefacts appearing in these locations alternate with one another: broken plastic dolls missing limbs or eyes, forgotten clothes catalogues bulging with old rain, shattered windows lingering amongst pools of mud.

For ten minutes at a time the film might follow the gradual drift

76

of objects caught in the Thames, or the billows of smoke curling away from the chimney of a crematorium. Abruptly the viewer would then be jolted into a montage sequence of furious cross-cutting in which a flurry of images might be accompanied by cascading sheets of electronic sound or the rousing campfire songs of a Cajun folk singer. At times the only thing that seemed to join two sequences together was the fact that somehow they existed side-by-side within the boundaries of the same film.

At any given moment things might shift into a more playful mode. There are irreverent abstract interjections. There are jokes. In one sequence, a series of stylized tableaux is created from hundreds of bright-coloured clock-faces, assembled in Maximilian's living room and placed into a number of patterns and shapes, then filmed from a great variety of angles. Whenever it seemed to him that his film was in danger of becoming particularly dour or depressive, he would liven the tone with some stock footage of circus performers or tap dancers.

Without warning he might cut in images that had been appropriated from newsreels, public information films, cartoons, or old advertisements. Snippets of archive material showed how locations he had filmed at a later date would once have appeared. He included frames dominated by the Day-Glo colours of corporate logos, extracts from interviews with deceased politicians, rows of flashing lights in fairgrounds, footage of tower blocks being constructed or demolished. These insertions came from the history of the city, or rather the history of images of the city, reminding audience members that many of the same spaces the city's current residents traversed so regularly were once occupied by multitudes of both Victorians and Edwardians. In one instance the flickering ghost of a cab driver and his horse passed in front of the camera, confronting the cameraman and audience directly with a shared sinister gaze before disappearing from sight for eternity.

Intertitles were also used, in a variety of fonts, sizes, and colours, sometimes acting as pieces of concrete poetry, or quoting from a variety of texts in often oblique and surprising ways. These quotations included sentences taken from newspaper articles, tourist brochures, and political manifestoes, as well as fragments of handwritten advertisements discovered in shop windows and portions of letters found lying in the streets. These words could transform what had been previously described only in images, deepening and broadening the scope of a given sequence, so that parallels were drawn between a variety of disparate subjects, until the film seemed to have branched outwards, touching upon hundreds of different issues and themes.

In the late 1980s, Maximilian began to devote his attention to the soundtrack for his film, setting out to construct a complex, layered background that would shift the entire focus of the finished project. Long stretches of the final cut were to remain silent, while others were soon provided with blasts of strange music, waves of natural sound, voices from radio plays, shrieking dissonances, and static.

Eventually he began to compose and record segments of voice-over monologue. In the finished film, his own voice breaks through the other effects from time to time, often engaging in lengthy speeches, providing a sense of continuity, as well as an elusive fictional narrative ostensibly involving a number of persons who are never actually seen in the film. Teasing descriptions of the activities of these persons are frequently given in the voice-overs, but their identities are never formally stated, and the relationships that they maintain with one another are only ever hinted at, their precise motivations (or, indeed, actions) never being made entirely clear. All that we are definitively told about them, apart from various examples of their thoughts and behaviours, is the fact that each person mentioned in the film is a practicing photographer.

The film attempted to interrogate the meaning of photography, the extent to which it is or is not capable of recording memories, of successfully describing the world. The various characters discuss these ideas and related issues, often illustrating their arguments with photographs and pieces of footage, which tend to lead only towards further questions and lines of thinking. This mysterious state of affairs is compounded by the fact that almost everything of importance to these people seems to occur away from the screen, in hidden rooms, behind obscured windows, often at parties where all of the characters would congregate, where they themselves would be unsure of what was being spoken of barely a few footsteps away.

Ultimately, however, the film could not be reduced to the particulars of story. The narrative, such as it was, was only one element in a morass of conflicting signifiers. The idea was that repeated viewings would always reveal new layers, fresh insights into what was being said or shown. At times Maximilian felt as if his film merely consisted of a compendium of other possible films, a catalogue of styles and approaches, shifting in tone from a plateau of lofty seriousness to playfulness and irony. Many of the scenes felt to him like nothing more than tentative sketches, brief illuminations that could become starting points for other films, perhaps films of similarly extended length, heading down different roads, but all arriving at last at precisely the same place in which they had initially originated.

Views of a Forgotten Building

(1963–1981)

This photograph became Maximilian's favourite image of the city. A relatively insignificant location, emptied of people, captured in the midst of winter.

Whenever he saw the image he felt that the church was drawing him in, inviting him to enter through its dark doorways. Somehow it felt as if important occurrences or meetings must have taken place within its vicinity. This was a place that suggested a fragment of a story, a scene from a forgotten film.

Perhaps an important scene, from either the beginning or the end of the film, a film that few had watched and which had rapidly disappeared from public memory. Perhaps the camera would move inside the church, observe the few solitary figures huddled in prayer, the backdrop to secret exchanges. A large funereal organ drone might accompany the drifting camera. Sinister occurrences would surely ensue: silent gunshots, or a strangling, a knife silently falling into the bulges of flesh lying above the hips. Or perhaps there would be nothing more than orders given or received on this neutral ground, a slight nod of the head between one man and another, resulting in the murder of another man elsewhere, in another city, on another day.

In another film the same location might be used for different purposes. Perhaps two characters, people who the film has followed for some time, strangers to each other, finally come to meet outside this building, exchanging a few words before entering the church in silence, the camera following them, observing their responses to each other and to the church, before they separate, never to encounter one another again.

Maximilian first came across the photograph by accident, searching for something else at the library. Any image of the city was suddenly of interest to him, could potentially lead him to some new, secret location, could provide some sort of insight into how he might make his own film. Amongst the hundreds of photographs that passed before his eyes within the space of a few days, this was this one that spoke to him. Turning a page, it was suddenly before him.

He identified the church almost immediately, only a few days after he first saw the photograph. It didn't take long for him to find himself disappointed with the actual location, a place which could never inspire him in quite the same way as its image had done. Somehow the photograph was quite divorced from what it depicted. Despite having an undeniable beauty, it seemed to him that all feelings of mystery were absent from the church itself. Afterwards, he took to grasping, vainly, for his sense of the original image, for many years to come.

In reality, these were streets, walls, windows, trees that were just like many others in the city. They contained nothing particularly remarkable for him when seen or touched. Observed in colour, in the cold air, surrounded by people and cars, the church no longer seemed to him unusual or worthy of note.

After placing a copy of the original photograph in a frame above his bed, he would often find himself staring at its forms, trying to decide what it was that he felt he could see in the image, why he found it so fascinating. He liked the steeple, shaped like a wizard's hat, placed at the top of the structure, the grandeur of the large windows in the buildings that framed the church on each side symmetrically. The trees in the park behind the church bereft of leaves. There was a sense of the city sprawling onwards beyond the frame, into a manifold profusion of other buildings and rooms. Equally, there was a sense in which the city seemed to have been emptied of its people, leaving only buildings and deserted streets behind.

Reasoning with himself, he came to the conclusion that the religious character of the building was of no interest to him. Religion had nothing to do with his attraction to this place. He would attend services in the church now and then, over the years, slipping away before the end of proceedings, having no desire to meet either the parishioners or the priest. Whilst he discovered little of interest to him on these occasions, the sporadic views of the interior that he thus obtained satisfied a strain of curiosity that he could not seem to expunge.

He would frequently return to this location with one of his movie cameras, filming the church and surrounding streets from many angles, capturing many different qualities of light, on occasions when the streets were crowded with groups of tourists, and on other occasions when the streets were deserted and ringing with silence.

Shots of the church appeared at many different moments in his finished film, the result of many attempts to capture the spirit of the building. He was to find that despite all of these efforts, he could never recapture the initial attachment that he had developed for the place. The strange excitement which the image had provoked in him soon wore off, leaving only an insistent desire on his part to live through the past once more, to return to the place in which he had originally found himself. But such a desire was of course, and despite all his efforts, still impossible to fulfil.

These streets, this church, this image belonged for him more firmly within the realm of myth and fiction than most other places. It seemed to him that possibilities for extraordinary narratives linger within certain locales while remaining entirely absent from others. Why this should be the case, he could not say, but he found it a difficult truth to deny.

Eventually he realised that he no longer needed to know why the photograph appealed to him. Attempts at explanation only led to the formation of false answers, which at best contained only partial truths, being for the most part ideas that had happened to take precedence at a specific moment in time, on a particular occasion, with no relevance even minutes later. Finally, Maximilian understood that he was the sort of person who could derive more pleasure from *not* knowing specific answers, who thrived on uncertainty, chance, ellipsis.

On What Has Been Discarded

(1964–1992)

It was in the late spring of 1964 that he caught glimpse of a trail of scrawled black writing coating the surface of a white tissue, blown and billowing profusely against a row of black iron railings.

This particular object drew him with an uncanny power. He crossed the street with haste, snatching at what he could now see was a paper napkin, claiming it as his. The markings on the paper were legible, but soon stood revealed as a shopping list. Maximilian's excitement deflated at once.

Still, he stuffed the curious article into his suit pocket and took it home with him, a decision he couldn't entirely explain at the time. This was to be the inauguration of a new and great collection, the first of several thousand paper napkins that Maximilian would come to appropriate, label, and conserve.

His collection would include paper napkins of almost every species imaginable. Cloth napkins never had any particular appeal for him. At first he was solely interested in examples of the form that held either drawings or text, this due to a wish to explore the impulse that had led him to appropriate that first, chance object, to somehow justify the hope that he had felt on that day, the momentary belief that he had stumbled upon something of note. What he most wanted, he decided, would be to find evidence of some genius toiling in obscurity, inscribing napkins with brilliant asides before throwing them to the winds, for the delectations of who knows what audience.

Over the decades that followed, there would only be two or three occasions when Maximilian found new exhibits for his collection that seemed to affirm his initial stirrings of hope. For the most part, however, the writing he came across in this fashion could be dismissed as junk. Not to be dissuaded, Maximilian came in time to be fascinated by the simple fact that these objects were so readily dismissed. To his delight, he was to discover that if one actively sought out napkins bearing writings or drawings, there was never any shortage of such artefacts on hand.

Almost every instance of "napkin writing" he discovered was of no interest from a literary perspective. Jottings and notes dominated, along with a number of lists and reminders, calculations of sums, and shorthand directions to particular locations. Only rarely did he discover anything striving for what Maximilian would have considered as depth or posterity to be found on a paper napkin, a sorry state of affairs that was yet another trial for Maximilian's desire to think only the best of his fellow citizens. However, when he did on occasion turn up a piece of napkin-writing possessed of even the vaguest merit, he became elated, repeatedly analysing the author's syntactical choices and attempting thereby to deduce information about his or her face, lifestyle, personality. Maximilian would fantasize that the author was a kindred spirit who had also come to understand the inherent perfection of paper napkins. Admittedly, this seemed a sad impossibility and ultimately his sense of isolation from other human beings was only strengthened by his fervent collecting.

With some tenacity Maximilian was eventually to find drafts of poems, song lyrics, entire paragraphs belonging to no-doubt unfinished novels, strange descriptions of states of being, lists of names of famous persons, football statistics, messages never sent to girlfriends—versions, in miniature, of just about every form of writing that had ever existed. Maximilian especially loved the absence of all metaphysical urgency pervading so many of these opuscules. Frequently too there was the profound absence of any density, importance, or talent. Occasionally he would take it upon himself to mail envelopes filled with examples of this new "genre" to the addresses of prominent writers.

Drawings were less common napkin-fodder than poetry or prose. But Maximilian felt that the general artistic standard of the drawings tended to be much higher than that of the napkin-writings, even if the vast majority of the images found were of simple matchstick men and what he could only think of as figurative fumblings. The advantage of the form, as he saw it, lay in the spontaneous nature of the drawings; by transforming the first suitable object which lay to hand into works of art, Maximilian felt that those responsible had discovered a certain freshness, often childlike, lending their creations a levity which could not always be achieved using more conventional materials.

On a café table he had once found a drawing of a tree with limbs sprouting outwards until they had invaded the entirety of the square frame that contained them. Unusual species of birds perched on particular branches, with speech bubbles containing musical notes emerging from their beaks.

A few years later he discovered a full comic strip left behind in a laundrette. Its protagonist aged drastically from one panel to the next, these making up a series of tableaux representing the essential parts of his existence: work, marriage, friends, hobbies, and retirement. Finally he was blind and bedridden at the age of 108, being refused a glass of scotch by a nurse.

Maximilian had found tentative sketches of budgerigars, policemen, offices, and disc jockeys. Little jolts of euphoria would always pass through him when he discovered another example to add to his collection. He loved to see the beautiful naïveté of the napkin-drawings—their inconsequential, spontaneous nature cheered him immensely.

After some time he became equally enraptured with blank, white, unsullied napkins. These were napkins existing prior to being used for any purpose, preserved in their initial phase, as purely utilitarian objects, incapable of aspiring to any deeper significance, solely intended for wiping mouths and other surfaces. Maximilian was increasingly amused by people who saw napkins as "simple" objects. He believed that their inability to form an adequate conception of the possibilities that lay suspended within a single white square was a symptom of terrible ignorance.

It wasn't long before his collection came to be dominated by these "empty" napkins, obtained at many different sites, and indexed in the alphabetical order of the locations where he'd found them. These included every part of London in which he had once stopped to drink a cup of coffee or eat a meal. Many of the napkins came to be imbued with memories of wasted time, and so to seem emblematic of the tragedy of all squandered potential: frames in which so much might have happened, but did not, their white forms lingering, unused, perhaps forever. He marvelled at how many things in this world were wasted, how much was destroyed.

There was also the question of napkins bearing decorative designs, of which there were many and varied examples. Maximilian felt it was his *duty* to collect samples of these, given the extent of his other work in this field. And so he seized upon napkins bearing tasteful floral borders, as well as those emblazoned with robots, those commemorating historical events, those that bore outlines of reindeers and snowflakes. These were not Maximilian's favourite napkins, but he supposed that they were representative of certain tendencies in the history of graphic design, and that they would preserve the traces of their particular era. He felt that there was a good chance this portion of his collection would prove to be of great significance to someone else, one day.

His napkin collection was stored in the same room as his newspaper collection, in his warehouse overlooking Hackney Marshes. Often he wondered which of these collections would ultimately be of more significance. Many heavy volumes served as napkin albums, with transparent plastic pockets inside them holding one exhibit per page. Each was accompanied by a typewritten text, although in no case were these more than a paragraph in length.

His preference for paper over cloth napkins could be attributed to the fact that the disposable napkin was a quintessentially modern object, inexorably bound up in his imagination with the onset of mechanization, the growth of cities, the generalized fragmentation of modern experience. In contrast, cloth napkins belonged to the realm of the antique, feeling heavy with dubious "significance," with the cleanliness and decorum beloved of a vanished social order—a state of affairs that he had no wish to preserve or uphold; only to extinguish.

Furthermore, Maximilian was taken with the fragility of the paper napkin, its flimsy body, liable to be torn or crumpled, to dissolve or become irreparably stained. They seemed to him such tentative objects, always on the brink of extinction. Reproduced infinitely, identically, they were taken for granted by virtually everyone living within advanced industrial economies. Their presence was thought to be as natural and inevitable as that of water or air, but this was of course an illusion: they were made, and many resources were taken up with their manufacture, only for them to be disposed of without a second thought. Maximilian also loved that paper napkins had become kitsch objects on a par with bubble-gum. They were widely considered to be ugly, when they were considered at all. Maximilian was haunted by the millions of neat stacks of napkins lining the insides of mechanical dispensers—objects so easily reached for and relied upon without their origin, meaning, or potential being considered. First brought to the mass market in America in the 1930s, the paper napkin was in fact a cultural artefact existing at the margins of Modernism. Silently it would come to lurk in the corners of films and modern novels. Maximilian felt it was a more elegant entity than certain other forms of tissue paper, perhaps because each napkin was always separated and removed from other, identical examples of the form, making each square a clearly delineated frame, an individual object that in every instance possessed the potential to be of great individual significance if transformed by social forces. He also liked the way that it mimicked what could be seen as an obsolete form— the cloth napkin—and could therefore be understood as a pretence, garish and yet somehow delightful to him for precisely this reason.

Maximilian loved the transformative possibilities of the medium of paper, its eternal invitation to make marks and leave inscriptions, to communicate with strangers, to add to the great swollen ocean of print. Paper was the medium in which nothingness was forever conquered by new statements and representations, lines representing new regions and fiefdoms.

He would never entirely recover from the hope that he had felt, the hope that he had come upon some marvellous and inexplicable message when he set his eyes upon the first napkin of his collection. But, its pleasures aside, his quest to find a napkin, *the* napkin, at last providing the consummation he had initially envisioned, was to yield no results. He would need to look elsewhere for his ecstasies.

Time Signatures Affect Desires
(1965)

Outside it was snowing.

He softly played a sheet of glass with a violin bow.

An Unexpected Encounter with Trevor

(1966)

That year, Maximilian was to have his first conversation of any substantial length in fifteen years. In that time, he had frequently needed to put himself through the paces of the usual pleasantries required of him by shop assistants and waiters, but he had never once engaged in a real conversation, that is to say any sort of dialogue involving a legitimate exchange of ideas, however rudimentary the thoughts expressed. This might be considered an unusual state of affairs, but it was only rarely that Maximilian was reminded that he no longer spoke to anyone; for the most part he was too preoccupied with other things to notice.

Whenever it had seemed to him that certain situations might threaten to develop into a conversation, he would sidle away without a word, without a thought for how rude or strange such an action might seem to whoever had tried to engage him. Eventually he reached the point of feeling that he needed to maintain his silence at all costs, or else face unbearable consequences. What would happen to him, he didn't know; but neither did he want to find out.

Relationships were replaced in his life with solitary actions and abstract ideals. Continuous immersion in his art was necessary; to slow or stop would expose himself to possible attack by such feelings as loneliness and anxiety; thus, he would work for twelve hours a day, only breaking off to eat, wash, and sleep before getting up for another day's work. The trick behind this unceasing diligence was to engage only in those activities that were, for Maximilian, purely pleasurable. As soon as a project became tiresome, he would abandon it for an indefinite period until the idea of it became interesting to him once more (if ever). Following this plan largely ensured the eradication of boredom from his repertoire of sensations and emotions. Solitude was his natural state, consuming him entirely. He couldn't imagine any other way of living.

So it came as quite a shock when, one evening, he found himself drawn into a conversation with a young man named Trevor. They were both sitting alone, drinking pints of ale at adjacent tables in the Widow's Son, at Bromley-by-Bow, during a tawdry Thursday evening of heavy and relentless rain. Much to his surprise, Maximilian found that after a few awkward stumbling moments, he was after all perfectly capable of engaging another person in conversation.

At first they talked about the difficulties of employment; the dreariness of waking up and forcing yourself into the workplace each morning, the tense exchanges with colleagues, the feeling of one's life gradually disappearing into a mass of tedious repetitive activity until your life was wrung of all value and seemed to recede into the far distance, like the shoreline of a country observed from a boat moving out into the sea.

Trevor, at that time, was working as an estate agent. He'd long since come to wish that he had chosen another career path, one that involved more creativity and freedom. Frequently, indeed, he would long for freedom, but he did not know how to go about finding it. Maximilian claimed to understand this predicament very well, and related some of his own experiences from his own brief period of employment (which had at this time concluded thirteen years previously). He applauded Trevor's attitude and stated that he hoped his situation might change for the better in the near future.

Maximilian went on to ask what forms of freedom Trevor would most like to engage in, if he could. At first this caused Trevor to stare into the middle distance and hold his head between his hands, giving out a series of ummms and ahhhs that successfully communicated a sense of confusion and indecision about how best to answer this question. Finally he responded that he really did not know, that he just felt that he would somehow like to be doing something else, whatever it happened to be.

Hoping to develop things a little further, Maximilian asked

Trevor what made him happy. He responded that football made him happy and that whenever West Ham, his team, won a match, that was enough to make his day seem worthwhile. He went on to say that the most important thing to consider in terms of his happiness, however, was women. On the few occasions that he had been fortunate enough to take a girl out on a date, he had found himself to be very happy indeed. Maximilian, having had extremely limited experience of this particular subject, remained silent, whilst Trevor was busy discussing the wonders of holding hands with women and even kissing them.

This being one of Maximilian's least favourite subjects, he was at pains to alter the course of the conversation as swiftly as he could, and he did so by taking advantage of the fact that they had both nearly finished drinking their respective pints of bitter ale. He offered to buy Trevor another one; Trevor having agreed, Maximilian moved temporarily to the vicinity of the bar to make the order, and, upon returning, launched into a lengthy disquisition on the subject of insects. Maximilian related the joy that he felt at contemplating the size of those creatures, the fact that they lived a nearly secret existence almost entirely neglected by human beings; that they were present everywhere, invisibly crawling and flying and scuttling, in immense profusion, although only rarely noted. Furthermore, he went on, was it not worth considering the difference in size between a human being and an ant? He began to expound in great detail on his sense of joy at being so much larger and more complicated than an ant. Apprehension of this fact, he felt, could make even the simplest attributes of the human being seem endlessly complex and fascinating.

Once Maximilian had finished his monologue on the subject, there was a moderate pause, followed by Trevor's beginning, with startling rapidity, to lament that his existence was worthless, that it would lead him nowhere, and wasn't life unbearably depressing? Why, in fact, should he go on? This went on for some time and elicited a certain amount of disgust on Maximilian's part. He seriously considered, and repeatedly, simply getting to his feet and walking wordlessly out of the premises. Why, after all, should he now be punished for his friendliness by being made to suffer through these impractical thoughts and observations? He came to the conclusion, however, that to abandon Trevor at such a juncture would be hypocritical, considering that Maximilian had nursed similarly negative sentiments himself, in the past. And yet, he reasoned, he had worked himself out of such thinking, albeit with a great effort of the will— Trevor would just have to do the same. He would have said as much, as soon as Trevor stopped talking, but Trevor did not stop talking, and so Maximilian remained there, listening, feeling that it would be impolite to do otherwise.

As soon as he saw an opening, Maximilian was immediately at pains to communicate certain things that he had learnt to this young man. He exhorted Trevor to be creative, to find any way of exploring the world, the human imagination. To find any way of escaping his sadness. He told Trevor of the excitement there was to be found in the process of accessing the vast body of knowledge which was available, for example, in his local library, and stressed the fact that this privilege was open to anyone. After this, he turned to his strongly held belief in the mystical properties of art. In creating artworks, he claimed, it was possible to have transcendent experiences, occasions that could prove entirely transformative for any individual, as long as they were prepared to devote themselves wholly to their work and the medium which it formed a part of, enduring great confusions and uncertainties, until finally, with patience and time, a sense of understanding might be reached, and the world might appear freshly, taking on a different character altogether.

Trevor responded with more than a little indifference to this advice, as if, Maximilian thought, he could not even muster the will to be excited, or to attempt to change his circumstances. By this time, he wasn't really listening to Maximilian. This was because he had become extremely drunk. He complained that he couldn't find the time to read, and that art didn't generally interest him very much. But he did say, mostly out of politeness, that he would try to have a look at some of the things that Maximilian was telling him about.

Oblivious to the sheepishness of this response, Maximilian felt encouraged to continue advising Trevor, in grandiloquent tones, recommending he engage, for another thing, in contemplating the infinite. He suggested that when one sat at a table it was possible to consider every table in the world, as well as every person who sat at every table, their vast variety of appearances and mannerisms, all engaged in a series of conversations or silences, which would inevitably range across most of the possible subjects addressed by human beings on this planet. He urged Trevor to consider that each table would necessarily be found in different surroundings and would have different objects placed upon it, would initially have been crafted from specific, individual pieces of wood or metal or stone, before becoming someone's property, and taking on its own distinctive history as certain people, and not others, sat around it, placed things upon it, spoke to one another in its vicinity, and perhaps even wrote or drew things directly onto its surface. When a table was considered in this way, said Maximilian, it became another entity altogether, and indeed a much more interesting one.

It was then that Trevor decided, for whatever reason, that he could not remain seated for a moment longer, and so said hurriedly to Maximilian that he was really sorry, but he was afraid that he had to be leaving, that he had work in the morning and that he needed to get some sleep, but it had been a pleasure to meet him and he hoped that perhaps they would run into each other again some time. And with that he swiftly shook Maximilian's hand, got up, and left.

Overall, Maximilian found their conversation underwhelming. He was reminded of his reasons for giving up conversation in the first place. At the same time, Trevor had sparked a desire to enter into the company of others once more, even if only in a limited capacity. In the nights to come, and even though he hadn't enjoyed the experience very much, Maximilian went over his talk with Trevor again and again, remembering certain things he had said, marvelling at the fact that he had managed to say them, feeling pleased with certain word choices and turns of phrase, still smiling at the thought of them many weeks later, even repeating them to himself in a low murmur as he took strolls around the city in the fading evening light.

For his part, Trevor soon put the conversation with Maximilian out of his mind. Now and then, for a few weeks after their meeting, he would consider Maximilian for a brief instant before immediately putting the experience of their dialogue behind him, shrugging it off as a strange and ultimately minor occasion, the likes of which he would most probably never see again. A few months after their meeting he met his future wife, Jill, and settled down to a life of servitude and domesticity. They had two children (Nick and Tracy) one cat (Ginger) and one dog (Bruce). Every now and then he would feel a sense of contentment with his life.

To Be Accepted As Truths

(1967–1968)

(The following aphorisms were composed by Maximilian one winter during a brief period of philosophical reflection. Originally he had intended this to be a project on a much larger scale, but he became distracted by other concerns, irrelevant to the following account. He recorded these thoughts in a 5½-by-7½-inch hardbound notebook containing ninety-four pages, with a pale green linen cover and dark brown leather elbows supporting the corners. Various pages were adorned by a number of stains believed to be spilt coffee. Each of the entries below was copied onto the notebook's pages in a precise hand and executed with green ink.)

Human society exists only as a consequence of happenstance, and so therefore there is nothing particularly noble or dignified about its social conventions.

Genuine states of liberty are always founded upon acts of destruction.

Our aesthetic configurations are so often a consequence of limited ideologies.

Words used in conversation often stray closer to a state of nakedness, and are more powerful in their blunt and awkward connotations, than they are when presented on the page.

There will always be tensions between the desire for individual freedom and the need for social organization.

The proper state of mind for any freethinking individual is one of frequent and delighted bewilderment.

Most of the standard measurements of human achievement indicate only the whims of a certain historical moment.

Our notions of justice should be flexible enough to allow for certain immoral practices.

When larger and larger numbers of possible forms of appropriation and consumption are available to us, our judgements can become so refined and individualised that they end up becoming minor tyrannies.

In future societies, a parade of abstractions will present themselves, accumulating in intensity over time, forcing everyone to merge with them.

Traditions maintained purely for their own sake can become the most sophisticated forms of decadence.

The creation of Utopias involves the stalling of all essential progress.

The denaturing processes of society which we encounter everyday can be appropriated as tools to fight innocence.

Every form of writing is interchangeable with every other one.

The widespread dissemination of photography causes the intricacies of physiology and anatomy to be forgotten altogether.

Nothing significant can be achieved without the presence of humour.

Sound is the most easily deceived of the senses because it is the subtlest.

A place is not a singular entity but a conglomeration of energies, histories and mental formulations.

When the imagination is exercised to its greatest extent, new possibilities for praxis will always emerge.

Playfulness is a more important and potentially *dangerous* quality than it is generally considered to be.

Mobilizing the Labour Force

(1968–1993)

One day Maximilian decided to set up his own employment agency. The only jobs on offer would be creative and intellectual ones, positions that hopefully stood a chance of being beneficial and enjoyable to the individuals who filled them. As it seemed obvious to him that the prevalent economic system would not be radically altered in the near future, he thought that he ought to at least attempt to help those who wanted to change society.

By the end of 1968, having followed the newspaper accounts of radical unrest during the period with great fascination, Maximilian came to believe wholeheartedly that the opening of an employment agency was a far more constructive form of political behaviour than rioting and protesting. Whilst he had enormous sympathy for the generation of students and young people who were engaging in demonstrations, he felt that, ultimately, they had no real plan in place for instigating real progress. Few of the young people of the day seemed ready to accept that it would always be necessary for humans to perform certain acts of labour. The problem, as he saw it, lay in the fact that the available forms of employment were with few exceptions unsatisfactory to anyone in possession of a properly functioning intellect.

Paying considerably more than most employers of the day, Maximilian invented a range of temporary positions whose duties included library research, the preparation of exhibitions, visits to museums, scouting expeditions across the city, the formation of political debating groups, as well as anything else that happened to pass through his head.

The day-to-day operations of the agency were overseen by two undergraduates recruited from Hornsey Art College—Chris Jenkins and John Groves. That autumn, Chris had come across a tiny note handwritten in purple ink and pinned to a neglected corner of a college notice board. As the two young men were the only respondents to this notice—one of a number left in a variety of locations—Maximilian had already decided to give them the job prior to their interview, without a thought as to their actual qualifications. However, he had stressed on his notice that those candidates selected for the positions would have to abandon their studies immediately. Chris and John were quite ready to make such a move.

Their interview was conducted in a café on the Kingsland Road and lasted for just under a quarter of an hour. No specific "skills" or forms of "relevant experience" were required for the positions. Maximilian told his applicants that he merely expected to see a reasonable display of enthusiasm and gentility, combined with a genuine interest in both radical politics and the avant-garde. During the course of their meeting (the only one that they would ever have with their employer), Maximilian had asked the young men a few brief questions about their artistic preferences, their general aspirations for the future and the political stances that they would take in a series of hypothetical situations. After this he handed them two large brown paper envelopes, each of which contained an eighty-three page document prepared especially for the occasion. Grinning, he told them that both of their interviews had been successful. Muttering, almost to himself, that he had some business to be attending to elsewhere, he then rose from the table, shook both of their hands at length and told them that he would soon be in touch. All of their subsequent dealings with him would be conducted either over the telephone or via the postal service.

Inside the eighty-three page "briefings" Chris and John were to discover some imposingly detailed directions for commencing their work. The following Monday they were to move into an office in Mayfair, and there they would begin to promote the agency and process applications. Not a single CV would pass through their hands without being given serious consideration, and, likewise, all materials would be forwarded to a P.O. box belonging to Maximilian. Chris and John might make recommendations, but ultimately the decisions as to who would be employed and in what capacity were to be made by Maximilian alone.

Outwardly, the office looked like any other. Many individuals arrived and departed under the impression that they had entered an altogether ordinary and legitimate business in which people were being quietly exploited, just as they were anywhere else. No pictures or ornaments decorated the walls. At all times the desks were cluttered with tall piles of paper. At first, in order to please their employer, Chris and John always wore suits and were at pains to appear fastidiously professional. Yet office hours were only to be from 10:30 A.M. to 3:30 P.M. Monday to Wednesday, with an hour reserved for lunch in the middle of the day.

From their first meeting on, both young men were convinced that Maximilian was clinically insane. Never once did it occur to them that there might have been a philanthropic basis for his peculiar behaviour. They thought that he was simply amusing himself. Not that they minded, especially, seeing as their salaries were generous enough to ensure their complicity for some time. There was no question whatsoever of their acting contrary to his wishes. In any case, he didn't really expect all that much from them.

After a while, they took to ignoring any part of their job unrelated to Maximilian himself—keeping him happy, as it were, for the brief periods they were actually in direct communication. Everything else was considered a waste of time. For example, they soon discovered that they could not afford to stay home during office hours, because Maximilian would phone them almost every day at random intervals merely in order to check that they were present, even cheerfully informing them on occasion that he was studying their actions through a pair of binoculars. Having finished all of their work for the week, come Wednesday they would put their feet up on their desks and smoke a little hashish, whilst waiting for the familiar voice of

Maximilian to arise at the other end of the telephone line.

One of the first things they did, as managers of the agency, was to ensure that all of their friends were employed. These friends in turn brought their own friends to the office, who in turn brought their own, and so on. This cycle continued for a few weeks until precisely one thousand people had been placed on the agency's books. At this point Maximilian decreed that it was necessary to stop collecting names, as the number already amassed was as much as he could comfortably administrate. He would have liked to employ many more people than this, of course, but that seemed to be too perilous an exercise for him to seriously consider: it would take so little for the enterprise to dissolve into chaos.

With a sense of humour that he hoped was not lost on his employees, Maximilian ensured that they were kept busy with a series of tasks that were frequently absurd in character. An employee might spend the day investigating the physical properties of plastic geese, or have to consider the scale of chewing gum use in particular train stations in the north-west of the city. Still, Maximilian was careful to be sure that, however ridiculous, his invented assignments usually had an intellectual component. Hundreds of people were sent to libraries to do research into inexplicable but precisely delineated topics, generally in aid of one of Maximilian's other on-going projects. And then, other groups would be tasked with investigating certain sites in the city, their purviews often restricted to a single street or building, on which Maximilian would demand a detailed "report." This meant a combination of photographs, a dossier of facts (contemporary geography, historical notes) and prosaic description. These reports became Maximilian's bedtime reading. Flipping through them, he would start with the photographs, giving them not much more than a glance, mainly in order to see if they depicted anywhere that seemed especially attractive to him, or else anywhere he could not recognise. If he happened to pick out a report that he felt had not been researched properly, or else didn't make any real sense, according to his own standard, then its author would be reprimanded with a stern written warning, stating that they would only be given one more chance, and if their next report contained the same mistakes, they were to be struck off the list immediately.

As a consequence of their newfound economic status, Chris and John came to enjoy highly privileged social lives of a most unusual kind. Without exception they were adored by those they helped to employ. Their inner circle became extremely tight-knit, meeting regularly to throw parties and generally cause mayhem. But as the years wore on and everyone became more or less dependant on the income provided by Maximilian, certain members of the circle developed a tendency toward paranoia. In many cases it was now necessary for them to provide for children and make payments on mortgages. It was hard for them not to wonder who their anonymous benefactor was and how long he intended to continue to ensure their survival. Nevertheless, the payments went on—for a time. And if anyone needed a reference to show to any sort of real employer then Chris and John would supply it, though lying about the nature of the work they'd done.

After a few years of this, Maximilian decided to let his employees request particular jobs. Once a month he would receive a flurry of forms on which outlines of these were written, with suggestions of possible wages placed in brackets. Any ideas that struck Maximilian as being excessively flippant in character were responded to with a flippant note of his own. But requests deemed "sensible" by him were often granted for short periods before he reassigned those individuals back to his own projects. In general he would only allow a request to be granted if he believed that it would be of sufficient value to the "growth" of the person who had suggested it. All requests of a lewd nature were discarded immediately.

Maximilian often considered the agency to be his most significant achievement. It was the epitome of effecting direct and positive change in the lives of others. While this endeavour was unlikely to have any lasting importance—unlike, for instance, a work of art—he felt proud that he had given a handful of individuals a taste of something very like freedom. He believed this was about as much as anyone could hope to accomplish for another human being.

One day, early in 1993, Maximilian's telephone calls to the office ceased without warning. At first Chris and John hardly noticed. Soon enough it occurred to them that they hadn't heard the boss's voice for a fortnight. As it turned out, they were never to hear from Maximilian again. Their aloof employer had now vanished entirely.

Many times over the years, Chris and John had attempted to engage Maximilian in a proper conversation, but they found it was impossible for them to lead him onto any subject that did not in some way involve their "business" together. At first they had felt some bitterness about this, but they had later come to accept it as one of their employer's many eccentricities. After his disappearance, however, that bitterness revived and became rage. Maximilian had provided routine and sustenance for so long, and for so many people, and now all of them had been cast into the void.

Abandoned Projects of Minor Significance

(1969–1983)

Amongst the more important of Maximilian's abandoned projects during this period we can include the following:

– For three months he took up playing Bar Billiards with the intention of entering a national competition, but he found himself giving up hope that he would ever achieve a high enough standard to make his efforts worthwhile.

– After spending a number of years practising the art of walking on his hands he considered the possibility of embarking upon a long voyage undertaken in this manner, but he suspected he was at risk of becoming famous.

– He collected examples of mammals that the General Public of the British Isles was extremely unfamiliar with. These included quolls, tarsiers, solenodons, bandicoots, and lorids. He had hoped that he might open a small zoo dedicated to these little known species, but he found the experience of having the animals in his home too disturbing to endure for long and so abandoned the project altogether.

– For a while he attempted to form a system which would ensure continuous success whenever he played bingo. Merging together strands of research he had undertaken in the fields of statistics, anthropology, and telepathy he believed that he was beginning to discern a variety of patterns which might eventually enable him to make considerable financial gains, but his researches never progressed beyond the preliminary stages.

– Occasionally he would return to the project of inventing his own ice cream flavours. Gastronomy was generally of very little interest to him, but ice cream was an unusual exception. His flavours included quince, zabaglione, sherbet, and brown bread. Whilst the results were very interesting, they were rarely exceptional.

– In 1973 he studied for a degree in Philosophy at the University of London without being enrolled on any of the courses. After diligently attending every lecture for many months the common assumption was that he was evidently a legitimate student, even if a slightly old-looking one. But as it would not be possible for him to obtain the degree, he gave up his studies after two terms.

– He left tiny slips of paper all over his bedroom. On each of them he had written messages in scrawly lines of black ink to potential future versions of himself. There were so many slips of paper that it would be impossible for him to remember the precise contents of all of them. Bewilderment and surprise would surely be inevitable. Despite intending to write 1,000 of them he stopped at 587.

– Reading through nearly every book available on the subject of levitation he discovered to his disappointment that none of them seemed to lead towards any real methods of flight.

– He took to making his way onto the roofs of public buildings, visiting locations that often possessed superb visual panoramas. In the aftermath of every successful ascension he would feel victorious and elated, usually feeding off this energy for some days. He successfully reached the roofs of Somerset House, the Criterion Theatre, Alexandra Palace, and the Brent Cross Shopping Centre, but he gave up this pursuit after being forced to flee security guards on a number of occasions.

– Inventing his own onomatopoeic words, he began to create an entire dictionary of them. Coming upon the realisation that words were always an abstract entity, separate from the things that they represented, he first of all learnt of the many different words for "woof" in a number of European languages, discovering that it could be translated as "au" (Portuguese), "jaff" (Bulgarian), "ghav" (Greek), and "haf" (Czech). So he took to inventing his own terms for describing the sound of a door opening, of wind passing through trees, of footsteps pattering against a floor. In the end he abandoned the dictionary, as there were too many sounds to contemplate and eventually the experience had become maddening.

– In 1978 he purchased a double-decker bus that was no longer in service. That summer it became his home as he followed roads running parallel to the north-east coast of Scotland. A part of him had firmly intended to travel all the way to Hong Kong the following year, but he never found the confidence to leave the country.

– He attempted some primitive experiments in composing his own electronic music. Bleeps, crackles, and blips echoed against the walls of his living room, occasionally reaching the ears of his neighbours, who generally felt quietly threatened and alarmed. All in all, he could see that this project had not been any sort of success.

– He wrote the first draft of a realist play that was to be performed on board a submarine at the bottom of the Pacific Ocean, but finally he felt that given his lack of first-hand experience of the subject, he was incapable of achieving any kind of authenticity.

– In 1983 he spent hundreds of hours inscribing Socialist slogans across the walls of public toilet cubicles all over the city. Disappointed at the lack of societal change that his actions seemed to be causing, he gave up despondently and returned to other concerns.

Brief Communications with the Populace

(1970–1980)

Every last morning during the 1970s, after eating his breakfast, but before performing his ablutions, Maximilian would sit himself down in his armchair, where he would spend approximately half an hour writing postcards, to thousands of people across the city whom he had never met.

Whilst composing his messages, he would never have any particular person in mind, but, rather, would focus on a different area of the city every month, tailoring his communications to his ideas about each place, forming a secret dialogue with London based upon words overheard in pubs, contemporary films set in the relevant locations, and articles read in local newspapers. Carefully attending to the nuances of a given neighbourhood, Maximilian would meditate upon the attitudes that had seemed most prevalent on the appropriate streets when last he'd passed through them, as though he were in fact addressing these mindsets themselves, made flesh. Names and numbers were practically an afterthought, only added once it was time for the postcards to be sent.

No two of his messages were ever the same. His mind would range across a vast array of subjects and ideas, jumping with ease from one region of thought to another, condensing years of musings into short paragraphs, sometimes single sentences, in the hope that some of them might provoke further thoughts within the minds of others, perhaps even the occasional moment of joy. Each postcard was written out twice, so that he always had a duplicate in his files. These were placed inside one of hundreds of large linen albums arranged in orderly rows along the floor opposite his bed. He also kept a ledger in which he would carefully copy down the date, the area to which he intended to send a given card, and then, in shorthand, a few indications of the general subject matter employed in his missive, so that he was sure to never repeat himself. After a few years of practice, he became proficient enough to be able to finish five cards within the space of three minutes.

Each postcard took the standard size: a rectangle measuring about 150mm x 100mm. For the most part, in terms of the "fronts" of the cards, he favoured those with photographs over reproductions of artworks in other media, believing that this was not the ideal way in which to make one's first acquaintance with a drawing or a painting. In his opinion, already striking photographs became even more so in this form, and would be all the more likely to lead his recipients to take notice of them and then read what was written on their backs with attention. Inevitably, he reused certain images many times over, as the postcard manufacturers of the time couldn't keep up with Maximilian's appetite for their product; even so, he tried to vary his images as much as was possible, a policy that resulted in his sending many postcards he wouldn't otherwise have employed: cards that might, he worried, court too quick a dismissal, thanks to their obvious ugliness or banality.

Maximilian's messages touched on almost every topic he had ever thought or imagined, at times veering towards the very edges of rationality in an effort to instigate any sort of sincere response. Each of his cards began with the words, "We don't know each other," in order to clarify the social terms of the communication. After this preliminary, Maximilian often liked to assail his readers with questions, forcing them to confront themselves, the world, their situation. Quotations also featured regularly, and on some mornings he would launch into his task with arms laden with esoteric literature, which Maximilian would proceed to open at random, choosing sentences that happened to appeal to him at the moment of composition. On other occasions he would record whatever thoughts came to him while considering the image on the front of his current postcard; on others still, he would indulge in fragments of narrative, descriptive paragraphs, tiny dialogues, impromptu aphorisms.

Inspiration rarely failed him, as there were always more subjects to discuss, other ways of defining, exclaiming, elucidating. On the rare occasions he was feeling a bit lazy, he would rewrite old messages, changing the wording of a previous postcard ever so slightly to create a message that, strictly speaking, could still be considered unique. A single thought might be repeated in thousands of different ways before Maximilian finally exhausted whatever interest it had originally held.

From the very beginning, he made the firm decision not to send any of his postcards until the '70s had come to their conclusion. He wanted to see how it would feel to repeat an activity for the duration of a decade—not a day more or less. The exercise, he thought, would serve as a method for gauging the meaning of mortality, at least as it related to him: it would force him to pay continuous attention to the fact of time's passing. He also hoped that the practice of writing would focus his attentions usefully each morning, exercising his mental energies in a way that he would be able to apply elsewhere.

All of the postcards would be sent out on the same day, in early January, 1980. This singularity would unify all of the recipients, even if they were unlikely to be aware of this fact. Maximilian's intention was that his cards would send out a series of subliminal psychic waves, spreading silently through the metropolis, reaching out to gently usher the populace in the direction of his cherished concepts of "freedom" and "imagination" by, paradoxically, employing a sort of mass hypnosis to bring the citizens of London under his beneficent sway. In this case, Maximilian accepted in advance that his ambition was destined to fail, but did not let this interfere with carrying out his plan.

Gradually he came to find himself compromising his living space merely in order to continue with the project. In the end the postcards took over three rooms in the bungalow, stacked in hundreds of gigantic towers that were at risk of toppling to the ground should the slightest motion ever occur in their vicinity. He could not help but remonstrate with himself from time to time for taking on this particular scheme.

So many times over the decade he imagined how it would feel once he had sent all of the postcards. They would reach households in every last corner of the city, at every social stratum, speaking to every kind of personality and temperament, in every possible situation. They would reach people who were waking up to difficult circumstances, whilst others would be merrily celebrating their birthdays. One sort of person might be delighted by his or her message, while others might conceivably feel disgust. Maximilian felt certain that many, perhaps most of the cards would simply be thrown away with a grunt, never to be seen or thought of again. But, then, inevitably, some of the recipients would be interested in what he'd had to say, and he wondered how many of these there would be, persons who felt that they had gained something from the experience.

In sending them at the turning of a decade, Maximilian's intent, as much as to edify or confuse, was to have the cards serve as a form of greeting, marking the onset of a new and significant, if arbitrarily delineated, period of time, with an act of friendship and community. Somehow, he persisted in believing that a few of the recipients would manage to recognise what he had done and see it as a statement, a declaration of the importance of the imagination, a condemnation of cynicism and alienation. At the same time, considered as a series of individual communications, it was such a small gesture, only a very minor occasion in most people's lives, if they noticed it at all. It would be a fleeting moment of confusion or pleasure, almost certainly destined to be forgotten long before the new decade reached its conclusion.

When 1980 finally arrived, a date Maximilian had wondered if he would live to see, he found himself feeling more than a little daunted by the logistics of sending all of the cards. He spent many months preparing the day of their release, planning every last detail, tracing lines across a succession of maps, working out an extremely precise route, taking careful note of the traffic patterns in certain places at certain times of day, and any other potential hazards that he might encounter. Batches of the cards would be deposited in thousands of different postboxes around the city. He was worried that if he didn't distribute them equally between the different postal regions, the postal service was likely to become suspicious or angry, thanks to the sudden and enormous influx of work, and even refuse to carry the cards to their destinations. Eventually Maximilian even decided to memorize the names of every street that he would follow during the day, in the order he would take them, so that he might lessen the possibility of getting lost or falling behind schedule.

When the time came, his journey commenced at 11 P.M. on Wednesday, the 2nd of January, 1980. Working his way through the night, he had already deposited batches of postcards into 482 different postboxes before the first post was collected in the morning at 6 A.M. Driving through the abandoned streets, Maximilian encountered a strange nocturnal realm that felt as if it were almost his own creation. Surely, he thought, no one could ever have seen London in quite the same way before. He could not help but think of all of the slumbering figures lying everywhere around him, hidden behind heavy walls and locked doors, oblivious to his presence, even though in many cases they would soon come to be the beneficiaries of his present frenzy of activity.

The subsequent hours were immensely difficult. In all of his years of working diligently at obscure schemes, Maximilian had never before experienced such tiredness. It was a day of relentless hard work. As he travelled from one postbox to another and then another and another and another, he was reminded of the long-forgotten monotony of his first and last proper job. Once more he found himself gazing into the abyss of identical actions, the infinite series of repetitions that eventually led to an inevitable emptiness and conformity, until the possibility of anything actually changing seemed so remote and obscure as to be a laughable prospect, one perhaps even worthy of contempt.

Moving from one district to another all day long, Maximilian found himself increasingly at a loss for places in which to park his car; more often than not he would simply leave it running in the middle of the road whilst he rushed to the pavement, stuffing his postcards through the mail slots as rapidly as possible, hoping that no one would notice, before hurrying back to his car and progressing, sometimes only a few hundred metres, towards his next destination.

It proved to be exceptionally difficult for him to keep up his concentration. At one point in the late afternoon, he was attempting to find his way from Shepherd's Bush to Putney; after taking a wrong turn, he realized with some desperation that he had no idea where he was. Maximilian was astounded that, despite his intimate knowledge of the city, he was still susceptible to such mishaps. He lost nearly an hour, navigating through unknown streets, so consumed with nervous agitation that he began to make further wrong turnings, after which he became genuinely worried that he would never again find himself back in his own familiar city. Finally he discovered a route back to Notting Hill, and he compensated for his wasted time by stuffing the last postboxes he visited with a greater number of his postcards than planned.

When at last he went home, he had left batches of postcards in 1,958 different postboxes, inciting the anger of 631 motorists and three policemen, not to mention postal workers, who of course noticed what he had done, in time, and reported it to the tabloids, where it ran as a minor story, being described for the most part within the length of a single paragraph.

Maximilian felt exhausted, spent. He suspected he would be incapable of strenuous activity for some days to come. Retreating back to the bungalow, he sank into his armchair, where he listened to melancholy records for the rest of the evening. Drifting towards sleep, he reviewed all that he had accomplished that day, the endless succession of streets observed at numerous points of time, seen in a great many different gradations of light, until night had finally descended once more. Although he was excited by the idea of people waking up to discover his messages, his sense of loss was considerable. He was still not altogether sure how he would fill the gap left in his life by abandoning his postcard work. From now on his mornings would surely feel bereft of activity. The time he had invested in the project could not now be recovered, despite the extensive records Maximilian had kept. He had never really considered how painful this particular evening might feel.

Watching the records revolve upon his turntable, he weighed up his achievement. He had managed to communicate with many thousands of strangers, a feat that few could claim. Now, too, he felt that he really did know more about what it would mean for him to die. However, in the end, perhaps there was nothing much to it. Perhaps it was foolish to attempt any grandiose justification of his actions. He shouldn't forget, he admonished himself, that the whole exercise had been based upon the whim of a single distant afternoon. A part of him believed that he had only behaved like this for his own perverse amusement in order to make himself smile for a moment or so once he had finally reached old age. Wasn't that all it came down to, really? An ephemeral act which would probably never be appreciated or even noticed by anyone, almost certainly resulting in no sort of reaction, no reply, and consequently being entirely futile. Yes, at the decisive moment, when he should have felt pleased with himself, Maximilian could only feel a sense of disappointment. He was convinced that the entire scheme had only been a way of wasting a little time each morning for many years. Perhaps it had only been an act that was tantamount to yawning.

Things He Made no Record of

(1971–1973)

(His sudden longings for days walking up and down hills, his various encounters with the aroma of frying onions, the tiny buttons which so frequently fell from his coat, unknown species of crustaceans discovered when strolling through the stalls of Billingsgate Fish Market, the tendency of his pocket radio to miraculously discover mysterious broadcasts from distant countries, the many sublime uses of vinegar, the ways in which plastic globes are touched and surveyed by children, his desire for the eradication of all worthless municipal bylaws, the cheerfulness of colour-coding systems, expeditions undertaken on foot for several miles solely in order to view particular plaques, imagined arguments between ornithologists, beautiful stratagems and schemings and manipulations, an old man in a pale green suit shuffling in the street, voluminous supplementary appendages contributing nothing to that which they supplement, peeling wallpaper with exquisite floral designs, the precise recollections of dentists, the wetness lingering underneath the tongues of pumas, an umbrella unfolded and scattering rain, intimations of the daydreams that might be encountered at high altitudes, cloudy thumbprints left on a windowpane, certain pairs of brightly coloured spectacle frames noticed on the noses of young women, the lack of profound historical events associated with zebra crossings, the pleasing aspects of T-shirts decorated with horizontal stripes, consolatory contradictions, appreciation of kite flying and its various practitioners, an encounter with a blind accordion player inside a pub bearing the odour of moths and old teeth and which resulted in a misunderstanding about the rightful ownership of a tumbler of rum, noting a moderate decline in the already miserly percentage of men who wear hats, considerations of almost any manufactured commodity as a microcosm of a given nation, the places in which shadows fall gravidly upon wooden shutters, silver encrustations formed in white laboratories, navigations of the city undertaken with a brass compass, vestiges of fallen epochs lying resident in steam-rooms, quiet urinations in the vicinity of public monuments, the process of the enculturation of ornamental glass objects, the ranking of publications in order of smallest total circulation, thoughts concerning the precise number of brands of breadsticks available to the restaurants of the West End, the magisterial air of eminent librarians, the density and quality of pillows, the inevitable problems that arise from refusing to sing, a yellow starfish placed on an oak dresser, nocturnal divagations and peregrinations, street corners and their atmosphere upon one's first standing at them, congregations of secret parliaments, arrangements of converging lattices, crowdings of barely perceptible memories, the vastness of oblivion represented by a valley of stones, the stench of steam and clean white linen, a cat with milky green eyes following him dutifully through a neighbourhood and staring at him imploringly with a look so inquisitive it could almost have passed for speech.)

The Repository of Words

(1972–1989)

Frustrated by the scarcity of print resources available to the public, Maximilian decided to found his own library. Once completed, it would be by some distance the largest free lending library in London. Admission would be open to anyone who had not yet proved themselves to be a troublemaker. All in all, it surprised him that such an important project hadn't occurred to him sooner. In the midst of his furious researches in the British Museum Reading Room, he had discovered that the vast majority of published books were kept well hidden from public view. Knowledge was an asset extremely difficult for most people to acquire.

There were, after all, so many obstacles in place. Maximilian became very cynical when he took a moment to consider that this state of affairs was enforced by governments who routinely spent enormous sums on training and equipping their militaries, on building civic infrastructures more than a little harmful to the environment, on maintaining police forces that (as an aside to their other activities) helped to keep the population in a state of docile conformity; not to mention the fostering of economic systems which barely gave individuals the time or the energy to read—should many books even be available to them. As far as Maximilian was concerned, it was no mere accident that so few books were available at the public lending libraries of the British Isles. This was a subtle, probably unconscious method for exercising an instinctive and very powerful form of mind control, an activity perfected long ago by the ruling classes.

Maximilian firmly believed that books were the key to all genuine advancement, whether personal or societal. He created the library in order to enable a few more individuals to achieve forms of personal liberation one day, once his actions had been discovered. He firmly believed that it was only by presenting readers with row after row after row of inviting volumes that the full scale of existence could be successfully communicated to anyone. It was really only when books could be glanced at, picked up, flicked through, and smelt, that an individual might begin to piece together some idea of their metaphysical situation. He knew first-hand, from his own experiences as an adolescent, that a single book could bring miraculous transformative powers to bear on one's life, leading towards the next text, and the next, until the contours of one's world had widened.

As soon as the idea for the library had taken hold, he began to gather together copies of as many books as he could get his hands on, ignoring any obvious criteria for selection. Purchasing from all available sources, in enormous quantities, he often took to certain titles over others for what even he considered very dubious reasons. He might buy a book merely because the author's name happened to appeal to him at the moment that he saw it printed on the spine, or because the cover illustration reminded him of the details of an afternoon from his childhood. Precious antiquarian volumes were placed beside modern illustrated DIY manuals; slim political tracts rubbed shoulders with books describing the habits of goldfish; there was an abundance of anthologies of Dutch anthropological writing, and various nineteenth-century dissertations on what ought to be considered the proper forms of social conduct when seated at table. Careful to include anything that anyone might have even a passing interest in, the collection soon expanded to include vast numbers of forgotten and unusual works.

So many titles passed through his hands that he developed a vertiginous dizziness. When enormous regions of knowledge are constantly hidden from view, the experience of discovering them can be quite a disconcerting one. All he had once taken for granted was now thrown into doubt. Words could no longer be relied upon to designate specific meanings, such was the previously unsuspected scale of their potential use. He could no longer think of the medium of text as he once had. Often now he felt absolute indifference towards authors whose work he would once have appreciated, and many "great" authors' voices now seemed minute to him, like tiny islands possessing only a single inhabitant.

His collection was stored in a warehouse in Clerkenwell. He had a series of small rooms built up within the space, each of them holding different numbers of books, some with substantial holdings based around a particular theme, others containing just a few chairs and only three or four titles on their otherwise empty shelves. Each room was painted in a different shade; each had a different painting framed upon its wall. These few small rooms gave way to the enormous, largely unconverted spaces in which hundreds of books were piled on top of each other and could only be reached by ladders. Handwritten signs in ornate calligraphy encouraged different forms of loitering, browsing, dawdling, and mingling. Hammocks and sofas were scattered across the space so that visitors might feel invited to read for as long as they liked. Figurines, bowls, and plants served as a series of "real-life" adornments amidst so many words. Certain areas were set aside for serious forms of work and scholarship and these were to be entirely silent. Millions of volumes came to line the shelves, and Maximilian suggested (in a bound document entitled *Proposed Rules of Conduct for the Library*), that every ten years, on New Year's Day, the majority of the books should be given away by lottery, to be replaced with a range of new, unexpected titles.

It was not meant to be a comprehensive collection. Whilst it would point the way towards the vast totality of printed matter available in the world, those seeking definitive collections would have to venture farther afield. Maximilian wanted the library to focus on the "random," the masses of ignored authors and subjects that formed the basis of the majority of the collections in the world's libraries. (When he had finished assembling the first catalogue of his institution, Maximilian realised that there were hundreds of volumes about the history of Hawaii, but not a single work that could be attributed to William Shakespeare.) Likewise, by making only haphazard acquisitions, Maximilian hoped to ensure his institution's impartiality: it should, he believed, reflect no one's taste and embody no sort of agenda. This was not something that he came even slightly close to achieving, but he thought that to at least aspire towards this aim was noble.

There was no question of using any of the standard methods of classifying and organizing the books. As far as Maximilian was concerned, the Dewey Decimal System made very little sense, with its frequent reliance upon obscure designations in order to create more and more precise, but no less arbitrary, categories. He gleefully put together a list of categorizations that he felt certain had no equal in any other library. His method was based on instinct; he would set aside groups of books, titles that he *felt* must exist beneath some as yet unknown heading that would in time occur to him if only he gave it enough thought. The essential ruling principal in his library's organization was this: that all categories be as arcane as possible, even—perhaps ideally—meaningless. All other considerations were quite remote from Maximilian's thinking.

There were, at the simplest level, the books that happened to have similar images on their covers, or which had been published during the course of the same year; but then there were the collections of books catalogued as "pleasurable articles devoid of all real suffering" (.2874639), books that "have most probably been read by fewer than one hundred people" (.9478250), that "may contain several references to tigers" (.6478933), that "could be used as evidence in support of the hypothesis that all human beings are secretly embarrassed by their bodies" (.0578239), or as "templates for future societies that our mothers never dreamed of" (.7826347), and then those that "might be worth a glance . . . but I wouldn't know for sure" (.2784091).

Gradually he catalogued everything, typing up all of the details carefully onto individual file cards. Anyone who searched through the catalogue with care would discover that most of the categories merely involved the grouping together of titles that Maximilian had never read, but there were a few that involved highly personal and thoughtful selections of books that he evidently loved.

Books—as he had cause to consider, with deep sadness, at regular intervals—were crucial arbiters in determining class roles. Knowledge of the true scale of literature was often dependent on the social strata that you happened to belong to from birth, the levels of education which you passed through, the pitch and style and content of the talking voices which you mingled with from childhood to death. Books would have to appear on the shelves in the rooms that you inhabited, would have to be read by those in your vicinity, forming an accepted part of the social interactions taking place around you whilst you were brought up. Otherwise it became more and more difficult to enter the labyrinth of words.

Again and again during the process of setting up his library, Maximilian found himself marvelling at the veritable endlessness of the medium of writing, of books and the writing of books. The body of literature was so vast that it could never be fully known; its character could never be clearly discerned, even its outlines could barely be grasped with any coherence. Nevertheless, and despite the state of near-continual neglect accorded most books, every one of them was of potential interest to *somebody*, and their authors could always be discovered in some form, living resident within the pages, where, for better or worse, so many people had deposited aspects of themselves for the duration of history. Their jokes, insights, prejudices, failures, and marvels lay there on the page waiting to be encountered. How remarkably unlikely it was that anyone had ever managed to communicate anything of value amidst such a gallimaufry, such a wild profusion—how incredible that anyone had managed, indeed, to convince readers like himself of the *importance* of these works, had managed to make readers see their own lives reflected in these texts. This struck him as a highly unlikely fact about the world.

On the Planet Everybody Calls Home

(1973)

(Maximilian was responsible for the composition of only a single song over the course of his career, which was performed on only one occasion, the 17th of August of the above year, in the immediate environs of Wimbledon Underground Station. Passers-by responded with a generosity that took him entirely by surprise.)

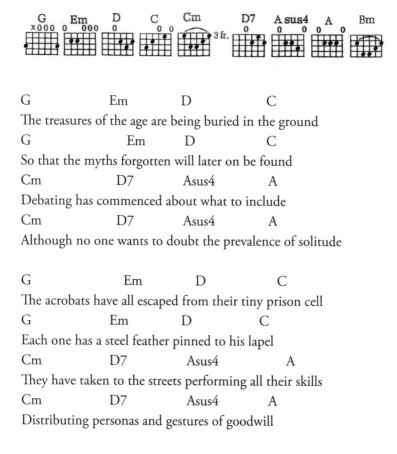

```
G          Em         D          C
```
The treasures of the age are being buried in the ground
```
G          Em         D          C
```
So that the myths forgotten will later on be found
```
Cm         D7         Asus4      A
```
Debating has commenced about what to include
```
Cm         D7         Asus4      A
```
Although no one wants to doubt the prevalence of solitude


```
G          Em         D          C
```
The acrobats have all escaped from their tiny prison cell
```
G          Em         D          C
```
Each one has a steel feather pinned to his lapel
```
Cm         D7         Asus4          A
```
They have taken to the streets performing all their skills
```
Cm         D7         Asus4      A
```
Distributing personas and gestures of goodwill

Bm   D   C   Em
CHORUS: On the Planet Everybody Calls Home (x 2)

Vehicles of transportation are zigzagging through the night
Carrying abstract sentiments all glittering and bright
Moving towards small villages selected only for their names
Sent there by a gentleman pointing an old Malacca cane

In the temples groups of storytellers gather with their wares
Their reverberating voices ringing loudly in the air
The crowds that listen at their feet are hanging on each word
Afterwards they'll re-enact all that they have heard

CHORUS: On the Planet Everybody Calls Home (x 2)

Plans for new state institutions are created every day
By the powerful and noble the one's who have to have their say
Fantasies operational for one week at a time
Before tumbling into chaos having never reached their prime

The reporters are all busy gazing through long telescopes
In the process they discover they have become misanthropes
The visions that they're seeing, have led them to believe
That from many different angles they had all been quite deceived

CHORUS: On the Planet Everybody Calls Home (x 2)

In the thickly crowded taverns of forgotten villages
The patriarchs and young men exercise their privilege
In small rooms lit by lanterns they are rolling on the floors
Sleeping under tables and breaking into snores

The Escapologist is trapped inside a giant silver bell

Her time is nearly over she is not feeling quite well
Remembering her past in thick and urgent waves
She considers the mistakes she will be taking to her grave

CHORUS: On the Planet Everybody Calls Home (x 2)

Cities of the sacred hold great visions of allure
Maidens line the alleyways all pouting and demure
An opalescent tomb is lying in a hidden chamber
Battalions of clowns are busy sweating with their labours

In the crystalline-blue bathrooms in the palace of the queen
Take nothing for granted, things are not quite as they seem
In the folds of the vast mirrors are the imprints of the dead
Hiding traces of the men she killed for things that they had said

CHORUS: On the Planet Everybody Calls Home (x 2)

The streets are filled with signs that illustrate malaise
With symbols formed from circles or a calculated phrase
They appear at random junctures held aloft by metal poles
Representing forms of warning, subtle systems of control

When a cat crosses a courtyard at the same time as a goat
This is said to be propitious, a secret antidote
To the evils that are spoiling, the lives of those who'd seen
And for fifteen days they'll prosper, becoming things they had not been

CHORUS: On the Planet Everybody Calls Home (x 2)

The prophecies of shoeshine boys spelt out with a trembling hand
On a Ouija board at midnight in a brokendown bandstand
Verbose communications causing bewilderment

Provoking transformations leading to enlightenment
Children run in circles, over an empty beach
Making handstands and cartwheels, sprinting out of reach
After building vast sand castles, crowned with seaweed and white shells
They've agreed to leave their parents, without saying their farewells

CHORUS: On the Planet Everybody Calls Home (x 6)

Acts of Industrial Sabotage

(1974–1995)

From that year on, Maximilian commenced an impassioned and sustained campaign to sabotage the workings of capitalism. Of course, while he realised with some disappointment that it would probably be quite impossible for him to dismantle the entire edifice of capitalism single-handedly, he felt that he should at least make his own private protest. There was no reason he could think of, morally speaking, not to create as many problems as possible for the various big business concerns that he had chosen to target. He discovered that he had a positive genius for acts of deception and, broadly speaking, mischief. Making the lives of other people slightly more difficult proved far easier than making them slightly less so, and indeed helped Maximilian to achieve an equilibrium of his own, after several other projects failed to come to satisfactory conclusions.

Employing his customary discretion, Maximilian was again successful in keeping his involvement entirely secret. Over time he would come to compose many thousands of letters to business executives, outlining his deep disgust at their behaviour. Whilst he was aware that the majority of these communications would never reach their intended recipients, being seen and destroyed first by any one of an army of secretaries and other interceptors, he persisted in sending his letters, feeling that in forcing these sentiments into the grand organs of commerce, and with such regularity, he was despite everything pushing certain ideas into places where they would not otherwise be encountered. Short of engaging in direct or violent protest, which, as he had already noted, did little good, and often only encouraged oligarchs in their various vapid assumptions, he felt that this letter writing might if nothing else disrupt the thought patterns of those who worked within these influential organisations. To be told, he thought, on a regular basis, that one's actions were corrupting the very nature of one's soul, could surely not fail to have some sort of impact?

So much of his life seemed reducible to just such futilities. As some people are in the habit of speaking to dogs much as they would to other human beings, laying clause upon clause as though the canine species were fully capable of parsing such intricacies, so too did Maximilian continually persist in calling upon the deaf and uncomprehending, believing despite all evidence to the contrary that perhaps the essential spirit of his words would somehow be grasped. His letters were a veneer of diplomacy and politesse painted over a furnace of rage—though the former would have done little to hide the latter, had anyone given the letters their full attention.

The project soon evolved. Maximilian became a collector of secret information. In particular he began to enjoy compiling long lists of employees' home addresses and details of company accounts. To gather such intelligence, it was necessary of course to break into factories and offices at night, evading the attentions of slumbering security guards, before rifling through sheaves of documents held inside enormous stacks of filing cabinets. Ever immaculate, he left no evidence and was never so much as suspected, although there were nights marked by the necessity of hiding in webs of shadows with a rapidly beating heart whilst probing beams of torchlight sought for his features in vain. On occasion there was the interesting experience of jumping out of a window in order to flee from what might have been a scene of no small tension; this accompanied by the awful piercing crash of shattering glass, a sound in which he did not often find occasion to indulge.

Before leaving any business premises to which he had gained entry, Maximilian would deposit a variety of objects meant to be discovered the following day by the employees of the organisation in question. He did this in an effort to enliven what were otherwise staid and colourless environments. Particular favourites included inflatable palm trees, volumes from his library touching upon the intricacies of breeding duck-billed platypuses in captivity, and a variety of paraphernalia related to one or another aspect of Ancient Egyptian embalming practices. Still, he was careful to form no definitive rules about what was and was not a suitable artefact to leave behind. Different things appealed depending on the occasion. After his break-ins he liked to imagine the facial expressions of those entering as normal the following day. He wanted the executives to feel the horror of intrusion, as if someone had left a trail of muddy footprints behind them upon an unblemished white surface.

Pretending to work for a variety of organisations, Maximilian made use of public telephones, requesting that many units of product be transferred from the premises of one company to another. He was soon to discover that as long as the shipments were not *too* large, they would frequently be authorised without any questions being asked. Often he liked to order many such shipments on behalf of a single office during the course of a single day, so that in one afternoon a given company might find itself under siege from lorries bearing many thousands of harmonicas, snooker chalks, zips, balloons, nail clippers, and all sorts of other examples of the wonders attainable by simply speaking into the mouthpiece of a telephone. Whenever he engaged in this sort of behaviour Maximilian was always sure to round things off by sending boxes filled with copies of the sort of socialist literature generally published by small presses barely able to pay their bills. With great amusement he wondered if he might be causing various accountants to experience a certain amount of sleeplessness. He saw frenzied nights of paranoid tossing back and forth within clammy crumpled sets of bed sheets. He believed that worse crimes had been committed.

Late at night, when the streets were deserted, Maximilian would drive around in his car, often drifting with no particular destination in mind, searching for advertisement hoardings to vandalize, and armed accordingly. Squiggly moustaches would appear on faces that had hitherto been barren of hair. Unusual colours were added to make jarring conjunctions. Slogans written in highly critical, politicized language were daubed across photographs of refrigerators and automobiles. Whenever his imagination failed him, or Maximilian found himself harbouring a particular anger towards a piece, he would simply destroy it.

He objected to the fantasies of idyll and purity found in the many pristine, inescapable images presiding over so many street corners. As well as detesting the fact that they taunted the populace with dreams of inexcusable consumption, he felt that they contributed to the glaring physical ugliness of contemporary life, polluting the places in which they were erected, their presence alone retarding the likelihood of a better society emerging. Nothing could validate their placement amongst a population evidently incapable of comprehending the power that such stark, unsubtle monuments possessed. If the people would not tear them down of their accord, Maximilian would give them a little push.

From the early '70s onwards, Maximilian began to haunt trade union meetings on a sporadic basis. He paid particular attention to those unions whose activities were being actively discouraged. Sidling into the back of busy meeting halls, he would lurk alone, listening diligently to the proceedings, and then take care to leave before the discussion had come to an end, so that he didn't risk detection. After having obtained a suitable number of employees' addresses from burgling a given company, he would send them leaflets promoting these union meetings, as well as a variety of socialist causes. Of course, this resulted in considerable bewilderment amongst certain union leaders, who wondered who it was in their organizations frittering away their already insufficient postage budgets. Maximilian thought he could see attendance increasing at the meetings, and, as such, wondered if he might take credit not only for improving membership but also instigating a variety of important reforms as a consequence.

He also got into the habit of championing small businesses that he admired. When a business didn't make any effort to expand, but instead operated on a local level, engaging in a minimum of exploitative working practices, as far as he could tell, it seemed to Maximilian that a moderate contribution had been made towards the progress of civilization. Frequently he felt that he could detect glimmers of genuine humanity resident within the eyes of the proprietors of such businesses, and it was to these individuals that he turned his attentions. He would pay to have advertisements printed and then deliver them by hand in the residential areas that the different businesses served. Negotiating terms with distributors over the telephone, he would sign deals on behalf of whoever he happened to be supporting that particular week, in some cases managing to reduce their costs considerably. On a few occasions, when a shop or business was working from premises that seemed to have fallen into disrepair, he paid for refurbishments. Workmen would appear, announcing that a secret benefactor had underwritten repairs and redecoration. A few proprietors were offended and sent the workmen on their way, but the vast majority were more than happy to accept their unexpected gifts.

In 1975 Maximilian opened a "free shop" in which clothes, bedding, furnishings, and electrical appliances could all be obtained for no cost, although a number of cardboard boxes were placed by the entrance, politely requesting that those who could do without leave behind other such items whenever convenient. By locating the shop on Old Cavendish Street, immediately adjacent to the roar of commerce on Oxford Street, he told himself that he was making an obvious statement to the flourishing business community by showing how blatantly ludicrous and exploitative their behaviour actually was.

Maximilian rarely made an appearance at the shop, after the initial work was done and it was open for "business." Almost immediately, then, a gang of squatters moved into the premises with their sleeping bags and a not inconsiderable amount of marijuana recently smuggled into the country from the foothills of the Himalayas. On the few occasions that Maximilian did visit, he wouldn't utter a single word. Walking through the door, to all appearances a short middle-aged businessman from the suburbs, Maximilian cut a curious figure in his suit and spectacles as he pretended to browse through the ragged commodities now presided over by the squatters. When he arrived, no one thought for even a moment that this could be the person responsible for the shop's existence. They eyed Maximilian warily, as if he might be capable of destroying the secret kingdom that they had discovered. Between them the squatters ran the place successfully for a number of months, and it was extraordinary how infrequently any of their number questioned the origins of the enterprise. However, it did not take long for them to be forcibly ejected by various members of the police force, who had heard about their activities, and did not take kindly to the ways in which they were behaving. After their intervention the premises were to lie empty for some time.

Window, Bicycle, Lamp Post

(1975)

Maximilian gazed out upon the street, noticing a bicycle that was chained to a lamp post.

• This was the street upon which Maximilian had lived for many years now. At one end it commenced with a garage with a roof ringed with barbed wire and shards of broken glass. Beyond this the rows of housing consisted of semi-detached pebbledash houses and bungalows.

• The bicycle had a blue-and-yellow fluorescent aluminium frame, with five-speed derailleur gears, a black plastic saddle, dynamo lights, and translucent yellow handlebar grips. Drops of moisture had settled onto its cold, hard surface. A few pedestrians passing it had felt envious of the owner.

• Seeing the bicycle, Maximilian was reminded of his youth, when he would ride for hours to distant locations, a practice he had given up in favour of driving. These memories made him wish to pedal around London once more.

• The owner of the bicycle was a man who was fond of both arm wrestling and playing darts. Jogging was his principle form of exercise, an activity he engaged in about five times a week. Habits directly related to his mouth included cheery whistling, the prolonged savouring of sticks of chewing gum, and the tendency to forcibly spit on the ground in public venues.

• The lamp post was a tall, steel, contemporary one. It rose towards the sky, and once reaching an apex, moved abruptly outwards, in the direction of the road, forming a right angle. Emitting a sodium-orange light, it stood, imperious, its light beyond the reach of human arms. Placed in the street by Hackney Borough Council in 1973, a number of local residents had failed to notice its presence.

• In recent times this lamp post had witnessed a poster being attached to its exterior, a piece of paper advertising a competitive quiz that would shortly take place in some community centre. A week ago a child had attempted to wrap its arms around the lamp post and encircle it completely, but without success. Two days ago a dog had urinated against it.

• The dog who had been responsible for said micturition was a diabetic Yorkshire Terrier, who answered to the name of "Petey." He was twelve years old, had an uneasy gait and a coat of black and tan fur. Around his neck was a light brown leather collar and a circular bronze nametag engraved with his name. He was fond of attempting to steal chips from his owner's dinner plate. Despite his advanced age and modest size, he would bark incessantly at any other dog he encountered.

• The dog's owner was an elderly woman who was fond of eating chocolate truffles and drinking glasses of brandy. She was a member of a local group that met regularly to play poker. None of the group could persuade her that it was a bad idea for her to continue riding her motorcycle every day.

• As it happened, this scene of Maximilian's gazing through the window took place on a morning in autumn. Dead brown leaves like flakes of parchment had settled into heaps on and about the pavements. Perpetually overcast skies glowered onto nothing but grey, pallid objects. But these things were not at the forefront of the observer's mind at the time.

• Maximilian was standing at the window at this precise moment because he had realised, in the midst of one of his lapses in activity, that he had not taken the trouble to gaze out of his living room window for some years, and that when he looked upon the street he was no longer seeing its reality, was no longer seeing with any curiosity or scrutiny.

• Only rarely did he stand, observable, framed within his window. He spent many hours gazing at other London streets, but this was the one from which he kept aloof as much as was possible, a tendency that extended to his relationship with his living-room windows.

• On the other side of the road, in the direction of Maximilian's gaze, lived a family with whom he had no contact whatsoever. The father worked as a mechanic in the garage at the end of the street, and in his spare time constructed model railway sets. His daughter was in the process of training to become a hairdresser's assistant.

• In his position beside the window, Maximilian was a dimly lit figure, semi-concealed by a thin white lattice of net curtains, a barrier that removed him from the scene to an extent which he almost found acceptable.

• A figure intruded upon his state of quiet reverie. A young woman, with short blonde hair, a white leather handbag dangling from her shoulder, was at that moment walking from one end of the street to the other, appearing first on the right-hand side of Maximilian's window frame.

• In all, Maximilian had stood in front of the window for approximately eight seconds before seeing the form of the young woman approaching, which led him to retreat and walk into the kitchen, where he drank a glass of milk.

• A few minutes after Maximilian left the vicinity of his window, a car sped by, hurrying a middle-aged man to a meeting of the British Association of Synthetic Rubber Manufacturers, an event to which the man was looking forward with great and sincere anticipation.

Habitual Practices that Cannot be Ignored

(1976–1998)

The longer that Maximilian spent in isolation, the more his personal habits became erratic and strange. Eventually he found it difficult to conform to any of society's preferences in even the slightest way. As far as he was concerned, he was surrounded on all sides by a society continually engaged in the practice of utterly irrational activities he did not have the slightest hope of understanding.

The truth was that he could hardly even bear to brush his own teeth in any sort of ordinary way. Once he had discovered the existence of the electrical toothbrush, he became one of its most eager advocates. The sensations that this strange device gave rise to often seemed so spectacular that he felt as if he were truly engaging with space-age possibilities, the hopes of technological transformations that might in time genuinely alter the course of history. Then, somehow or other, he came upon the information that a small company in Japan had begun manufacturing pistachio-flavoured toothpaste. He began to order regular shipments of what he already regarded as a very precious substance. With the inimitable taste of this paste in his mouth at the beginning of each day (an experience, he knew, that must differ radically from that of his fellow citizens), it felt to Maximilian as if he was declaring his opposition to society from the very beginning of his day, to the extent that it no doubt affected his subsequent outlook in subtle and mysterious ways, sometimes having a profound influence over his entire day.

Every Friday morning he would get his hair cut at a barber's shop in Surbiton. Whilst it was not strictly possible for his hair to grow to any great extent over the space of a week, he still persisted in making these regular visits. They helped him to feel confident in assuming his customary posture of anonymity. Even if there was no new hair to be cut, it was extraordinary how Harry (for that was the name of the barber) would always manage to do something or other behind Maximilian for several minutes, often humming a little tune as he did so. Cutting only tiny strands of hair away, applying an electric razor with great care to the back of his customer's head, he would make a great performance out of the act of barbering, all in all making what amounted to no discernible difference. All that mattered, to both men, was that an appearance of genuine labour be created, maintained, and executed with dignity.

A tacit understanding had sprung up between the two men soon after the beginning of their relationship. After various primitive attempts at conversation, it was instinctively understood by each party that beyond the usual minimal greetings and good-byes, no communication of any depth or significance should ever pass between them and interfere in the matter at hand. Once this had been definitively established, they took up their respective positions each Friday morning for the following twenty-four years, until one day Maximilian did not return, and his chair sat empty and forlorn.

The only form of exercise that Maximilian took during these years was to ride a unicycle through the streets of Bermondsey, a ritual that he began to perform every Saturday at the beginning of the 1980s. Years of practice were necessary before he felt comfortable riding through the streets and braving any obstructions that might come his way, or vice versa. In general he could practice this art form in relative safety, but there were still the odd occasions on which gangs of delinquent adolescents ridiculed him and taunted him and threatened to visit upon his person various recherché acts of violence.

As soon as they caught sight of him, small children would smile and wave as he cycled, sometimes asking him why he was behaving in this manner, to which he responded differently on almost every occasion, until most of the children resident in the area had their own idea of who the mysterious figure on the unicycle was, and where he was going to. Many of them would think about this at night whilst they were lying in bed and trying to fall asleep. Locals got to know the sight of the unicyclist very well, as he circled the streets over the years—sweating, his heart racing, experiencing the strange exhilaration that can be brought on by exercise. Stories about Maximilian would often circulate amongst the men sitting in the public houses in the vicinity of his rides, and over time this talk became so refined and intricate in its references to references that considerable insider knowledge was needed to unravel the many aspects of what was being spoken of on such occasions.

As soon as Maximilian began exercising regularly, he also became extremely fastidious in all culinary matters. Every day he would estimate the precise number of grams of all the substances that he ingested, noting down the quantities of vitamins, salts, and acids contained in each known ingredient. With regard to foodstuffs, he favoured the metric system to the imperial and used it exclusively. He took to doing his food shopping every week in Wembley, the place that inspired him the most, thanks to the South Asian population who were increasingly resident there. When preparing his meals, Maximilian always felt as though he were entering some exotic domain, embarking on rarefied states of a sensual nature, experiences that he found were capable of satisfying him as much as any artistic project. Improvising with every herb and spice available, he was determined to enjoy the full range of the palate that nature had provided him, seeking out flavours that were rare in the country at this time, glutting himself with jasmine, caraway, sassafras, tamarind, cardamom, saffron, turmeric, and aniseed.

Complimenting these other habits was an even greater fixation on cleanliness. Each evening, before retiring, Maximilian would attend to every object and surface in the bungalow, making certain that not a single mote of dust had settled upon any given inch of his abode. Eventually Maximilian took to donning a blindfold, a length of black cloth that he would bind around his forehead, winding it slowly around his eyes until his field of vision had been obliterated and he could comfortably scour each surface by touch for traces of pollutants. Doing this so frequently, he came to be intimately acquainted with all of the rooms and objects that lay within his jurisdiction, adding a further layer of complexity to his apprehension of everyday existence. Within this meditative exercise he discovered something of the sense of balance and calm that he had long been seeking, but had never quite attained successfully.

Every night this process would be followed by Maximilian's listening to the same record in order to encourage sleep. "Raga Mishra Piloo" ("An Evening Raga") was a long, sprawling piece by Ravi Shankar considered by Maximilian to possess a rare and tranquil beauty. The music induced a pleasant numbness; he welcomed it into every fold of his body, which let its stresses dissolve away one by one. After months of listening to it every evening, Maximilian found that from the first few moments of the needle touching the rim of the record, he would begin to drift towards sleep, succumbing soon after. This was repeated with such reliability every evening that Maximilian had no idea what the last ten minutes of the piece were like.

He kept the volume knob fixed in the position that he considered to be optimum, producing at most a distant hum, but this was enough to induce the trance state required. The music lulled Maximilian into a womb-like serenity in which his mind was cleared of all confusion, to the extent that it became absolutely devoid of both pleasure and suffering. It was under these conditions that he never remembered his dreams.

Notes on Inconsequential Occasions

(1977)

July 1st

To commence a diary, record of a brief period of time, one particular summer, a collection of hours.

July 2nd

I have few urgent preoccupations for the time being and feel content to see what happens when these entries become my sole creative activity.

July 3rd

Wandered over to Islington from Hackney Marshes, eventually coming upon a television crew in Wilmingston Square. Sat watching them for half an hour. Leafed through newspapers in the Westminster Reference Library. Drifted towards the river and ambled all the way to Chelsea Embankment before returning home.

July 4th

Visited the Sir John Soane's Museum. It remains my favourite place in London after all these years. Coffee and newspapers in Holborn. A stroll in Green Park. Various drinking establishments in Marylebone.

July 8th

Riding a merry-go-round in the afternoon rain. Only a handful of children joining me. Pleasant sense of peace amid such melancholy, although all of the parents looked at me a little suspiciously. By this time I'm so used to feeling that I've been painted as a dubious character in other peoples' eyes that I think very little of it. What exactly is wrong with a grown man earnestly riding a pink-and-gold horse?

July 9th

And so it seems that most of my activities have ground to a halt. This has happened before, indeed seems to happen from time to time, so I can't say I feel enormously worried, but nevertheless there is always the fear that during one of these periods I might become overly complacent and drift into lassitude permanently. On some recent days the lethargy has been so overpowering that I wonder if I am about to fall into some sort of permanent state of inaction.

July 11th

Boredom. Hours in a cafe watching the customers and staff, all of whom seem considerably more cheerful than me. No real interest in anything much. Fiddled with the salt and pepper shakers for a while. Tried to spur myself on and generate some enthusiasm for something or other, but nothing doing. How long can this go on?

July 12th

Only aardvarks and peppermints seem to interest me today.

July 14th

Have found temporary solace in crosswords. Began in the morning with a couple discovered in tabloids lying around in the cafe. After finishing those fairly quickly I then progressed to a more serious crossword in *The Times*. Not being used to the form at all it proved to be a real challenge. Confidence increased after a couple of successes, and by the onset of evening I felt certain I had successfully completed about two thirds of the puzzle. A feeling of minor triumph.

July 15th

Sitting on a bus approaching Trafalgar Square, I felt the need for company, strangely—at least for a short time. Just to begin a conversation with the old man who sat next to me. I know this is impossible, that I've invested too much of myself in my many forms of solitude, that to enter into any sort of relationship right now would destroy me. And yet . . . this fantasy of easy camaraderie lingers. Find myself amazed at this.

July 19th
Walked through Selfridges for the first time in many years, marvelling at the great ridiculous display of products and the monumental appearance of the building and its spaces. Found the grandeur to be quite seductive, not that I bought anything. It made for a good stroll, if nothing else.

July 21st
The mysterious clustering in cities, whereby human beings pack themselves together into such limited spaces, leaving enormous stretches of the surface of the planet unoccupied. What perversity.

July 22nd
A day-trip to Brighton. Walked along the beach. Played the slot machines. Passed through antique shops in the Lanes. Sat in the gardens of the Pavilion listening to a Salvation Army Band.

July 23rd
Visit to the Westminster Reference Library. Sat next to a man who fell asleep repeatedly and who was told off for doing so by the librarians. An air of desperation pervades the place. Old men who have nowhere else to be gather there in weather-beaten clothes and sit for hours with few thoughts of the future in mind. Whenever I stop working I find myself coming here often. Sad and slightly ashamed that I fit into this company so easily.

July 25th
Spent the night camping in Epping Forest. Reading under torch-

light undoubtedly has a quality of its own, being a state of artificially induced unreality intimately related to memories of childhood. Enjoyed the darkness and emptiness, the sense of removing myself from the city and hovering above it—a place I could return to whenever I wanted, but which I was choosing to keep at arm's length.

July 26th
Time is always disappearing, but it's impossible to always worry about this.

July 29th
Fantasy of living on one of the islands in the midst of the Thames. In particular Eel Pie Island at Twickenham or Oliver's Island at Strand-on-the-Green.

August 1st
I think there is pleasure in the abruptness, the superficiality of these entries. Reading back I feel they evoke the previous month quite well. Fragments are of more interest to me these days than entire stories or epics. Contemporary life seems to demand concise statements, a certain brevity.

August 4th
Whenever I pass a hospital, lately, I find myself filled with an unbearable dread. I project myself into the future in which I will be a patient.

August 6th
Riding buses most of the day. Seeing the entire length of a given route, the landmarks that one comes across, a sense of the city shifting as you move from east to west or north to south. Surprises in the form of unknown places that I find intriguing—at which point I either disembark for a few minutes to investigate or jot the street name down in my

notebook. A perfectly pleasant way to spend the day.

August 10th

Looking forward to autumn. It suits the country so much better than summer, a season that occasionally promises to arrive but rarely does with any substance. In contrast, autumn never fails to provide the melancholy of brown leaves, overcast skies, and overdue library books.

August 12th

Followed the Regent's Canal all the way from Camden Lock to Victoria Park. Hard to avoid the enjoyable fantasy of living on the houseboats that you pass. The snug cosiness of the cramped quarters within each. Equally, the fantasy of drifting down canals for months on end.

August 13th

Have developed a fascination with horoscopes. Enjoy the idea of a project that would involve assembling all of the thousands of horoscopes printed for one star sign on a given day. This would include newspapers and magazines from all over the world. What a beautiful array of clashing sentiments would arise!

August 15th

Purple and scarlet streaks flaring above the dome of St. Paul's as dusk was descending this evening.

August 16th

Took a tour of Highgate Cemetery, where a guide showed a small group of us the grave of the man who invented the dog biscuit. Crumbling mock-Egyptian tombs. Dilapidated stonework. Beautiful sense of unkempt profusion, forgotten desolation.

August 17th

A day spent in a few of the most dismal areas of the city: Tottenham, Redbridge, Barking. Wandered through the streets for many hours merely to try and discover a single redeeming feature. I feel that there must be something of interest in these places, but so far I have failed to find it.

August 21st

Visited the Windmill Museum in the middle of Wimbledon Common. The museum is housed inside a windmill that was built in 1817. Lord Baden Powell wrote parts of his book *Scouting for Boys* when he was staying there in 1902. A fine eccentric monument.

August 24th

I can no longer imagine any kind of ordinary life for myself. If I had given in to the demands of the workplace then my life would have been one of slavery and emptiness. Such a fate seems both impossible and odious to me now.

August 26th

Followed the river between Brentford and Kew Bridge. This stretch is one of the most beautiful parts of the city and feels all the more appealing for being largely hidden and unknown. Large houseboats moored permanently have their own gardens along the footpath.

August 29th

Not for the first time, the idea of leaving London. To depart from the country altogether, perhaps, in order to take up a new life elsewhere, one of an entirely different character. I love the idea of selecting my new homeland when browsing through travel guides in a bookshop. To see a single photograph of a distant city and then proceed to make arrangements to live there for the rest of one's life—that would be a terrific way to leave. Actually going through with the scheme is another matter however . . .

Broadcasts Received in the Outer Regions

(1978–1991)

From that year onwards, every Sunday evening, as dusk began to fall, Maximilian would make his way to his garden shed in order to broadcast a radio programme. This was the one place within his abode in which he always allowed himself a moderate amount of disorder. Amidst shelves crowded with oily work tools, boxes of various mementoes, and files crammed full of disordered papers, lay his hidden radio equipment: turntables and tape machines, large boards covered in buttons and dials, enormous black speaker cabinets, a spider-like mass of black-coated wires spilling out from a profusion of sockets. It was in this place that Maximilian felt most comfortable, relaxing into a blue-and-white striped canvas deckchair, a bottle of ale by his side, listening intently to a great variety of recordings as he broadcast them to a tiny minority of obsessives and misfits.

His programmes consisted of carefully chosen selections of natural sound, mixing recordings he had made himself with those discovered in record shops and lending libraries. Focusing entirely on examples of what has been called musique concrète, he played a series of sounds formed spontaneously in a great variety of environments, with occasional interjections of speech included in its many myriad forms, whilst only rarely straying into the domain of traditional musical composition. In his opinion, the ordering of sounds permitted by the government on its radio waves restricted the range of recorded sounds heard by the population to a staggering degree. There was barely any place within this scheme of things for radio shows that were not venues for either speech or music, that is to say for programmes taking into account the majority of naturally occurring sounds in the world. Maximilian was at pains to change this tendency.

Long ago he had made the startling discovery that sounds,

divorced from their immediate contexts, were transformed, became clearer and more definite, much in the way that photography transforms the visual environment, whilst also taking on more abstract qualities, to the extent that they could become impossible to identify. Maximilian wanted his broadcasts to be difficult to listen to, at least on occasion, just as they were nearly impossible to locate on a radio dial, so that only the genuinely dedicated would continue to listen and be forced to think about what they were hearing, a rare agenda for any radio programme.

After years of secret broadcasts, he discovered, somewhat to his surprise, that he *did* have listeners. He learnt of their existence after setting up a P. O. box which he read out over the airwaves one evening, inviting anyone listening to contribute "suggestions" or to simply get in touch for any reason that they wished. Repeating this invitation a number of times resulted in a small trickle of mail, ranging in substance from the extraordinarily banal and literal ("I am writing to tell you that I enjoy your programmes very much . . .") to what could only be described as rare and inexplicable ("Considerations of goats are rarely far from my cerebellum . . ."), but Maximilian felt tenderly towards everyone who wrote to him and would often keep certain individuals in mind when preparing his broadcasts. At first he did not feel inclined to respond to these letters in written form, partly because he felt that he was far too busy with his other activities, but eventually he could not resist the temptation to enter into correspondence with the few listeners he found to be particularly interesting.

Over time, he began to receive many hundreds of cassettes, all from just a handful of sources, containing field recordings from over the world. He placed a world map above his transmitter, marking the locations of his "sources" with coloured pins, each colour representing a different mood or theme. Before long he got into the habit of requesting sounds from listeners who lived in places that he happened to find intriguing. Constructing running orders around particular locations became another fixation. Following a series of precise spatial patterns, he would create playlists that moved across the surface of the globe, covering many kilometres in lines or circles, or else focusing exclusively on the sounds of a single village, street or field.

Many of his programmes took months and even years of slow and meticulous preparation to reach the stage at which Maximilian was comfortable transmitting them: he gathered together the necessary materials and experimented with different timings and juxtapositions between clips. On pale afternoons in winter he would play a number of tapes in the various rooms of the bungalow whilst he wandered from one to another, bathing in the different palettes of sound, forming close acquaintances with certain pieces, so that he could best decide upon the position that they would take within a certain programme, jotting down his observations, notes that would often develop into monologues which he would deliver on the airwaves.

Years of solitude had sharpened his senses; whilst the majority of the city's populace hurried to workplaces before hurrying home as soon as it became possible, frequently quite oblivious to what was occurring around them, Maximilian had given himself the opportunity to meditate, more or less endlessly, on his environment and all that it contained. Entire weeks might be devoted to wandering through London in order to attend to the panoply of sounds he would encounter. Sound became, for a time, the principal way in which Maximilian related to his surroundings; he would hear an object or space before seeing it.

Monday mornings might find him dressed in a suit, eyes hidden behind a pair of sunglasses, intently holding a microphone up to air-conditioning systems and radiators; or else attempting to capture the "flow" of a particular street with a series of different tape recorders, shifting his position frequently, the better to take in every nuance. Such practices even saw him leave the city, unusually; he would travel the length and breadth of the country picking through the sounds he collected along the way. He would spend five or six hours at a time recording the sound of rain falling on a fallow field, or the clatter of feet as they progressed up the steps of a cathedral.

Before going on air, Maximilian always took a good while to prepare himself. He would rehearse, strolling around the bungalow, going through a series of voice exercises, producing a selection of incomprehensible nonsense, bursts of babble incorporating the entire phonetic range of vocal gibberish. These exercises would take about an hour. Once they were finished, he would strut before a tall mirror, adjusting his clothes, taking in his features, attempting to project onto them the persona that he wished to assume. He suspected that, when speaking on the radio, he became a different person entirely, a less inhibited one who didn't mind talking at length about his beliefs and activities, who didn't shy away from employing esoteric words and phrases, breaking off into strange digressions, and revealing a substantial amount about himself in the process.

Anticipation of his broadcasts brought out a nervous excitement. It was often his favourite moment of the week. Once a programme began, he would imagine his broadcasts spreading out beyond his house, a vast net sinking into a darkened sea, reaching the ears of who knew what stray individuals, most of whom would be residing in solitude not unlike his own, sitting in armchairs, or else underneath heaps of blankets in their beds, or else driving in cars along motorways.

They might be listening to the insides of a hole cut into the ice of the Arctic Ocean, as drippings and splashes of water fell amongst glittering specks of snow. Winds surging across the empty roaring bitterness of the plains. Slow movements of light melting the cold wastes, vague stirrings of summer.

The growing swollen oceans, teeming with innumerable tiny bodies, including many that have never received human names. Enormous landscapes of rock, grass, and sand. Clusters of buildings. Webs of roads. White frothing rivers. Craters of dormant volcanoes.

Cool shady clearings in forests. Hoarse voices calling in teeming marketplaces. Old men mumbling in ancient temples. Yellow lizards scuttling across the dirt-stained walls of ragged rooms, darting into crevices.

Trains clattering towards forgotten destinations. The steady rhythm of their wheels revolving. Glimpses of fields and houses far in the distance, cliffs falling and crumbling into the sea, villages gathered on lofty hilltops. Long idle conversations drifting through afternoons, the meetings of strangers. Journeys through obscure provincial cities, each containing an old woman on a bench in a train station with her dog sitting attentively beside her.

A campfire blazing on a hill in Scotland. Branches crackling and snapping apart. Flames wavering and smoking, licking against the sky. Indistinct words sung over the patter of a soft-strummed guitar. Finger cymbals, hand clapping, rough rhythms beat out upon a tambourine. Muffled voices. A burst of whistling. Pockets of laughter.

Las Vegas casinos. Jangling coins and the electric chime of the slot machines. Trumpets blaring from elaborate stage shows. Peacock feathers and sparkling bikinis. Blunt, commanding voices of gamblers huddled around gigantic tables covered in green baize. Crowds wandering in swathes, murmuring as they move through the giant neon-bright hallways.

Conversations overheard at café tables in Paris. Elegant men wearing black waistcoats and bowties, immaculate white shirts. Arms aloft bearing drinks on circular metal trays. Light curling against buildings, shining across rooftops, detectable in the movement and levity of the voices. Clattering of coffee cups and spoons. Cats tiptoeing around table legs, nuzzling against feet with soft purrings.

Street interviews conducted with pedestrians. The original questions erased or replaced with other questions. Disjointed statements, new thoughts and images. Suspended voices. References to events that have not yet taken place, ideas that no one has thought. Words without images, words refusing to describe.

Clicks and crackles. Whining of seagulls. Grinding of engines and machinery. Shoes clacking across pavements. Winds shrieking across a field. A room of wooden rattles. A room of wineglass rims ringing from the rub of wet fingers. Balloons filling up with air. Children playing in a garden in summer. A harmonium on a pebble beach. A patter of whispers.

A Speech Delivered to a Small Audience Gathered Inside an Abandoned Ballroom

(1979)

Good evening ladies and gentlemen, and welcome to an occasion that will no doubt cause you some dismay.

I don't believe in speeches. In fact I don't really believe in speaking at all. It's not as if there aren't many other methods of communication available. Frankly, I think that there are better ways of making a point than by delivering orations. I frequently go decades at a time without speaking, and it's never done me any real harm. People dedicate so much of their time to speaking, losing hour after hour of their lives talking about entirely insignificant subjects whose mention makes no difference to their—or anyone else's—lives. What an absurd waste of time it all is.

There is no good reason for me to deliver this speech. No one asked me to speak this evening and I have no particular subject in mind. It might be added that this is the only speech I have ever given. Perhaps it will be the only speech I give in my life. Thus, it might well be a good idea to listen most intently to every word I say. There probably won't be another opportunity to absorb these riches.

Preparing a lecture is a tedious venture. One has to read books that are of no interest, compile pages of notes, prepare one's material, condense it, pick out the important elements, place them in the best order, make difficult concepts digestible to your audience. Each stage in the process is laborious. As such, I have skipped these preparatory steps. With regard to the way my words may or may not effect you, I may be said to occupy a position of total disinterest.

155

If you stay here to listen, there will be no relief. Boredom will contaminate every last particle in circulation in this space. The air will become clammy to the point of being unbearable. You will shift about in your seats uncomfortably, discovering aches of which you were not previously aware. Syllables will drawl from my mouth continuously until it will seem I could not possibly persist. But, nevertheless, I will persist. Your attention will wander, you will think of other things; indeed, you will desperately, gratefully, seize upon *anything* else that might distract you. And still I will drone on.

Whatever positive qualities my words might have, I assure you these couldn't possibly add up to much of substance. Of the already small number of individuals present to listen to me tonight, perhaps only five or six will manage to follow my thoughts through to the end. Of *those*, perhaps only two or three will be able to remember what I have said in a week's time, whilst no one at all will *act* upon what I have said, as indeed they would not act upon what anyone else might say, if they were to stand here, and deliver a speech, as I am doing, to an audience of this size, of this kind.

I know very well the pall of tedium that can linger in a room in which a speech is being given. The speaker on top of a platform or dais, speaking and gesturing, sometimes with great animation, whilst his audience is seated below, distracted, thinking, indeed, of anything other than the matter at hand, whatever that is, anything that might bring with it the hope of some sort of pleasure or significance. Surely every public speech should be delivered in consideration of this fact. This one certainly is.

Movements of interminable grind. The extraordinary profusion of characterless, flavourless topics. The repetition of actions inimical to thought. Blank, inert, vacant persons and occasions and places. The forces that reduce the things of the world to empty vessels lacking in all sensuous qualities. These are the things that this lecture will, for your benefit, embody. For as long as you choose to remain here listening to me, this is the place that we will inhabit together. If I were you I would *definitely* leave now.

Yes, I urge you to stop listening to this speech. Make haste. Perhaps a number of you, dear listeners, might approach me, bind my hands with rope behind my back, stuff a handkerchief in my mouth, tie me to a chair and then proceed to make me listen to whatever you deem it necessary to say to me in reproach. Perhaps, after this, you might destroy the room. If you were to do this, you would then be behaving as active individuals, rather than the passive spectators you have become by dint of sitting and putting up with the things I am in the process of saying to you. You are anonymous to me, you men and women seated before me, persons with whom I will probably never speak in an informal way, whose faces I will glance at for barely an instant before moving onwards, to another room in another building inhabited by another collection of undistinguished faces.

Rather than listen to me, you might rise up from your seat and walk out of the door. You could walk for three miles without stopping to rest. There need not be any specific destination. Perhaps it is enough to go walking. You might even find yourself making friends with a cat. Perhaps it would be better to choose a direction leading to a place with which you are unfamiliar. To see new streets and buildings. Or, at least, places that you have never stopped to examine with any real care. I urge you to find something, anything preferable to this speech, something that will be truly engaging and nourishing.

It could well be that on the other side of the city, another lecture is taking place. A man, of a similar age to myself, might be on a platform, before a canvas screen, on which he is projecting a series of slides. He may be pointing towards various shapes and colours on the screen with his wooden cane, pointing to signs that he believes will inform and entertain his audience. The things that he is saying, the facts that he is busy relating, the choice of descriptions he has made, the quality of his chosen slides—these things make him stand out as an individual, make him worthy of attention, make him almost glamorous, by contrast. His powers of communication are doubtless far superior to my own. It might be worth your while to locate the room in which he is speaking. You would certainly be better off doing that than staying here, where you are simply going to hear more of the same. If you've enjoyed yourself so far, I suppose, then keep listening, because you will not find what follows to be a disappointment. I may even choose to repeat everything that I have already said.

You could continue listening to me in order to find out what happens, to see how this will progress, before it peters out, or stops abruptly, or extends—it's possible—to marathon proportions. No one will know until that point has been reached. You could stay for that reason—to engage in an act of spectatorship, of voyeurism, simply following a series of events from beginning to end. That, at any rate, is the task that lies ahead of you. But I would like to give you another warning, if such is your intention: nothing of interest is going to occur here. Nothing will change. There will be no movement or progression. Where we are is where we shall wind up.

You may well feel disappointed. Somehow you expected this speech to *contain* more. It sounded so interesting at the outset: you expected that perhaps you might walk home in a state of exaltation, refreshed and invigorated by the words that you heard this evening. Spurred on by the excitement of new ideas, branches of knowledge that you had never before encountered. You hoped that you would walk home with gleaming eyes, thirsting for the company of other people with whom you could share word of this experience. But instead you have found yourself here, still here, only here, listening to me talking about nothing much of consequence, and doubtless you are already thoroughly disheartened by the experience.

Why give a speech of this sort? I don't really have any clear idea. And, perhaps, hidden within my casual attitude is the answer to your question. I am giving this speech precisely because there is no reason to do so. I am saying these things because they are irrational, because they will only lead to an emptiness of all purpose, all significance. Nothing will be achieved. Barely anything will even be spoken of. And it is that, I think, that I most believe in. In doing things that barely qualify as having been done; in saying things that hardly qualify as having been said. No, that isn't true. I am not concerned with belief, this evening. There is nothing to believe in here.

Indifference like this can't be taught, can't be effectively communicated in a speech. One has to grasp it instinctively, or, better, inhabit the state naturally, as a matter of course. No conceptual apparatus is required. All that you need to know on the subject could be learnt in less than a second. There is no point in thinking through the issues I've raised—if I've raised any—with what might be laughably referred to as "depth." Anyone attempting to formulate a concrete understanding of the views and ideas under discussion here is going to fail. All of us are going to fail anyway, in so many ways, and that is all we have to look forward to. But that isn't my point—if I have a point. Which I probably don't.

There is no end to boredom. Think how remarkable this is. It contains infinite possibility. One can be bored for a very great length of time; in fact, it is possible to be bored from the moment you are born until the moment that you die. It has no boundaries. It has no centre and no edge. Potentially it can inhabit anything and anyone at all, as we can inhabit it. Entire cities, entire countries, even entire continents can seem boring, at times, to certain bored or boring people.

One could argue (and I shall) that I could talk about any subject in this manner and it would still wind up being boring, purposeless, lacking in meaning. Of course, we recognise that all human affairs can seem meaningless if one considers the size of the universe, the age of rock formations, of oceans and trees. In comparison with these elements of nature, human beings live for but a tiny length of time. Consequently, our concerns are empty of any real and lasting significance. It does not matter what one chooses to deliver a speech about. Before the reality of the cosmos, your lecture is no more significant than the tiny dot upon which we live.

I could not possibly know how it feels to be an individual listening to this lecture. If it is a lecture. There is a definitive, probably unbridgeable gap that lies between lecturer and lectured. I can only project myself into your place; it is a fond, romantic sort of gesture, and so falls outside of my purview. I can only guess, therefore, at the tedium you are now experiencing, the sense of waste and futility. The outrage and disgust, perhaps, that must be fomenting within the juices of your gurgling stomachs. I expect that you have never felt repulsion to this degree towards what ought to have been a light entertainment.

And so, finally, one arrives at no conclusions. After considering nothing much, one is only left with nothing much. One doesn't really discover anything along the way. There is no adventure. It is a case of one foot following another, in order that a journey take place, but ours is a journey without purpose, and therefore, no rewards will be obtained, no insights enjoyed.

No help is coming. You are on your own. No one else can rise up from your chair, no one else can shout insults and slam the door behind you; no one else can storm out of the room in your own particular manner, with your own indelible personal signature. No. The responsibility is yours alone. And how many other times should you have made your presence known? When else should you have risen up against the oppression of politeness? Look around you. Is it not a sort of synchronized narcolepsy that forces individuals to endure such terrible forms of theatre? Surely you should have declared your feelings before, made your opposition known. As they say, it's never too late. Until, of course, it is.

I'm sure it would have been better if I'd never said a thing. I should not have got up on this stage. I should not have started to speak. All of this could have been avoided. There would have been no endurance test, you would not have had to experience this or any of its consequences. That would have been best, I'm sure. At least, then, something worthwhile might have taken my place. Some small joy, at least, to make the day. But, alas.

Of course this lecture need never end. There could be further instalments. You could all return evening after evening to check in on the progress of my thoughts about nothing whatsoever. I could stay on this stage until my throat was so dry that I could no longer speak, or until it became impossible for me to stay awake. All the while I would still be here, talking and talking, with no hope of an end in sight. The subject would remain the same, the tone would remain the same, even the order of the words in certain key sentences. I don't believe in speeches.

The Rebuilding of Ickenham

(1980–1986)

Throughout its long history, Ickenham has always been condemned to official neglect. For centuries it was a tiny village where very little of consequence occurred. Swallowed up by the north-west suburbs of London during the course of the twentieth century, Ickenham became a commuter base after the opening of the Metropolitan Railway in 1905. Gradually it turned from a grey, overlooked village to a grey, overlooked part of the city. Maximilian, intrigued by this historylessness, undertook a review of the possible transformations that could be visited upon such a locality.

Over the years Maximilian had developed a fascination for the fringes, the forgotten margins, places whose appearance remained perpetually unknown, where anonymous figures shifted from one point in space to another with little of significance resulting from such movements. Places like Ickenham are, paradoxically, capable of obtaining a strange allure when they are visited from afar and infrequently. In such conditions, for brief periods of time, such destinations can seem to have the air and character of foreign countries, feeling entirely removed from the main thoroughfares and arteries of the greater city to which they nominally belong. Maximilian would spend days on end drifting amongst gigantic industrial buildings, empty expanses of school playing fields, relentless rows of houses. There was, he thought, a strange sense of calm there.

Whilst he enjoyed these places in their current form, Maximilian could not but dream of tinkering. He loved best those scenarios in which these margins would ascend to a sudden international prominence as a consequence of elaborate permutations in culture and architecture. Ickenham became the nexus to which these fascinations always led. One day, in the throes of the boredom he did not like to believe he still experienced, Maximilian took to imagining

Ickenham as a genuine arena of possibilities, a dream space behind whose windows and in whose cabinets who knew what fictions, as yet indefinite, were lurking? Easy to lose sight, Maximilian felt, of the fact that the miraculous could emerge from here as well as from anywhere else.

He began to walk down every street in the neighbourhood, taking photographs of every surface. Stepping through the doors of local businesses, he made preliminary enquiries regarding a range of goods and services before disappearing without making a purchase. Consulting the telephone directory, he rang hundreds of private residences, succeeding on a few occasions in engaging individuals in conversations about a number of subjects, ranging from the state of the weather to the eternal problem of infidelity. All of these actions were attempts to grasp the psychic co-ordinates of Ickenham, to gain some knowledge of the area's habits and preferences, its rhythms and forms.

Head bowed over a pint of ale in the Coach and Horses, he would eavesdrop on conversations, making himself as inconspicuous as he could, whilst he heard of petty rivalries and a variety of schemes that were all probably destined to end in failure. Never lingering long enough for his features to leave any sort of lasting impression behind, he nevertheless became constantly frightened that he might one day be recognized by Ickenham's residents. As a consequence he employed his usual tactics of camouflage and disguise, walking the streets only late at night, or during the hours of the afternoon when the area was largely deserted. It was only occasionally that someone mistook him for a potential thief.

Delving into books of history, he discovered that Ickenham was first mentioned in the Domesday Book of 1086, where it was referred to as "Ticheham." It had grown up as a settlement in the environs of the great estate of "Swakeleys," a property originally named after one Robert de Swalclyve, who was recorded as owning property in the area in 1326. The estate was to have many owners over the years, but the most famous was Sir Robert Vyner, a banker and goldsmith, friend to both Samuel Pepys and Charles II, who became the Lord Mayor of London in 1674. When Pepys visited Vyner in September 1665 he recorded that: "He [Vyner] showed me a black boy that he had had that had died of a consumption, and being dead, he caused him to be dried in an oven and lies there entire in a box." Maximilian was periodically haunted by this statement for some months after discovering it.

Perhaps the other most significant resident in Ickenham's history was living in the village at the same time as Vyner. This was one Roger Crab, a hermit who dressed in sackcloth and lived in a hut that he had built for himself. For the most part his diet consisted of water, dock leaves, and grass. Serving in the parliamentary army, Crab fought against Charles I during the English Civil War, eventually retiring to open a haberdashery in Chesham. After two years there, one day, digging in his garden (whilst facing the east) he suddenly saw "the Paradise of God." Promptly selling his shop, he gave all his proceeds to the poor and then settled in Ickenham, where he gained some reputation as a mystic, doctor, and prophet. He was whipped on occasion for Sabbath-breaking and was forced to endure the stocks. In 1657 he took a journey into London in order to publish a book entitled *Dagons Downfall, or The Great Idol digged up root and branch*, a work that sees him lapse occasionally into verse.

At the turn of the twentieth century, the annual village fair hosted a "greasy pig" competition. Only women were allowed to take part. Assembling at one end of the village, competitors awaited the aforementioned pig, who was covered in grease and released at the opposite end of the village whilst being steered towards his potential captors. The object of the game was to catch the pig and then hold on to it until a significant period of time had elapsed. Apparently there were many arguments as to who had been the victor, each year.

Later, in 1917, Ickenham was the site for an R.A.F. base which came to account for much of the area's population and which provided housing for its employees, an arrangement that led to the construction of many identical dwellings, with "standard issue" furnishings, décor, and even cutlery. Later the base was taken over by the U.S. Air Force and so many Americans moved to the area, along with a number of C.N.D. protestors.

Once his initial investigations were complete—investigations that proved largely valueless—Maximilian took to producing a series of life-size painted polystyrene replicas of various portions of Ickenham. Learning how to do so was another arbitrary challenge. He spent over a year training himself to sculpt with this new material. That a substance essentially vulgar and industrial in character could be utilized in this fashion—to make, he hoped, something beautiful—was especially satisfying.

Maximilian worked on these pieces in a large studio space that he had hired close to the scene. In each instance he selected a fragment of Ickenham and then proceeded to finish, first, an "accurate" model, and then revise its forms and structure until he felt that it had been sufficiently "improved." Making both "before" and "after" models, he wanted to illustrate the range of utopian formulae that were available—but, sadly, unrealized—in suburban life.

Taking, firstly, the local fish and chip shop, he reproduced its contemporary form with as great an exactitude as possible, paying attention to its sign with its different shades of brown, the pale brown tiles covering the floor, the brown, circular sticker on the front door stating that Luncheon Vouchers would be accepted here, the mural of fish swimming amongst streams of brown bubbles underneath the counter, posters announcing the various forms of produce available on the premises, steamed glass counters holding brown pies and sausages, bottles carrying quantities of salt and vinegar standing upright on the counter.

After toiling to capture this scene with as much authenticity as possible, Maximilian then built his own version of the fish and chip shop, with fluorescent fish dangling from wires attached to the ceiling, a much larger and brighter mural placed underneath the counter which now also included both a mermaid and a submarine, an array of fairy lights attached to the walls, and fish-shaped stickers placed on the door bearing a series of quotations on the subject of fish, attributed (perhaps correctly) to one or another famous writer or personage.

He next made a complete replica of the Ickenham Village Hall notice board, with its posters announcing the coming of the spring fair, the ploughman's lunch soon to be held at the church, a floral arts society, a bowls club, a miniature railway, as well as minutes for the Village Hall's Annual General Meeting, which at the moment of replication was due to be held in a fortnight's time. For the purposes of accuracy he added some stray articles of litter on the ground, as well as a couple of cigarette ends which had been stamped out and flattened by a boot, not to mention a small clump of weeds sprouting from the ground.

This he revised by building a frame painted in lurid shades of red and yellow, with posters announcing a reading group intending to focus its attentions upon newts, a Dadaist bowling union, an evening of Inuit food and poetry recitals to be held in a nearby café, a nude wrestling association, various descriptions of dreams recently experienced by members of the local population, as well as minutes for the Village Hall's annual general meeting due to be held in a fortnight's time.

After this, he turned his attentions to a house of a kind quite common in the area. He strove to capture its gravel driveway, the fresh-cut lawn, the bed of marigolds and azaleas, an old tennis ball lying forgotten in the soil, a row of heavy stone pots with pink geraniums, a cat yawning and stretching, a red car of recent manufacture, a front door with the numbers "4" and "9" rendered in brass and fixed to the blue-painted surface, two storeys giving way to an attic, six windows looking out onto the street with curtains drawn across them, the roof rising upwards into a triangle, the pine trees towering above in the back garden.

Attempting to subvert this, in the "after" model, he placed sculptures of indistinct snail-like forms across the spaces of the lawn and driveway, which he left overgrown with a variety of weeds. In place of a car there was a very large vehicle with no antecedent in human history, bearing a number of levers and dials of indistinct purpose, seats that rose high into the air and enormous but impractical wheels. The roof of the house was flat, with a number of triangular and trapezoidal chairs and tables arranged around various species of cacti. Above the front door he had added a large nose.

In all, he was to create twelve different polystyrene sculptures of Ickenham. After 1986 they were to remain locked away and forgotten. Having probed the depths and many possibilities of Ickenham, Maximilian felt exhausted, incapable of returning to the area ever again. There were, as they say, "too many memories" for him there, too many places capable of inducing unpleasant emotional states. For some years afterwards, he was to find certain houses and street corners, first seen in Ickenham, now placed into strange new contexts, within the many tangled layers and narratives of his mind.

Rumours of the Neighbourhood

(1981)

Pauline (57) had heard that the man in the bungalow used his home for regular meetings of an Anarchist terror organization. Apparently they were responsible for attempted attacks upon a range of targets including gardening centres, bowling alleys, village halls, and post offices. Their pamphlets were said to contain appalling essays that held the power to influence and corrupt even the most upright citizen. She deeply regretted that she had to live so close to such people. Whenever she passed the bungalow she stared at its exterior with fear and curiosity, and produced an inward shudder.

Gary (6) had heard that the man in the bungalow was a magician. His friend had told him that the man could make things disappear or change. One time he had turned a cucumber into a limousine and another time he had taught pigeons to speak just like people! All the man ever ate was red liquorice and he wore purple pyjamas all day long and in the middle of the night you could sometimes hear him talking to aliens through a long plastic tube.

Reverend Michaels (72) had heard that the man in the bungalow was a practitioner of the black arts, the leader of his own cult, one in which thin white cotton robes were worn and in which mysterious group chanting was undertaken, along with the drinking of goose blood and the printing of texts backwards so that they needed to be read in a mirror. In particular he was concerned about the possibility that ritual human sacrifices might be taking place in the bungalow and he was considering establishing official contact with the police over the matter.

Enactment of an Unknown Epic

(1982)

That year Maximilian devoted himself to writing and staging a play entitled *The Unusual Adventures of Methuselah McGanaghan*. Work on the project commenced in early January and after a few days of writing he began to devote much of his time to completing the piece, which he was adamant had to be performed before the termination of the year. The play's sole performance took place in a cramped room above a pub in Camberwell on the evening of December the 30th and was attended by a tiny audience made up of men and women who had for whatever reason been intrigued by one of the posters that Maximilian had hung up inside the few theatres in London whose management would allow him to display one.

The performance lasted for six and a half hours, with no interval. It described, in immense detail, the life of its titular protagonist. During the course of the piece, Maximilian played 143 different characters, assuming a different tone of voice for each and performing a frenzy of movements for his audience, as he jumped from one portion of the stage to another, generally on tiptoe, sometimes portraying semi-improvised five-way conversations which lasted for hundreds of lines. These were interspersed with long monologues delving into the richness and fury of McGanaghan's life as it unfolded throughout the 1920s and on into the '30s. Moving across a number of continents, McGanaghan met up with a great sweltering mass of humanity, including a chorus of shambling beggars and quick-witted conmen, lascivious sailors and alcoholic journalists, not to mention cameo appearances from a vast array of other individuals including a number of tennis players, anaesthetists, and international telephone operators. Furthermore, especially for this performance, Maximilian had undertaken several months of study mastering the art of vocal imitations, for example musical instruments and the sounds of nature—bodies of water, animals, weather—in order to suggest aspects of the environment that his protagonist would be passing through. Bubbling and rushing sounds stood in for rivers, oceans, lakes, and so forth. Pressing his tongue tightly against his teeth, he could create a buzzing that resembled a harmonica. His trumpet was a particular success. More than once, during the play, he attempted the sounds of an entire teeming marketplace, complete with a cloud of babbling voices and a frenzy of footsteps.

Oil lamps and fairy lights were laid out across the stage, casting slanted shadows and pools of luminescent light, Maximilian's attempt to project an aura of mystery, to imply a space in which mythology might possess a certain reality and in which the contemplation of supposedly impossible pursuits would become as natural to the audience as silence. Upon an enormous backcloth, shades of olive, vermillion, and gold alternated within depictions of a variety of key moments from the life of McGanaghan. Maximilian stood before it with pride, gesticulating wildly, chin held high, modelling a series of hats that changed with every new profession or pursuit that McGanaghan embarked upon, although at all times the star of the show was bedecked in a white cloth suit with red braces, a red handkerchief folded into a triangle and tucked conspicuously into his breast pocket. In such a costume Maximilian felt that he could adequately convey his ideas about centuries of English gentility and the odd relationship it possessed with the no less significant desire to dominate other nations.

Brought up in conditions of dire poverty in the East End, Methuselah was determined to escape his background. Each of his fifteen brothers and two sisters made a brief appearance during the early scenes. They would be together in the street playing interminable games of football and cricket, occasions that would often collapse into violence, with fist fights and headlocks becoming increasingly common amongst the young men at the onset of puberty. Of the various members of the McGanaghan family, Methuselah alone found these grunting displays of power and bravado to be repugnant. Crying or glowering by himself on the doorstep of their house, he felt no sense of fraternity whatsoever, and future decades of disgust began to brew within him. He vowed to himself that he would be free. At last he couldn't spend a day longer in the company of his family.

Following these instincts, Methuselah took ship to America at the age of sixteen, joining the teeming crowds at Ellis Island before spending two months hopping freight trains as far as the corn fields of the Midwest, where he briefly obtained employment as a farm labourer. After this, he began to dream of a life as a film star, so he travelled to Los Angeles, succeeding only in becoming an extra in the film *Foolish Wives* by Erich von Stroheim. Glimpsed for a fraction of a second in a crowd scene, obscurity claimed him soon after.

Depressed by his inability to make any real entrance into the world of film-making, he made his way to Paris. Trying to pass himself off as a poet in the cafés of Montparnasse, he soon made the acquaintance of a number of dissolute characters who led him into a life of criminality. Smuggling opium into the city and selling it to the city's artists, he soon began to make quite considerable profits, but after a number of run-ins with the authorities, he decided to flee the country.

After throwing a dart at a map of the world whilst wearing a blindfold, McGanaghan next chose to travel as far as the Siberian wastes by train, with the intention of learning elementary Russian and opening a cocktail bar. Instead, after enduring a series of long and barely comprehensible conversations with his fellow passengers, McGanaghan came to feel that he would very probably die there. In a monologue lasting nearly half an hour, he describes the many sounds that he thinks he can distinguish, listening to the winds at night as they whine and rattle against his window.

Standing silent and frozen in a tableaux for some minutes (representation of the passing of six years and McGanaghan's growing belief that Soviet Communism would be a failure), the play's action abruptly shifted to the Moroccan city of Fez where McGanaghan was now living in fits of desolation, penniless, whilst dreaming of becoming the owner of a wallaby farm somewhere in the deserts of Australia. These dreams came to haunt his sleep on an almost nightly basis and Maximilian enacted a number of such nights, including various conversations McGanaghan shared with several favourite wallabies, indicative—dramatically speaking—of the character's nervous collapse. He then became a goat herder on the blasted plains that lie between Marrakesh and Ouarzazate, but after a few months found that this life was no more tolerable than any of his previous ones. It wasn't long before he hid himself on a ship that was sailing from Casablanca to Uruguay.

After this shift in location, McGanaghan ran through something close to the entire spectrum of emotion that an individual might come to know during the course of a lifetime. On several occasions McGanaghan nearly died. In Venezuela, a waiter attempted to cut his nose off with a razor blade. In Peru, he suffered from the agonies of madness after licking the hallucinogenic skin of a frog. In Mexico, he was accidently buried in a coffin writhing with rattlesnakes. And on it went.

The stage came to take on the dimensions of the world itself. Jumping, shuffling and gliding from one portion of the stage to another, he traversed many regions of time and space, so that a single footstep would represent on occasion a movement of many thousands of miles, a transposition from one continent to another, from one era to another. Maximilian took cosmic leaps, defying (in pantomime) the constraints of earthly life and affirming his freedom as an individual fully in control of his destiny. Maximilian believed all this to be his own innovation.

Using the format of a one-man show, he hoped to investigate the manner in which an individual confronts society, the compromises he has to make in order to engage with the social sphere, and the complex range of tensions that arise whenever a strong-willed person defies the rules and conventions of the social order. He liked to see McGanaghan as a great individualist, a loner rebelling against the fate dealt to him by the whims of birth—who would come into his own as a human being through a series of decisive actions rather than the whims of fate, heredity, culture, and so forth. Better put, Maximilian saw the play as, principally, an examination of identity itself: the different masks worn by an individual over the span of a lifetime. These personae differed so greatly from one period to the next that it was unclear where the self was in fact resident, the role with which it had the most natural affinity—the play explored the fragility of the self, the way in which the mask has superseded the face. All the while, simultaneously, though his audience could neither have noticed nor much cared, Maximilian was presenting a sly self-portrait, a record of his own shape-shifting, chameleonic stroll through the darkened backstreets of history.

Of those citizens who had chosen to attend the performance, only three stayed all the way to the very end, but each who did so seemed to enjoy himself. Afterwards, in a doomed attempt to engage Maximilian in a discussion about his opus, these few spectators found themselves feeling no less alienated than those audience members who had abandoned the performance early, thanks to Maximilian's extraordinary coldness. Maximilian simply pocketed the small amount of money that the play had generated and promptly marched out of the front door, alone, silent, tussling with his demons in ways that his audience would doubtless find largely incomprehensible.

What Will Happen at this Juncture?

(1983)

A gradual movement towards the abstract in which any slender narrative you may have perceived to this point is abandoned in favour of dropping all recognizable characters and henceforth describing nothing but landscapes trailing off into secluded rooms and unknown corners of villages?

A descent into the quotidian where each object and landscape is grey and the emphasis is firmly placed on the precise routines involved in cooking a meal, in washing oneself, in walking down streets that are lined with houses, in watching weather forecasts, in generally experiencing boredom and toil, perhaps in the figure of a man stumbling onwards just as anyone does, in infinite cycles of repetition, whilst he waits desperately and vainly for anything to change, for anything of interest to ever occur at all?

Long sequences of portentous symbolism, littering the remainder of the narrative with clocks and shadows and dwarves, with strange melancholy descriptions of day and night that will be depicted as entities ruling over two distinctive temporal theatres, in which every character is wearing a mask and their clothing always corresponds to their status, a situation giving rise to multiple interpretations and (hopefully) long classroom debates, to further books filled with elaborate analyses of the tumbling profusion of (no doubt) significant statements and troubling allegories?

A sequence of memoirs, recollections of childhood, suggesting that the past matters more than the present, that a person is only a catalogue of his or her memories, of whatever they happen to remember, an accumulation of ways in which they have learnt to be themselves, in the process of which finally all the things they hoped to retain from this journey are lost irretrievably?

The book progressing and traipsing from one curious incident to another, maintaining the ever-present possibility that another street will be wandered down, in order to discover what lies beyond other walls, where perhaps acrobats will appear clambering on top of each other to create a pyramid, before suddenly disappearing, existing as an illustration of the notion that "anything might happen at all"?

A complete change of every element: character, tone, pace, rhythm, style, typeface, layout, situation, hairstyle, house, plumbing, outlook, paradigm, clothes worn, weathers observed, facts related, colours mentioned, items bought, rooms furnished, metaphors employed, religions preferred, events depicted?

A lurch forward in time of perhaps 859 years, a change of scene, with things no longer so simple and now possessing so many layers of historical meaning that it has become difficult to even perform the act of walking from one side of the street to the other, a place in which time travel is now a part of everyday life, thus irrevocably altering all societies, all histories, all politics, all memories, all ambitions?

A sudden enormous shift in the life of the protagonist, resulting in the remainder of his days being ineradicably altered in ways that he had previously thought were not possible, ensuring that his levels of happiness and sadness will increase, that his long-term interpretations of events both local and international will no longer seem as concrete and evident to him as they previously had done, consequently causing waves of bewilderment to affect the operation of many of his everyday actions?

It's Never Impossible to do Something for the First Time (If You Haven't Done It Before)

(1984–1985)

In the late summer of 1984, Maximilian took to attending lunchtime recitals of classical music held in a number of small churches in the West End. On these occasions he always liked to sit in the front row, a red carnation pinned to his lapel, a black fedora atop his head, his eyes firmly closed, so that he could more deeply engage with the reveries that the music induced. He loved the air of secrecy and seclusion that pervaded these events, that their sparse audiences were composed entirely of people immersed in private fantasies, persons living in retirement or exile or simply escaping from the demands of the office.

During one such recital he experienced a strange and somewhat remarkable encounter. At the end of the concert, Maximilian, in his customary fashion, stayed rooted to his seat, his eyes closed, as he spent a few minutes readjusting himself to the ordinary function of his senses, so that he might be able to walk upright in a manner befitting a citizen of composure and restraint. He was interrupted by sounds of shuffling and breathing in his immediate vicinity. Blinking his eyes open into the brightness he beheld the curious apparition of a young woman, tall and red-haired, with a yellow silk cravat tied around her neck, staring at him intently, her green irises twinkling at him with interest and amusement. After a few seconds Maximilian realised that she was the harpsichordist to whom he had just been listening.

Smiling, she greeted him. A lengthy conversation ensued, which lasted into the early hours of the evening, continuing for some time over a couple of gin and bitter lemons in a tiny bar in Soho. It became apparent to Maximilian that this young woman, who he had learned was named Ramona, had for whatever reason taken an interest in him, although he could not begin to understand her motives in this regard. Dispensing rapidly with all formalities, their talk soon ranged across many subjects, encompassing topics as diverse as the personality quirks of international chess players, the depressing nature of the government then in power in Westminster, and the extraordinary number of transvestites that both of them had happened to encounter in recent weeks. Ramona, who might have been said to "collect eccentrics," found Maximilian utterly bewitching, as he seemed to her to be quite unlike anyone else she had met before. Being still only twenty-one, she was at a stage in life that demanded the constant seeking out of adventures and this situation had presented her with a very tempting one.

They arranged to go out on what Maximilian would not have known to call a dinner date. In his favourite Korean restaurant, over plates of duck in plum sauce, they deepened their intimacy considerably by sharing further information about their pasts. Maximilian found it very odd that they seemed to have much in common. Both were "free spirits" (her term), prone to rebellious gestures that often caused them personal difficulties but, in recompense, a sense of liberation. They shared the opinion that music was the noblest of all art forms and that every last sound should be attended to in the same manner reserved for pieces of tonal music. Mischief, so called, was never far from either of their minds, and they both revelled in behaviours dominated by one or another mode of "aesthetic weirdness" (his term).

Not long after they had finished their meal, Maximilian, at the age of fifty-six, lost his virginity. It proved a shattering experience, particularly as he had assumed he would never have it. He had shut his mind to thoughts even tangentially related to the subject. Now, however, he felt that he had been in error. He had suffered a great existential loss. He had never understood that sexuality was the secret hidden at the heart of human life! Wandering through crowds, he looked at every adult that he saw in an entirely different way.

Ramona had coaxed him back to her room in South Kensington, where the crimson walls were decorated exclusively with broken mirrors, and where a four-poster bed, covered in white muslin drapes, was the undisputed locus of thought and deed. Throwing Maximilian onto the mattress, she had torn away at his clothes, an act he had read about but never imagined could occur in so literal a fashion, scratching her nails across his back and thighs, covering him with almost savage kisses, before impressing tiny bite marks into the skin at the base of his neck and making demands in crude language that Maximilian interpreted (correctly) as the final ritualized gesture she would make before expecting the initiation of coitus proper.

They saw each other often. During their meetings it became apparent to Maximilian that this woman was selfish, conceited, and consumed by an unsettling snobbery directed at anyone at all who spent their life engaged in commonplace activities. Frequently, in the midst of conversations, she would raise her voice in order to articulate obscure adjectives very carefully and slowly, doing her best, he imagined, to belittle Maximilian by using words that she presumed he would not understand. Whenever she encountered any earthly phenomenon that did not meet her standards, she would roll her eyes with great, exaggerated effect, and, lightly tut-tutting, would attempt to dismiss whatever lay in her direction . . . Pleasing her for an extended period of time was more or less impossible, Maximilian decided.

In addition to the harpsichord, she could play the piano, the oboe, the ukulele, and the hurdy-gurdy, not to mention a great variety of percussion instruments; yet it was the harpsichord about which she was most passionate, and to which she devoted the most time, nonetheless, she had also managed to find enough idle moments to become an expert tap dancer, a form of recreation that had come to dominate much of her leisure time from adolescence onwards, after she had been inspired by the example of the classic MGM musicals, privately re-enacting dance routines in front of her bedroom mirror.

Growing up in a family of academics, she'd been a highly educated and cultivated young lady at an age when most people have barely been given a chance to choose their own socks. After mastering a number of European languages and abandoning a likely career as a Classics professor, she began a prolonged descent into hedonism, glutting her senses with every experience available to her, focusing particularly, although not exclusively, upon explorations of her sexual temperament. Once this had become her path, she spent a number of years sampling almost every form of behaviour imaginable, socially acceptable and otherwise, making many hundreds of unlikely acquaintances, often of the sort who would vanish with the dawn and so make no further demands upon her time. There wasn't much in the world that she wouldn't be interested in trying at least once.

It took Maximilian some years to understand that this peculiar creature had been interested in the idea of him more than the individual. She had told him that she was attracted to his seniority and the status and experience that came with it. Flattered by these sentiments, Maximilian began, for the first time in his life, to walk with a proud, defiant posture. Only later did he realise that almost any older man would have been sufficient for her at that time. Put simply—she had used him.

She made sure that sex was never to be taken for granted. Frequently she would provoke him, arouse him profoundly before withdrawing her attentions entirely. He became afraid to make a move, to speak out of turn, to criticize. When she decided, finally, to return his affections, he felt as if he had won some kind of rare victory, although he could not have said how.

Nevertheless, it was clear that she derived a great deal of pleasure from their relations. They stayed "together" for a not inconsiderable length of time, perhaps—or so Maximilian feared—for no other reason than that he was more malleable than her other lovers, because so inexperienced. There was little that he would not do in order to try and satisfy her, but this compulsion was rarely reciprocated. Clicking

her fingers he would rise up and behave as required like a performing animal.

Ramona loved to taunt him. She made particular use, in this
regard, of his age, his mannerisms, and the fact that he had no sort
of social life whatsoever, aside from Ramona herself. She pitied him.
She would suggest innumerable possibilities for his engaging with
the world in more direct forms than he would ever have considered
on his own, telling him to "confront his fears." There was a very
fine line between torment and encouragement, as far as Ramona was
concerned.

Maximilian was overawed by her. He frequently thought of nothing and no one else when they were apart. He got no work done.
Images of her laughing and running played through his mind, perhaps inspired by certain pharmaceutical advertisements he had seen.
There was the time they spent together, and then the long barren
intervals in between. Nothing else. And yet, these were, without
a doubt, the happiest days of Maximilian's life. Whenever he and
Ramona parted, Maximilian would return to the bungalow and fall
asleep nearly choking on his tears of gratitude.

Of course, Maximilian did not tell Ramona the truth about his
life's work. She was never to know about the vast majority of his
accomplishments. He did take her to the bungalow on a few occasions, but despite his devotion, he felt profoundly uneasy about letting her into his domain. As expected, she had thought that the lack
of decorations and furnishings was foolish. Disapproving as she was,
she still regarded his dedication to this lifestyle as highly admirable.
He had told her at the outset that he was an artist, but he refused to
reveal even the slightest aspect of his work to her, saying only that
all of his work was done in a studio to which neither she nor any
other living soul had ever been invited. Despite feeling the inevitable curiosity, Ramona found his air of mystery highly romantic
and sought, in her way, to prolong it, rather than try and get Maximilian to acquiesce. Their relationship was based upon the erotics of

falsehood and concealment.

At first they did the things that lovers do. On winter Sundays they would take long walks across desolate windswept beaches. Gratuitous quantities of sentimental phrase would be exchanged in hushed tones. They would kiss each other with the intention of making little offerings of food at the same time. Each invented a dozen terms of endearment for the other on a more or less arbitrary basis. Dressing in each other's underwear they would parade across Ramona's bedroom in a series of spontaneous dance moves.

Once some months had elapsed in each other's company they began to play many different kinds of sexual game together. At first, they spent some time on role-playing—nothing revolutionary, but enjoying the frissons of subversion lingering in their personal interpretations of the classic bedroom personae. Father, Mother, Master, Slave, Teacher, Nurse, Policeman, Pilot, Secretary, Maid—they tried them all. Ramona was always the one to instigate these games, but the further that she drew Maximilian into them, the more grateful he became. When he and Ramona retreated to her bedroom, he felt as though he were fighting against the fact of his own mortality.

Between their meetings Maximilian would try to get on with his routine as best as he could but he found himself thinking about her constantly. During their lengthy separations, at wildly inappropriate moments of the day he would suddenly be possessed by the desire to masturbate (another recent discovery), and whilst engaging in yet another extended session of this activity he would picture his beloved and murmur her name to himself.

Eventually Ramona decided to introduce him to drugs. Roaming the streets together, high on amphetamines, they would lurch through a series of mental contortions, complicated by their rapid-fire chattering, enjoying the colours and forms of the tiniest observable objects, however simple they might appear on the surface. In this way Maximilian came to discover the urgent excitements to be found whilst attending to the fluctuations of a broken streetlight flashing on and off repeatedly, the conventions of decorum and behaviour that had become expected at the majority of delicatessen counters, not to mention the different forms of typography that were employed across the exteriors of pub jukeboxes. The terms on which he had based his entire conception of rationality were suddenly challenged, *mocked* by the very reality in which they had previously held firm. It would be quite impossible for him to return to the many assumptions which had previously ruled him.

Maximilian and Ramona spent epic days hurtling through a series of varied perceptions and identities, both of them attempting to follow the convolutions of the other's imagination, until each had become attuned to the mental co-ordinates of their counterpart. Remnants of memories thought long ago discarded were retrieved, often taking on a new significance. Maximilian and Ramona tried to invent new ways of speaking to each other in order to accommodate their sensory discoveries, until all known forms of conduct had to be forgotten and replaced. Together they vowed that they would enter the rarefied, sacred realm in which all desires are to be explored and fulfilled.

The kind of intellectual talk with which they had commenced their relationship continued, but now it formed the back-cloth of their conversation, the shared assumption lying behind their strange improvisations and excursions. Role-playing mingled with everyday speech until it was difficult to determine which "character" might be making what otherwise mundane comment. Identities merged with other identities, and one persona might dissolve into another within the course of a few minutes.

Much of their talk came to consist of in-jokes, secret messages, obscure references. Filtered through the frenzy of their amphetamine perceptions, they held on to old subjects that became manic little tics that each might throw into the stream of their relationship. Often their allusions were so subtle that their intentions were in danger of remaining secret even from each other. Playing in this manner helped strengthen the bonds of their intimacy enormously. Outsiders overhearing their conversation would likely have found it farcical, unless of course they would find it terrifying, given its lackadaisical disregard for both continuity and kindness.

And then, one day, she disappeared.

Transcription of an Afternoon Walkie-Talkie Conversation

(1985)

MAXIMILIAN: Smooth flow of black ink falls wetly from my pen nib scrawling across the surface of folded white paper. Red plastic receptacle on left hand side of desk holding assortment of pens and pencils. Heap of paper clips inside a small plastic box. Brass frame holding photograph of smiling wife and children.

RAMONA: I changed the flowers in the vase on the hall table. Red tulips. Daffodils. I held them by their stems and cut them with a pair of scissors so that they would fit into the vase. I placed them very carefully, with a measured exactitude, into the cool, transparent bulb of glass and water. I sang a little tune in the meantime. My mind was pleasantly vacant. Gradually I discovered the optimum arrangement of the flowers by arranging and rearranging them, thinking of other things.

MAXIMILIAN: I am wearing a suit. The shiny black polished sheen of the shoes. Black laces peeping through tiny silver-rimmed holes. Black socks. Pinstripe suit. Tiny white dashes arranged in long, vertical lines over a soft bed of well-cut, tailored wool. Straight, neat, silk red tie with a bulbous knot hanging beneath my throat. The redness of the tie flaring brightly over the white cotton shirt. The outfit says, I am one who commands. One who possesses a legitimate presence. One who will become very angry if provoked. One who will brandish a tool and use it with immaculate skill.

RAMONA: I made myself a cup of tea. Inside an empty white porcelain cup. I poured hot water into the cup. A white flurry of steam vapour drifted upwards, brushing against my hand. I placed the tea bag in the water, watched as tea doused the cup with an inky brown dye, a soft spreading cloud. The water was transformed, had become dark and bitter, a steaming murk. I poured soft tangled folds of milk from the jug, into the cup. I stirred the liquid in circles with a small silver spoon. The spoon gave a little ring against the edge of the cup. I sipped at the cup. Hotly, it trickled down my throat. It was quite pleasant.

MAXIMILIAN: We had a meeting this morning. Voices boomed across the room, back and forth, with a slight tingling reverberation. Charts filled with numbers were projected onto a canvas screen. The hands moved around the clock-face on the wall. I scrawled jagged abstract shapes on a piece of paper. Secretly, I took off my left shoe and rubbed the ball of my foot around in tiny circles so that I could feel the texture of the carpet.

RAMONA: I watched a soap opera. It fulfilled my need to follow the continuous tragedies of fabricated persons. I observed, once more, a fixed routine of events taking place in a well established setting. Very little that happened was surprising or unusual to me. The purpose of the narrative was to never end, to continue on into an infinity of identical days, stretching off blandly into the future. I like to see a middle aged woman who will silently speak to me from the screen saying: "I am an ordinary middle-aged woman. I suggest that you gauge your existence in relation to my own."

MAXIMILIAN: So another day is passing. There are tensions with colleagues. Particularly with those who have their desks in very close proximity to my own. We exchange a few curt words, restrained glances behind which we attempt to conceal our hatred for each other. But of course that is impossible; all of us are well aware of how we each feel about one another. We pretend that we are ignoring each other as we work, but really each of us is consumed with anxieties regarding our appearances, status, where our boundaries lie.

RAMONA: My friend Sarah rang me on the telephone. We exchanged gossip, just as we do most afternoons. As usual, we talked about our children's illnesses, purchases that have recently been made by mutual friends, simple domestic problems that we don't know how to solve, the state of the weather as it appears to us on the other side of our windows. Yes, we have a close-knit circle of friends. We are a great help to each other in our common depravity.

MAXIMILIAN: Many people fall within my sphere of influence. I like being reminded of this. I have hundreds of telephone conversations, write letters and memos, occasionally visit people at their desks on different levels of the building. I enjoy shaking hands with other men and making their bones crack whilst doing so. You might say that I spend all of my time making calculations of how I might best declare my sovereignty, how I might best demonstrate that I can mobilize large sums of money at a moment's notice.

RAMONA: I went shopping, enjoyed peering at the window displays, the possible purchases carefully arrayed on a series of pedestals, new forms of merchandise recently designed and created so that persons such as myself might have the pleasure of considering whether their interest in them is sufficient to warrant a purchase. I pick up these objects, hold them, turn them over in my hands, feel their weight, in order to decide how much they interest me.

MAXIMILIAN: I had lunch in the canteen. I spent the duration of the hour speaking to Colin. We talked about the way in which our shared obsession with football is related to a general regressive tendency that we both give in to wholeheartedly. A tendency that helps to stop us from possessing even the slightest aspiration towards reaching moral and intellectual adulthood. We agreed that we both use sport, in part, as a means of deflecting all attention away from our responsibilities and potential sensitivities. This led on to a discussion about the fact that we both like to act in a way that subtly pronounces our authority over our wives and children. We talked about how much we enjoy this mildly tyrannical power. Together, we came to the conclusion that we both love to set the limits upon what others can and cannot do, both in work and at home.

RAMONA: These actions, these afternoons define my existence. I do very little else during the week. There are slight variations now and then, but the fewer the better. The more that you are careful to follow a routine, the more that things are likely to run smoothly, without interruptions. The possibility of harmful ideas entering your mind is lessened. There is a kind of purity to keeping a household clean and orderly. I don't think all that many people understand how calming it can be.

MAXIMILIAN: I thumbed through a variety of documents, working my way down the pile stacked up inside my in-tray. Reading letters and reports, scanning rows of figures resting inside tables of statistics. Tedious, often impenetrable data that I do not always understand. And yet it goes on, so many years of quiet deception, always appearing to be such an expert. Will anyone ever see through me?

RAMONA: I dusted the shelves. I made the bed. I tidied up the conservatory. I defrosted the freezer. I looked through the mail. I ironed your shirts. I folded your socks. I took the rubbish out for collection. I fed the cat. I went to the supermarket. I cleaned out the oven. I baked an apple pie. I read the newspaper. I watched the television. I picked up the children from school.

MAXIMILIAN: I'll try to get home as soon as I can. I'll drive. In my car. Steering wheel. Gear stick. Windscreen. Brakes. Dashboard.

Speedometer. Fuel gauge. Airbag. Headlights. Wheels. Axles. Hub-caps. Exhaust pipe. Number plates. Tail lights. Central locking. Leather seats. 2936 cc engine. 170 mph maximum speed. Acceleration of 0 to 60 mph in 5 seconds. Titanium wheel nuts that add 0.00001 mph. Aluminium pivot bearings. 240 litres of boot space. I should be home in half an hour.

Relations with the Absolute

(1986–1988)

After Ramona left him, his sexual appetite knew no bounds. Yet it seemed inconceivable that he might meet another woman like her. He had no other choice than to pay for the company of prostitutes. Quietly, one after another, a series of women began to visit the bungalow. Undoubtedly, Maximilian felt guilty about this state of affairs, particularly as he could only afford their services as a result of his own illegal activities. Nevertheless, this indulgence soon became an addiction, and it wasn't long until he had drawn up a schedule of his preferred sexual behaviours, as well as their ideal timetable on a weekly basis. Women would arrive every single night of the week, each assuming the different roles that they had been assigned.

On Mondays, Elsa would visit. They had established a routine in which he would wash her from head to foot, slathering soap everywhere, running his fingers through her hair, massaging her scalp with shampoo, before applying a number of towels as she continued to stand upright and still. After blow-drying her hair and brushing it repeatedly in long, languorous strokes, he would perform a thorough manicure, followed by a foot massage. Covering the bed with pristine white cotton sheets, he would direct her to lie down upon them, still unclothed, her breasts and blue eyes and gaping cunt staring upwards at him, whilst he gradually coated every available inch of her flesh with a very thin layer of icing sugar, a substance that he would then proceed to lick away with an extraordinary slowness, lingering in some places for greater or lesser periods, often dabbing no more than the very tip his tongue onto the surface of her skin, so that only a few specks of the sugar could be removed by a single twitch. Her cunt was always his very last destination, and could only be explored—or so he had ruled—once all of the other sugar had been removed. The fleshly, sour human flavour of her sex was always

189

shocking to encounter after so much sweetness. Elsa would become quite wet, but would never have a full orgasm under Maximilian's ministrations, although he certainly attempted to make her do so on every occasion. They always parted very amicably.

On Tuesdays, Lucy would visit. He would be waiting for her, suspended from the ceiling, held aloft by a contraption he had assembled, a cunning torturing device of his own invention, consisting of an array of ropes, straps, buckles and harnesses. Whilst his naked form hovered amidst them, Lucy would alter his position on a whim, tightening the grip around one of his limbs until he experienced excruciating shudders of pain, perhaps to be relieved by a feather against his prick, or a fleeting stream of kisses travelling over the length of his belly. At any moment this feigned affection might give way to further smacks and slaps, dramatic insults intoned in a vicious gleeful voice, providing a steady ritual parade of torment and humiliation. He would savour the sense of anticipation, knowing that he was not allowed to take things as far as he wished to, and that if he attempted to he would receive inevitable punishments.

On Wednesdays, Deborah would visit. He expected her to read to him from whichever book he had left at the end of the bed. Shedding all of their clothes, she would mount him with her back turned to his face, giving very slow and gentle thrusts, whilst reading the pages of the book that had been marked up for the purpose. He would always know the passage well and begin to work towards his climax when the reading he had selected was beginning to reach the end. Ideally, he would always come whilst she was finishing the last sentence, but if this did not happen then he would attempt to do so as soon as he could. The texts that he chose varied greatly. Only occasionally were they of an overtly sexual nature, for the most part being poems or passages of prose that he believed constituted great literary works and which subsequently aroused him enormously. As soon as she uttered a single word, he would always find himself erect immediately.

On Thursdays, Olga would visit. She would provide an hour and a half of entertainment whilst he lay horizontal, masturbating, as she tantalized him with a variety of outfits, poses and manoeuvres, moving so close to his body at times that he could feel the warmth of her breath upon him. However, there was a strict "no touching" rule. She would shimmy and wiggle, waving her breasts in his face, shuffling back and forth towards the bed and then away from it again. After prolonged teasings with bikini straps and stockings, she would finally reveal herself, baring her breasts and massaging them with oil, before performing a series of cartwheels and handstands, always ending with her balancing on her head with her legs spread outwards in V-formation, her cunt fully visible and glistening, at which moment Maximilian would allow himself to reach his climax, spurting warm semen across his belly amidst a chorus of groans. Olga would then move into another room, quietly clothe herself and discreetly take her leave.

On Fridays, Rebecca would visit. After walking into the bathroom she would change into a white lace wedding dress. Once attired in this way she would meet Maximilian in the living room where he would caress her, burying his head into the folds of her dress, smelling its freshness, noting its stretches of smoothness, its unexpected creases, following the progress of its shape and length all the way to her feet, which were in white leather heels. Gently taking these off, Maximilian would put them to one side and begin kissing her feet, then brush his head against her calves and shins, before travelling up through her dress towards her thighs, where he would look above to see her white lace underwear adorned with swirling floral patterns and tiny ribbons, a dark growth of pubic hair underneath. At this point he would unzip the back of her dress and drag it down, letting it fall into a heap on the floor. Stepping out of it, she would stand still as he unhooked her bra and pulled her underwear off, sliding it over the length of her legs. He would bend her over on the floor, lower his trousers and penetrate her from behind, smacking her buttocks playfully before shifting after some moments into the missionary position, he would continue for some additional minutes and often come when both of her legs were resting on his shoulders.

On Saturdays, Lorna would visit. Maximilian would engage her in lengthy conversations. From the outset he had attempted to convince her that he was a private detective. Smoking in bed, he would recount tales of adulterers and businessmen whom he had trailed and on occasion even brawled with. Lorna had been chosen for this role because Maximilian believed that she was the most gullible of the girls that he was employing. She found his stories romantic, enthralling. The act of deception was itself a pleasing turn-on. Maximilian enjoyed embodying a masculine archetype of strength and virility. Playing this role once a week suited him. Other smaller lies would also enter his monologues, so that he used his time with her to explore a variety of fantasies of conduct. These many deceptions made their sessions an almost intellectual exercise for him. Even if the physical details of their relations held nothing unusual about them, he still felt that their sex was somewhat distinctive and rare.

On Sundays, Angelique would visit. As he lay on the bed, naked, Angelique would place caterpillars carefully on different parts of his body. With delicate, measured movements, she would place around thirty of them on his legs, chest and prick, before gradually taking them away again, equally slowly, so that the entire process would usually take about an hour to complete. The insects would proceed to crawl from one region of his body to another, and the sensation of having hundreds of tiny legs prickling across him acted as a thrilling prelude to the human caresses that would follow. The insects incited an urgent, hungry itching just underneath the surface of his flesh. At times during the procedure he would groan with the pleasure of deliberate aggravation and postponement. When his ordeal was finally over, with all of the caterpillars removed and safely locked away inside their case, Angelique would mount him. All would be over reasonably quickly, on most occasions, given the excitement that had built up within him by that point. Once they had finished, Angelique would always give him a light kiss on the lips (as instructed), whilst he lay back exhausted.

And so it continued, week after week, not counting the occasional holiday, for nearly three years. Maximilian missed the real tenderness that Ramona had occasionally offered him, yet he was amazed by his capacity to feel entirely fulfilled after an evening with any of these women. Indeed, he wondered if he had not stumbled upon his ideal form of existence. Desperate to satisfy a lifetime of desires in what little time he had left, Maximilian hurled himself into each situation with a febrile intensity, until his brow was beaded with sweat and his groin ached from thrusting. It seemed impossible that he would ever wish to cease, that he would ever feel his appetite had been satisfied.

But stop he did. Over time he began to feel that his desires were monstrous, that they seemed to loom over all of his other activities to the extent that they threatened to obliterate everything else in his existence. He became worried that he was losing his self-control and that he did not know how he would be able to contain these urges. So for the remainder of his life he confined himself to masturbation.

Instruction Booklet Discovered Inside a Large Box

(1987)

Introduction

"Time" is a game of skill for 4–6 players. It requires patience, initiative and stamina. Play involves undertaking a series of tasks that will themselves determine the movements of plastic counters upon a playing board. This then leads to the unfolding of situations encountered amongst a series of routines.

The object of the game is to solve, by means of deduction and elimination, the mysterious question of the movements of time. The winner will form a large "X" at the spot that is the correct point of the origin of time. Most methods may be employed to correctly identify this location.

Equipment Needed to Play

A Game Board
A Pair of Dice
Playing Pieces
Cards
Clocks
Alarms
Watches
Calculators
Dates
Calendars
Stopwatches
An Abacus
Sundials
Horoscopes

Hourglasses
Epochs
Aeons
Seconds
Zones
Sequences
Chronologies

Preparations for Play

(The rules of an intriguing and interesting game must inevitably seem to be slightly difficult to understand at first, but these rules have been drawn up as briefly as possible, and with a little concentration, should be easily assimilated by following out each act carefully and in its proper order.)

Act 1. Place the playing pieces on the starting squares marked for them on the board.

Act 2. All players should gather into a circle, hold each other's hands, close their eyes and collectively focus upon their perceptions of the nature of time.

Act 3. Certain players should place clocks around a variety of working environments at random intervals so that they will be encountered and discussed frequently by all who find themselves there.

Act 4. Each player should stare into a mirror, memorizing their features, the precise forms of hair sprouting and flowing from the top of their heads, the shades and colour within their irises, the clothes they are currently wearing, the texture of their lips, the angles formed by the protrusion of their nose. Attempts should be made to remember every detail observed with the clarity of a photograph. This should be taken as a starting point for one's awareness of "The Present."

Act 5. Shuffle the cards and place them facing downwards in small piles on to areas of sand, grass, snow, carpet, wood, and concrete.

Act 6. Each player should shake the dice. The highest numbers attained should be seen as indications of merit.

Act 7. One player should attempt to remember every occasion on which they have glanced at a clock. They should recall the time that they observed upon each face, the location of the clocks, their reason for needing to know the time, and the way that they felt after discovering what time it was.

Act 8. Each player should write 1000 words about an important experience in their life, focusing on the way in which their understanding of its meaning has been shaped by the passage of time.

Rules

1. Players must move in straight lines only, i.e., forward and/or crosswise, but never diagonally.

2. No other players may enter the game once it has commenced, whether for reasons of comfort, elucidation, or divination.

3. Players may consult any number of texts of their choice whilst preparing for their turn, up to and including pamphlets, newspapers, manuals, and leaflets. Still, each such item must be accounted for and noted on paper.

4. A player may move towards any destination deemed necessary as soon as such a movement is deemed needful. If permission to enter a given destination is not immediately granted, an adjacent location may be used as a substitute (if considered adequate).

5. Players are strictly forbidden to transform themselves into other players during the course of the game.

6. No move may be repeated.

7. If a player remains stationary for a prolonged period, their subsequent turns will be shortened.

8. Dice may be thrown only at the beginning of the game.

9. All encounters with unfamiliar ideas must be dealt with on a solitary basis until the end of the game.

10. Mathematical diagrams may be drawn in order to compliment intuitions and guesses.

11. Each player will only be allowed to contradict him or herself a limited number of times when attempting to account for themselves. A precise limit must be agreed upon by all players before play commences.

12. Players may not rub sticks together during the course of play.

13. If a player demonstrates exceptional abilities at any early stage of the game, it is appropriate that they be awarded a majority of points.

14. Players are encouraged to be considerate when touching upon the concepts of *age* and *aging*.

How to Play
(a) Players must assemble at a given point, bringing along the relevant equipment and being ready to commence play.

(b) Each player will pick one card at random from the well-shuffled deck. This will determine their role throughout play.

(c) Measuring instruments should be deployed at a variety of locations in order to attain knowledge of a variety of different rhythms and fluctuations. When possible, patterns should be formed which would only be visible from the air.

(d) Having reached a "room," a player may immediately make a "suggestion." Such suggestions could, for example, involve other players, locations or objects, and any interactions between these elements. In order to prolong the duration of silences during play, "suggestions" should be made using as few words as possible.

(e) These "suggestions" having been made, the player immediately to the left of the suggesting player must examine her cards. She must show one of these to the player who is to *her* left. If the player on the left is unable to show the same card from his deck, the enquiry passes on to the next player and so on, until *one* of the cards has been shown to the player who made the "suggestion." Once it has been shown, play passes on to the next player immediately to her left.

(f) Play continues to follow the movements of a spiral, circling inwards, moving towards a location that will remain concealed until it has been calculated and observed.

(g) When a player moves backwards, they must leave a trail of objects behind them—or, rather, in front of them—which can be used to follow them back to their starting/ending point. If discovered, the backwards-moving player may request an additional turn.

(h) If a player has provided significant evidence that her turn has been a success, they too may be awarded another turn.

(i) At irregular intervals, players may correspond with each other in a variety of insignificant ways provided that they have completed sufficient "suggestions" and turns.

(j) A player may formulate an "accusation" regarding the likely location of the point to be marked "X," provided that there is enough evidence in hand with which to establish a legitimate "suspicion" of said location.

(k) If an "accusation" appears to be unsustainable, all cards must be placed in a tidy pile on the floor. Players will stand in a circle around this central point.

(l) Bluffing may be taken up by a player at this juncture if a certain number of clocks have been successfully deployed. This may involve "inward-looking" bluffs in which a player secretly examines their interior for the purposes of malicious domination.

(m) If it is discovered that a player is in possession of a card which she has failed to show whilst they were making "accusations," she will be penalised by being denied any further turns, and will remain a player only in order to contradict the content of "suggestions."

(n) Should a gang of elk appear at this juncture, a series of precautionary measures must be taken in order to ensure that the game may continue.

(o) When a desirable location has been reached, players must discover its centre and appropriate methods for excavation.

(p) If enough points have been scored then a player may proceed to act upon the information that they have attained a certain number of points.

(q) As soon as all potential lines of enquiry have been exhausted, players may consider any new temporal conditions that may have come to exist since the commencement of play.

Winning the Game

✓ The winner is the first player to mark the spot agreed upon as the correct location of the origin of time.

✓ All players must concur, absolutely and conclusively, as to this being the correct location. If a single player will not accept every element of the testimony of a supposed "winner," then an ad hoc committee must be formed to resolve this difference.

✓ Once assembled, the committee must scrutinize all the claims of the so-called "winner." Magnifying glasses may be used to examine the evidence presented. Each piece of evidence should be considered in relation to every aspect of the movements of time.

✓ Any claims to victory are to be doubted from the moment that the claim first emerges from the lips of the player-claimant. If necessary, this feeling of doubt should be dramatized in such a way as to establish an aura of mild resentment, if not malice.

✓ In the event that the ad hoc committee is unable to reach a unanimous verdict, another committee should be formed (by the same players) in order to examine the motives and attitudes of the first committee. If this committee is also unsuccessful, then another committee should be formed (by the same players) to examine the motives and actions of *this* committee.

✓ If a definite conclusion is reached and a "winner" is unanimously agreed upon, then the game may be declared finished. All players should remember to withdraw any materials that have been placed within the public domain at any point during the period of play. The "X" should remain permanently inscribed within its correct position.

The Pleasures of Examining Ice

(1988–1989)

Much to his own surprise, for a couple of years Maximilian took to regularly visiting an ice rink. It began one afternoon whilst he was engaged in one of his customarily aimless explorations of the city. Without having a discernible reason to do so, he chose to venture through the doors of an "Ice Centre," perhaps because it was a species of institution which he had never paid any attention to before. In retrospect it would seem strange to him that he had never previously been inside one of London's numerous ice rinks, particularly as the one which he was to become attached to lay only fifteen minutes walk away from his abode.

When he first passed through the doors that day he was to find the ticket booth empty. Hesitant for a moment, he spent some time scanning the walls surrounding him, discovering framed photographs of curling teams. Trophies topped with gold-coloured pairs of skates moulded from plastic were displayed inside a glass cabinet. Deciding to move further inwards, he passed through the turnstile and heard a song from the radio reverberating against the walls of the palatial room that lay beyond. He tiptoed around the locker room, which was also empty, with its black rubber floor composed of small circles, and looked in interest at more photographs of local achievements in the realm of ice sports. He immediately noticed the wave of coldness surrounding everything and found it strangely inviting. A cluster of voices sounded, incoherently, from another part of the complex.

Shuffling towards the small cafe placed in a corner of the building, he found it to be open and functioning. He ordered a polystyrene cup of tea and a slice of sponge cake. As it was a week day, he was the cafe's only customer, and he looked out upon the expanse of ice before him to find it absolutely empty of human activity. For some reason he felt compelled to keep returning to this exact location, sitting in precisely the same chair, with his back turned away from the woman who served him tea, staring at the ice until he was lost in contemplations and daydreams. On average he would do this every fortnight for the next year and a half, fearing that if he were to come any more frequently the staff would consider him insane. They did anyway, looking upon him with pity, although to his relief they would always leave him to his own devices, a practice which began after they realised that when verbally approached he would barely speak at all.

He came to cherish the sense of inactivity which took over the space for some hours at a time. Entering the ice rink once more he would feel as if he were stepping into an entirely foreign jurisdiction, removing himself from London for somewhere that possessed slightly more glamour. Privately, so many details of this environment became strangely significant to him. He often liked to take note of the many frequently empty rows of blue plastic seats for spectators; the small shop which sold pairs of ice skates, sequined costumes and energy drinks; the weathered face of the woman who mopped the floors; the weekly appearance of the ice hockey goalkeepers who were so absurdly overladen with padded layers that they appeared to waddle obesely across the ice; the faces of children who would circle in the rink in imprecise circles on Saturdays, all of them equally thrilled and terrified by the prospect of falling.

On his second visit to the rink Maximilian was to find himself captivated by the pairs of figure skaters whom he watched training. In his many visits he never tired of following their intricate stances and movements acted out upon the ice. He would find himself marvelling at their virtuosity, as they formed long wavering patterns, breaking into catch-foot spirals, loop jumps, triple lutzes, or corkscrew spins. The pairs who had developed the most advanced techniques seemed as if they were attached to each other by invisible wires, making Maximilian wonder what proportion of the pairs were romantically involved with each other in one way or another. The possibility of romance seemed to be proposed, even necessitated, by all of their movements.

Maximilian loved to watch the many flourishes and exertions of the skaters, their extraordinary capacity for acting in parallel, commingling with tenderness, before separating and roaming through empty solitary spaces in which gestures that could not otherwise be given voice were played out through their limbs. He loved to see their supple, fluid movements, as they would glide over the rink, seemingly effortlessly, defying the harshness of both the ice and the blades pressed upon it. The skaters seemed so fragile to him, constantly on the brink of collapse, particularly when their manoeuvres took on very complicated forms, but it was reasonably rare for him to see anyone fall.

In the beginning, whenever he watched, all Maximilian could see was an array of abstract motions, impressive in their execution, but containing to his eyes only a confusion of jostling bodies. He wanted to be able to follow all that he encountered, to have insights into the skater's developments, understanding their faults and strengths with a clarity comparable to that of a trainer. So it was not long before he took to his usual thorough reading, examining diagrams and photographs, learning a range of specialist terminology and attending a number of competitions, finally deciding to write one of his last essays on the subject. In the end he acquired much of the knowledge that he desired.

When he questioned himself it seemed strange to him that he should have developed this new interest, because sport had never been one of his major preoccupations, interesting him only occasionally as an unknown realm set apart from his usual concerns. At times he could feel very negatively about it. But figure skating was different, and in large part this was because it was perhaps more of an art than a sport, being almost like a kitsch form of ballet, or perhaps a curious branch of show business. This was an art which claimed to be absolutely sincere in its earnest devotion to romanticism, a fact which did not lessen its beauty or attraction for Maximilian, but indeed only strengthened his convictions about its importance. He really believed that these people were unsung heroes, even the less successful ones. They seemed to him so much more than "athletes," although this was one aspect of their craft. He felt there was an expressive element at work here which meant that figure skating should be placed in an immensely appealing category—that of the forgotten art form. Considered as such, he believed that ice skaters ought to be placed beside puppeteers, stage magicians, and trapeze artists.

Maximilian would project himself into the role of the figure skater. He would imagine himself wearing a red silk shirt with florid white ruffs cascading down its centre, or a sleek purple spandex body suit for greater dexterity. In such clothes he would be accompanying a beautiful young woman to the rink, holding her firmly around the waist, raising her above his head with only one hand, or stretching her out upon the ground and spinning in charged, erotic circles. Unfortunately, he felt certain that he was now too old for such behaviour. Dolefully, he came to the conclusion that he should have taken to the ice many years ago.

Of course he *did* attempt to skate himself, and could hardly keep away from his desire to do so. Never having tried this as a child, 1988 saw what was to be his first and only effort to skate on ice. Unsteady, he just managed to keep his balance for long enough to form a complete circuit of the rink, but during his attempt at a second he was destined to fall onto his buttocks. (In the weeks that followed a small bruise developed there and he would eagerly follow its progress in the bathroom mirror.) He did not want to be dissuaded from continuing, so, despite being in a little pain, he went on and before retiring from the scene managed to complete a few more circuits without falling. However he did so wearing a face of pronounced anxiety, with his mouth left permanently ajar in an expression that was unintentionally redolent of an actor performing a slapstick routine. Afterwards, he vowed to confine himself entirely to the role of a dedicated spectator.

He was to discover that perhaps the most perversely pleasurable time to visit the rink was during an extremely hot day in summer. The feeling of having escaped his surroundings was then accentuated tenfold. Taking in slow, precisely measured breaths, he would relax into a deeply satisfying kingdom of fantasy composed of innumerable elements of ice, snow, and the cold. Much of his satisfaction with this could simply be explained by his delight at having created such an incongruous juxtaposition with the environment outside. He enjoyed discovering traces of the same sentiment in the faces of others who had chosen to come to the ice rink for the same reason. During this period Maximilian loved to watch the figure skaters train, but his principle reason for coming to the rink was always to flee from his life for an hour or so. In a number of ways this was more fully achieved when there was no one in sight. Even if all of his artistic projects were undertaken entirely due to his own volition, he nevertheless needed to escape from their maddening demands now and then, just as anyone needs breaks in their routine. Visiting the ice rink was to prove the finest method he ever found for doing this.

Occasional Wardrobe Combinations Discovered

(1989–1990)

(After many years of preserving his anonymity wearing very ordinary clothes, for the first and indeed only time in his life, Maximilian began to experiment with fashion, perusing the racks of second-hand shops for unusual items and fusing together a series of previously disparate styles in his own idiosyncratic way. Only rarely would any of these outfits be maintained for longer than a single afternoon.)

Brown flat cap. Sleeveless puffer jacket. Belt adorned with little metal spikes. Flares covered in graffiti scrawlings. Large black steel toe-capped boots.

OR

Sombrero. Blue-and-red cravat. Pinstripe suit jacket. Green-and-yellow striped t-shirt. Belt of white cowrie shells. Neon-pink plastic trousers. Sparkly silver glitter-coated slippers.

OR

Scarlet fedora. Purple cape. Yellow stars painted over forehead and cheeks. Tambourine, banjo, harmonica, and bells attached around body. Shirt made from pages torn out of comic books. No trousers. White Y-fronts. Large clown shoes.

OR

Long green hair. Swimming goggles. Purple lipstick. Cigarette dangling from left corner of mouth. Jumper depicting a canal boat scene. See-through clear plastic trousers. Flip flops.

OR

Rigid Mohican. Fake diamond necklace. Light blue shirt savaged with rips and holes. Purple leggings. A goldfish in a small round plastic tank attached to waist. Burgundy-and-white chequered bowling shoes.

OR

Deerstalker with long flapping ears. Aviator shades. Thin muslin scarf. Tweed blazer with camel-coloured elbow pads. White vest. Green corduroy trousers. Bare feet.

OR

Blonde wig. Monocle in left eye. White bowtie. Red-and-gold dragons emblazoned over a silk waistcoat. Trousers made from sheets of pink cardboard. Green socks. Slippers.

OR

Plastic cat's ears attached to head. Black ribbon tied around neck. Chest covered in an X-ray photograph of a chest. Plastic globe brandished in left hand. Purple satin trousers. Clogs.

OR

Hundreds of plastic replicas of flies attached to hair. Pince nez. White blouse emblazoned with a large black "M." Red plastic miniskirt. Black fishnet stockings. Feet inside two boxes with remote-control wheels attached to them.

The Invisible Expanding Galaxy Band

(1990–1995)

After a long period of suspicion Maximilian became a full convert to the medium of pop music at the beginning of the 1990s. For years his interest had wavered because he could not relate to what he saw as the largely adolescent emotions and stances of the music, but suddenly its aesthetics became appealing to him and he began to pay regular visits to record shops. Gathering together enormous quantities of vinyl, he became highly familiar with the ritual of record shopping, the smell of plastic and damp and old cigarettes that lingered in small shops, the act of flipping through endless rows of records at high speed in order to discover items of interest that lay amidst the thousands of forgotten and neglected acts, records that were condemned to merely be glanced at for a fraction of a second before being ignored once more and consigned to oblivion.

He got to know the frequently rude and obsessively territorial men who worked in record shops, sometimes finding himself marvelling at their often extraordinary higher knowledge of the subject, which they would casually display by playing a stream of unknown records to their customers on a daily basis, as well as by assuming an aloof authority whenever they were asked a question about a specific band or recording. Maximilian suspected that many of these men had become bitter when their own careers as musicians had floundered; once they were older they often seemed to cultivate highly arrogant mannerisms. Nevertheless, he could not help but feel a certain respect for many of these men, so self-assured and well-informed.

Towards the end of 1991 he decided to commence another project, having a number of LPs pressed, which he proceeded to secretly deposit at record shops over the following years. He paid a great deal of attention to the sleeves, but anyone attempting to listen to the records would discover that they were all blank, holding no music other than that of vinyl interacting with a needle, giving out a steady hiss.

The lavish sleeves had clearly been laboured on intensively. In each case he assembled a complex array of visual stimuli, using images that contained many thousands of miniature shapes, patterns created from repeated squiggles, lines, symbols, and indentations. Tiny grains were magnified, made immediate and visible. Bright colours shone like incandescent flames. The profusion was intended to be overwhelming, striking the eye in such a way that each sleeve would halt even the most hardened record-collector's usual frenzy of finger flicking.

Maximilian's LPs had titles like *A Mechanical History of Reduction* (1991), and *If You Don't Frolic Now You'll Never Have the Chance Again* (1994). They had all supposedly been recorded by a group of musicians known as the Invisible Expanding Galaxy Band. All of the tracks had been given the title "Anything," though the running times of each version of "Anything" varied greatly. Fictional group members and their instruments of choice were listed on the back of each sleeve, alongside often extensive notes detailing aspects of the production process, dates of composition, inspirations for particular pieces and the locations at which they had been recorded. There was no record label or contact address. On the surface, they looked like perfectly innocuous failures. Only the curious, the sort of collector who was always in search of the strange and unknown, looking out for records which had received no attention whatsoever, were likely to pay attention to these productions. Maximilian knew that his audience would be in the minority: the people likely to become interested in artworks simply *because* they hadn't been considered worthy of coverage. His records were his way of trying to speak to this demographic. For the most part he expected that it would be record shop workers who found them, but perhaps a few other intrepid persons would as well.

Sidling into the shops on Saturday afternoons, the time when the shop assistants were most distracted, Maximilian would pretend to be browsing, thumbing through records and pulling them out, setting a small pile to one side before replacing them in the stacks with examples of his own records. There was the usual fear of discovery, initially, which saw him nervously glancing around him at everyone present, wondering if he could sense any mistrust in the looks that were thrown in his direction. Eventually he came to realise that the customers never looked at each other, all being preoccupied with considering their potential acquisitions, whilst the shop-workers were all too busy reading magazines or talking with each other.

Maximilian had made a careful study of the posture and mannerisms of the casual record-buyer, focusing in particular upon the sort who never seems to actually purchase any records. After some practise, he became confident of his ability to remain anonymous, barely discernible from any other lonely browser who might stroll into a shop, lacking in memorable features to the extent that he might as well have not even been present.

He would only leave his records in small specialist boutiques, the places where genuine aficionados would meet and buy records that most people wouldn't even have heard of. Leaving a few examples of his work in each shop, Maximilian would never return to a given target more than twice, and then only after a significant period of time had elapsed.

By placing empty records within sleeves that were teeming with forms and incidents, he hoped to set up two aesthetic poles. Infinite presence and variation was set against absolute emptiness. He saw this as a way of portraying the whole potential that lay within the medium, a display of the primordial state from which all music had emerged. For the stretches of silence to take on real meaning, it would be necessary for a listener to consider why such an object had ever been created. An individual of this ilk would need to enter into the mind of the creator and feel their way around inside, engaging with ideas about the possibilities of sound. Maximilian believed that upon discovery of his records, it was surely inevitable that a series of thoughts of this kind would fall through the mind of anyone who was genuinely devoted to the medium. Perhaps the records would only be of passing interest to most people who found them, but he felt certain that they would be talked about, inspiring small clusters of people, which was really all that he had ever aspired to with so many of his projects.

He hoped that these works would be interpreted as a message to create, that the silences would be seen as a potential beginning rather than as a point of termination, that the whole project would be understood as half formed, needing to be *built upon* for it to reach some state of completion. In a subtle way he was attempting to urge the listener to fill the emptiness of his records with their own sounds, with any kind of sound, whatever they might be. He would wonder if he had in fact managed to inspire anyone to actually make any music of their own, and if they had, he formed speculations about the modes it would have taken.

From time to time he liked to listen to his creations on his turntable, often on Sunday mornings. Reclining in his armchair, he would place the needle at the very outer rim of the disc, enjoying the familiar stab of the point sinking into the vinyl, followed by the crackles and hisses that congregated near the beginning of every record, soon giving way to the emergence of a clear, perfect mirror of silence; a soft, lulling sensation pulling him inwards, black and glossy and translucent, moving in ever revolving circles towards the inevitable click, as the arm reached the end of a side, and the tiny low humming of machine-silence was replaced by the many silences of the room, by the infinity of sounds which would follow the record's conclusion.

As he listened he would invent movements of music in his head that would fill out the empty spaces. He heard elaborate orchestrations, sounds of gliding and clattering, abrupt swellings of violins, simple chiming melodies played on dulcimers, screechings and hollerings like animal cries, discordant electronic interruptions, wavering notes that were shattered and reformed and broken once more, notes that were sustained for such a long time that they seemed to stretch away into whole days and nights. On those Sunday mornings it seemed as if Maximilian heard all the music in the world, or all the music he could imagine, a teeming chaos of impossibilites.

Visual Responses to the Period in Question

(1991–1994)

(During these years, Maximilian produced many thousands of doodles in his notebooks as well as on the small scraps of paper that he used as bookmarks. Arguably these vary a great deal in terms of their accomplishment and interest to either the scholar or the casual observer, but the careful eye will note a number of recurring themes and subjects.)

The Museum of Contemporary Life

(1992–1997)

Having reached the official age of retirement during the previous year, Maximilian decided that it was an appropriate moment to embark upon his last major project. This involved the creation of an institution named the Museum of Contemporary Life. It came to occupy all four floors of a warehouse in Wapping. Displaying a vast miscellany of exhibits, he believed it would rival and perhaps even surpass some of the city's more famous museums in scope and ambition. Maximilian had written up detailed instructions for how he intended the museum to be run. If it was ever opened, after his demise, he wanted there to be no entrance fee and the public would be encouraged to roam through its spaces in any manner it deemed appropriate. Within its walls the curious spectator would surely discover much to savour and much that would enlighten.

In creating his museum Maximilian desired the achievement of nothing less than a complete transformation of the consciousness of the surrounding populace. He wished for his ideal museumgoer to enter the building with one idea of existence and to leave with another. Ideas of the "contemporary" were to be conceived here within considerably wider parameters than those which would be encountered in most public institutions, with exhibits being regularly replaced to keep up with the constant developments in the nature of contemporaneity.

As a visitor entered the building they would first encounter an area containing a selection of the newspapers which had been printed that day in London. These could be read at leisure whilst seated on a range of armchairs provided for the purpose. They were placed there with the intention of instigating ideas concerning the meaning and significance of the many things that might be considered "contemporary." The room was an attempt to directly challenge the enclaves of the media, vessels that had inexplicably become popularly associated with the act of telling the truth.

Maximilian believed that reading the newspaper was usually a spectator sport, a species of voyeurism for all but those who sought to directly affect the more important of the events described within their pages. He also found newspapers to be cultural artefacts that possessed a strange beauty, a quality he found in them when thinking of their often somewhat arbitrary designations of what might be considered socially significant. Above all, it was this latter quality that he wished to communicate.

Passing through a large hollow doorway, visitors would next encounter a room containing hundreds of identical circular clocks displaying the time in capital cities across the world. These were accompanied by many pieces of ephemera associated with different locations, including pages appropriated from tourist brochures, labels taken from tins of exotic foodstuffs, covers of books whose titles included the relevant destinations, not to mention examples of T-shirts with "Paris," "Tokyo" and "New York" emblazoned across their fronts. The room was steeped in an atmosphere of international intrigue and adventure, a feeling deeply indebted to the aesthetics of fictional espionage.

Beyond this lay a room devoted to statistics, in which calculations of different phenomena were arranged in a number of fonts and sizes, often with brief accompanying texts placed beside them which sought to elaborate upon their meaning. In large red numbers a digital screen held continuously evolving estimations of the population of the entire world. Oceans, deserts, mountains, and jungles were awarded approximate dimensions that were given in inches. Rates at which different nations consumed a number of universal commodities were compared in a series of coloured bar charts. A large piece of paper held a number of dots representing every last person who lived in Liechtenstein.

In the next room many "ordinary" objects were held upright by a series of white neoclassical plinths, including umbrella racks, fire extinguishers, plastic spoons, portions of carpet, paperclips, and road signs. Small typewritten cards described the exhibits in a number of ways. For the most part they held a solemn tone of high seriousness, possessing an air of objective authority, even when they were describing an exhibit that was plainly ridiculous. However, many of the "facts" related on the cards were deliberate falsifications, outrageous lies of the highest order. In some cases the cards made no attempt to describe the objects at all. Instead they proposed questions, made cryptic statements or responded to the objects in a number of poetic forms. With some of the less straightforwardly descriptive cards he had changed around their original locations after writing them, so that a card originally describing a painting was now underneath a clock, a flower was being described as a television set, and a wine glass had become a bicycle.

Opposite this display, crowding a number of antique mahogany cabinets, there was another collection of objects, artefacts that could not easily be come across in London, or indeed, anywhere else. Items of conventional beauty alternated with those that some would describe as kitsch. A wooden voodoo doll with straw hair and piercing eyes stared outwards, emanating a mesmerising force of weird unsettling splendour. A cigarette lighter crafted in the form of Notre Dame Cathedral was illuminated whenever asked to produce a flame. Ear trumpets from provincial towns in Scandinavia had been decorated with rustic scenes bordered with a motif of flowers and vines. A plastic telephone, manufactured in the '70s, bore the resemblance of Marilyn Monroe, who lay horizontally upon a chaise longue with one eye winking in invitation. Next to her a pine marten was suspended in motion, a victim of taxidermy who evidently intended to pounce on some prey that was unfortunately absent.

Another room held examples of the many different kinds of clothing being worn in a given year. They were placed upon a series of mannequins, each one manufactured in a slightly different style so that it almost seemed as if each was in possession of an entirely separate personality. Their limbs had been manipulated to form a number of unusual shapes and there was no evident pattern in their arrangement around the space. Certain of their number appeared to be excitable and others morose. Whilst one hovered close to the ceiling, seemingly engaged in the act of hang-gliding, another had placed her ear to the ground, evidently straining to listen to sounds that she believed would be of considerable interest. As fashions changed, their positions and gestures would also, but somehow, with an eerie persistence, their bodies would remain fixed in their exterior form, with identical physiques of an admirable quality, never becoming tarnished with the ravages of time. It would be impossible to predict exactly what they might be wearing in future years, but it was certain to involve choices that kept abreast of what ought to be considered suitable attire.

In January, each year, Maximilian would amble through the streets taking a series of Polaroid photographs that possessed only one factor in common: without exception all expressed aspects of the "contemporary" and in a myriad of ways tended to involve different forms of banality. He avoided depictions of all locations and objects that were obviously the consequence of previous eras, but besides this one criterion, which was haphazardly applied in any case, all he sought to do was to take as many photographs as he possibly could in rapid succession. They were to avoid all forms of aesthetic merit, embodying instead the pleasures of randomness. He attempted to discover scenes which would give rise to "bad" photographs. Poorly lit and framed, they existed without any overt forms of composition. Once enough had been taken each year, he placed them upon the walls without any ceremony or explanation other than the inclusion of the dates on which they had been taken.

During the course of 1993 Maximilian went out of his way to discover objects that heralded the name of the year across themselves. Calendars, diaries, annual reports, books, and T-shirts were all sought after and hoarded together. Once assembled in one place they formed a veritable collage of 1993 as seen from many different viewpoints, competing visions of a year that was shared by all who accepted this particular calendrical convention, but which could give rise to as many different experiences as there were people who lived through them. If the museum were ever to be opened after Maximilian's death, one of the duties of those running it would be to provide annual replacements of these objects.

On the second floor hundreds of television screens played a constant stream of footage taken from a number of stationary cameras that had been placed secretly within the confines of the city's many High Streets, picking up facial gestures of pedestrians who generally spent most of their time either shopping or going to and from their workplaces. They also recorded the occasional fight in parts of Hackney or along the Old Kent Road. Maximilian believed that in doing this he was providing an artistic response to the growing amount of surveillance taking place in the culture at this time, but there was also the blunt fact of the present day available within these images, clear evidence of the large amounts of vague shuffling from one location to another that most of the populace regularly engaged in. Nevertheless, he saw a certain amount of hope in the images and he believed that the voyeuristic desires they encouraged were difficult to dismiss with ease. There were undeniable joys to be gained from having simultaneous access to the evident visual and internal differences between, say, Chelsea and Greenford, or Hampstead and Rotherhithe, or Tooting and Saint John's Wood. Sometimes Maximilian would spend hours gazing at the screens absorbed and fascinated.

The third floor of the museum was entirely given over to a polemic against contemporary advertising. Appropriating examples discovered inside magazines and displayed upon bus shelter hoardings, Maximilian contrasted these with facts related to the realities of industrial production. Workers' hours and wages were listed beside photo advertisements for the products they had laboured upon, with their images of idyllic consumption. Pollutants that different companies were responsible for creating were named and described, with estimations of quantities and the effects of environmental devastation that these practices were causing. Unlike a number of the other sections of the museum the descriptions and captions provided were absolutely straight-faced and serious in their intentions. Maximilian saw advertising as the essential form of communication in the contemporary world, a medium stripped of all subtlety and nuance, a medium which propagated an outrageous series of lies. Because the bold, luminous colours of the forms that advertising took were so seductive, it seemed all the more important to him to oppose its insidious presence throughout contemporary life.

Once the creation of the museum was completed, towards the end of 1997, Maximilian locked the doors and abandoned the building to darkness. As with so much else that he had done, it would be necessary for others to find his work and choose to bring it to the attentions of the wider public. Afterwards, it was only occasionally that he thought of its spaces, the exhibits inevitably coated in layers of dust, throwing off shadows through days and nights of neglect, the mannequins and the photographs and the cabinets anxiously awaiting discovery, desperate for rescue from the oblivion that they would otherwise fall into. For his dream to be realised it would take a team of dedicated individuals to attend to it with great tact and care. But somehow he felt certain that such persons existed and that through a number of peculiar movements of fate, suitable people for the job would find their way to Wapping and decide that it was important to open the doors of the museum to all who cared to enter.

Thoughts Emerging from the Contemplation of Clouds

(1993)

" . . . honestly i think it's true to say that there are almost no basic questions being asked these days about origins and purposes . . . most people never come to a full apprehension of themselves . . . it's as if so many people are used to the saccharine comforts of childhood that we refuse to let go of our adolescence . . . have you noticed the way in which many thirty-year-olds seem to retain their adolescent physiognomies . . . think of the vast accumulation of images of youth, the bodies of fashion models, television presenters, film stars, the mass of lifestyle proposals distributed by all of the media outlets . . . collectively, these images cause people to aspire to the appearances and mindsets of adolescents . . . i'm convinced that their facial features are moulded by the continuous dissemination of images . . . believe me, this is important . . . staring for too long at a series of identical images, our bodies are naturally affected by them . . . and this eternal adolescence is further cemented by the clothes they decide to wear, their consumption choices, the cultural forms with which they identify . . . there's an enormous sadness in this . . . of course, their adolescence is a fake one, only partially successful at the best of times . . . thirty-year-olds can hardly keep the façade up indefinitely . . . finally, most of them look like rotting, overgrown children . . . sad, empty copies of images . . . " said Maximilian.

* * *

" . . . if you look at photographs or film footage from the '70s or earlier you'll find yourself thinking that there was more life in everyone's faces back then, somehow . . . yes, you can really see the difference, you can see that these faces are a little less eaten away by images, technology, mass production . . . and those people, they were so much more attractive, their eyes hadn't adapted to the act of staring at television and computer screens . . . their physiognomies look more lived-in, more aware of themselves . . . we form ourselves by staring into mirrors, you know, and not just the bathroom mirror, but the mirror of the stage, the mirror of the street . . . the mirrors of the faces of others, which we imitate, throwing our own gazes upon them and vice versa . . . a television set is a powerful mirror and a particularly poor one to choose as your model . . . of course this decline in self-apprehension isn't wholly due to the effects of the proliferation of media technologies . . . we are suffering from cultural and spatial displacements . . . the possibility of jumping so rapidly from one location to another, of living within a series of images that flip from one country to another, one object to another, one person to another . . . we aspire to impossible ideals presented to us in images . . . people mimic the pace of dialogue in television programmes when they speak to their intimates . . . their sentences become cut off before they are even realised in a form worth achieving . . . " said Maximilian.

* * *

" . . . most people don't actually live inside their bodies anymore . . . it remains an alien entity to them for most of their lives . . . there is the widespread expectation that bodies should remain youthful . . . any disease or deformity is taken as an affront to human decency . . . it's as if death and disease never occur . . . they are phenomena which should be safely confined to the television screen . . . plastic surgery represents a particularly outrageous form of this thinking . . . everyone forgets their own skeletons, their veins and muscles and organs . . . these are matters for medical professionals . . . food is ingested as if it's just another product from the production line . . . and of course that's what food *is*, from one point of view, but who aside from the people whose livelihoods depend on it give any thought to its relationship to soil, vegetation, sunlight, rain . . . food enters the body and leaves the body . . . in the same way that we simply expect a television to be regularly available to us . . . there's no exploration of the body's actual properties, its potentialities . . . " said Maximilian.

* * *

" . . . it seems impossible for so many people to imagine change at all . . . as time moves on and our social conditions remain dominated by the dictates of commerce . . . the urban environments devoid of community in which neighbours barely talk to each other . . . a reality whose rhythms and prejudices can plausibly be explained entirely in relation to the movements of money . . . yet it would be a reasonably straightforward task to begin breaking down this state of affairs . . . in a matter of a few months it would be possible to move things forward at least a little . . . but no one really wants to do that . . . the majority of citizens have come to believe that this form of living is entirely ordinary and even desirable . . . it isn't that we've reached the end of history . . . no, it's much more to do with our liking to deny that history has ever existed at all . . . whenever an individual purchases a mass-market commodity . . . an object identical in form to so many others . . . there is a comforting sense that this exchange will always be possible, that the shop where it was purchased will remain fixed in appearance and location for many years to come . . . for as long as the individual may find it necessary to return there and repeat his or her actions . . . the same motions of the body on the parts of both worker and customer . . . each without the least interest in the other as a human being . . . an interaction devoid of communication as our ancestors would have defined it . . . and the market-place demands that this be the case, that speech be kept to an absolute minimum . . . that we ignore each other's needs and propagate ignorance and silence and suffering . . . " said Maximilian.

* * *

" . . . we need to achieve a greater awareness of our relations with technologies . . . to avoid being dominated by them and see the degree to which we tend to use them in a state of utter blindness . . . i think it's ridiculous to simply dismiss technologies as negative entities, as so many of them obviously possess miraculous powers of transformation . . . they can provide us with fresh insights and new horizons . . . but this society is increasingly addicted to telephones and computers . . . we ought to be able to separate ourselves from them for a moment if it's necessary to do so . . . it should be possible for us to possess a nuanced view of the ways in which we use technologies . . . we should be able to see a telephone conversation, or indeed, any conversation, as holding thousands of potential divergent paths . . . we should attempt to form a better understanding of the ways in which our use of telephones creates and shapes our social world . . . to see that they help us to mould our identities and vocabularies and ideologies . . . and cause us to communicate with each other less and less, diminishing our inner lives and forcing us away from things of actual importance . . . it should be remembered that telephones do not allow eyes to meet each other and glimpse shades of colour . . . i think there is a great and unknown need for everyday encounters which presuppose these eye-to-eye exchanges as necessary . . . nevertheless, we cannot eradicate telephones, but it is surely preferable that we be aware of their effects and that we attempt to educate others of this . . . using subtle and devious methods if necessary . . . to constantly argue that the world is always more than you happen to think that it is . . . and that even the mouthpieces of officialdom and society . . . educators and politicians and journalists and writers . . . these people do not possess the truth, only splintered versions of available truths . . . " said Maximilian.

* * *

" . . . surely it is possible to imagine other ways of living, different forms of social organization and behaviour . . . what's needed is not some grand stratagem for renewal, the widespread assumption of a new ideology . . . we need new ideas and transformative actions to be adopted by everyone in a casual way . . . so that the majority of people start to take on board the idea that things can change from day to day . . . even *that* is a simple notion which eludes the majority of the inhabitants of this particular planet . . . the idea is stamped out of most people's minds with great invisible violence before it even has a chance of being born . . . and so often a hostility towards change results in the desperate clinging to dignity in the face of enslavement . . . nevertheless it remains perennially possible to educate and inspire understanding . . . to present people with the knowledge that they possess the power to mould their own consciousness given the limits of their situation . . . every teacher in every classroom should know this fact and attempt to act upon it . . . " said Maximilian.

The Ignoble Procession Backwards

(1994–1995)

When creating the Museum of Contemporary Life, Maximilian saved much of his energy for the fourth and highest floor in the building, the last place a visitor would reach when moving through the space. This floor was entirely given over to an exhibition that provided arguments against many of the political practices of the U.K. government in recent years. "Contemporary" in this instance covered the reign of the Conservative Party since it had first obtained a definitive stranglehold upon the political system at the 1979 General Election under the leadership of Margaret Thatcher.

Employing a large variety of charts, graphs, tables of statistics, pictures, and paragraphs of analysis, Maximilian sought to create an impassioned argument against what this government had done whilst in power, hoping also to make statements against reactionary politics of any kind. All information would of course need to be frequently updated in future years, but the exhibition was intended to be taken as a template to be used by any future museum curators.

Amongst his statements were the following:

That under the government of the Conservative Party the country had descended into an era of selfishness, in which the population began to aggressively pursue property and material wealth to an extent that had never been seen previously. Deregulation of the financial sector helped to foster a country dominated by capitalism, repeatedly destroying many possibilities for human growth. Foreign currency exchange controls disappeared in October 1979, meaning that pounds could now be moved freely throughout the world, encouraging businesses to expand and hide their assets in one or another tax haven. Banks were given the go ahead to ask the Treasury for enormous sums of money which would be taken on credit and never paid back. In 1981 house prices began to rise to absurd proportions after the banks were allowed to enter the mortgage market. Unprecedented levels of credit were sanctioned, often in the form of mortgages, so that vast quantities of pseudo-money circulated throughout the system. As a consequence of this increased credit, individual consumption started to grow by 6% each year, whilst overall production decreased, creating a major imbalance that resulted in huge amounts of hidden debt.

Throughout the '80s the Thatcher government repeatedly acted upon the belief that there should be a mass denationalisation of publicly owned assets. Little by little the interests of capital and business were put before the human need for workplaces in which fairness and equality are the rule. This strategy came to involve nearly every organisation that the government could manage to part with, including telecommunications, transport networks, refuse collection, the supply of gas, and even the provision of hospital meals. To make matters worse the general public was then invited to become shareholders in these companies. When Thatcher came to power there were three million shareholders in the U.K., but by the time that she left there were eleven million, meaning that one in five members of the populace now possessed a stake in the world of business. Ordinary working households had now become miniature capitalist investors.

The government then also began to limit the rights of workers by destroying the power of the trade unions. This was a genuinely poisonous move as historically it has only been through union organisation that workers can possess any voice at all regarding their working conditions. The Employment Act of 1982 allowed employers to sack all strikers. Unions could now be taken to court and fined enormous sums of money for "damages" of up to £250,000 depending on the size of the union. It was now necessary for 85% of the workers in a union to be in favour of industrial action for that action to be legal. Overall trade union membership fell from 13.5 million in 1979 to below 9 million in 1993, representing a massive cultural shift in favour of the interests of business.

In 1984 and 1985, the Miners' Strike had brought all of these trade union issues into focus. Thatcher had sanctioned the closure of mines, before government reports about their profitability had even been completed. In the midst of these actions the National Union of Miners called for strike action. 11,291 people were arrested during the disturbances. Certain police forces asked those under arrest about their political persuasions, a feature more often seen in totalitarian regimes. Many of the policemen fighting against the strikers were in fact soldiers who had secretly been told to wear police uniforms and often perpetrated acts of shocking violence, attacking miners on the picket line with truncheons, resulting in six deaths.

The 1980 Social Security Act had banned the dependents of strikers from receiving government benefits designated for "urgent needs," as well as bringing in compulsory deductions from the benefits that they were awarded. As the miners themselves earned no benefits whatsoever their families began to live for extended amounts of time in states of dire poverty. During the strike Thatcher referred to the miners as "the enemy within," a contemptible statement showing a complete lack of human understanding and sensitivity.

The Greater London Council, one of the few bastions of socialism then present in British public life, was destroyed by Tory legislation. Under the leadership of Ken Livingstone the GLC had brought down tube and bus fares, encouraging the use of public transport and saving the population money which was direly needed in the midst of a recession. The GLC had formed a constant series of campaigns in favour of minorities and the vulnerable. They stood for European integration and proportional representation when no one else would. Livingstone entered into talks with Sinn Féin at a time when they were essentially outlawed as a political organisation. These talks were a highly necessary move for the beginnings of any peace process in Northern Ireland, but it would be more than a decade until any politicians in Westminster did the same. In 1986 the GLC was abolished in a move that smacks of authoritarian control.

Arguably the worst actions of the Conservative Party during this period were those which saw the enormous increase in British arms sales, selling to regimes regardless of their human rights records. By the mid-'90s Britain had become the second largest arms exporter in the world after the U. S., being now responsible for 20% of global sales. Almost half of all government research and development funds were allocated for "defence." Thatcher repeatedly became personally involved in the completion of arms deals and encouraged manufacturers to increase production.

After attempting to gain independence in December 1975, the territory of East Timor was illegally invaded by Indonesian forces. Over the next two decades around 200,000 people were killed under the subsequent dictatorship, representing about a third of the population. 60,000 of these deaths came about in the first five months of the occupation, a period which involved a horrific series of tortures and mutilations. This was essentially made possible by the supply of American arms, but it was not long before Britain began to make a major contribution. In 1978 British Aerospace sold Indonesia eight military aircraft worth $4.5 million. The Labour Foreign Secretary of the time, David Owen, dismissed arguments against this action by claiming that "the scale of the fighting (in East Timor) . . . has been very greatly reduced." This was only the beginning of an extensive relationship. Between 1986 and 1990 Britain supplied $522 million worth of weapons to the Indonesian regime. By the '90s Britain had become Indonesia's largest supplier of arms.

In 1975, East Timor had been the site of an attempt to create a Communist government. Therefore the American supply of arms and silence in the face of atrocity can be seen within the pattern of the U. S. destruction of Communist governments, including those which had been formed for example in Chile, Nicaragua, Grenada, and Guatemala. East Timor was an example of the British collusion in these actions.

In 1994, Alan Clark, who had served as the Conservative Minister for Defence Procurement from 1989 to 1992 made the following statement on British national television: "My responsibility is to my own people and my own constituents, and I don't really fill my mind with what one set of foreigners is doing to another. One has to say, what is it that is so terribly special about the people of East Timor to the people here?" Such statements betray an insolent, callous disregard for the sanctity of human life. When paying a visit to Indonesia in 1985 Thatcher bluntly stated that "East Timor is not a matter for Britain." This small-minded indifference to the wider world seeped through into many spheres of British life during this period.

The Iran-Iraq War lasted from 1980 to 1988 and was instigated by an Iraqi invasion of Iranian territory. Despite this, throughout the '80s, high-ranking members of the British government repeatedly visited Iraq to discuss, amongst other things, the sale of arms. A Joint Commission was set up, meeting annually to make trade agreements. As a consequence Thatcher gave Iraq a £250 million loan to help its ailing war-time economy. This was followed by a meeting in Baghdad in 1988 which resulted in a deal that allowed £340 million of export credit.

During these years only "non-lethal" military equipment was to be sold to Iraq, although this definition rather obviously ignores the fact that *all* military equipment is lethal. Tanks, land rovers, radars, and uniforms were all dutifully supplied. Computer-controlled lathes and high precision machine tools were also sold. These were used to make components for shells and missiles. Sales to Iraq of this equipment totalled £31.5 million in 1988. Throughout the Iran-Iraq conflict the British government allowed Iraqi military personnel to be trained by the British armed forces or at Ministry of Defence establishments. At one point in the early '80s around 4,000 members of the Iraqi military were being trained in the U.K. yet despite this long term support of the Iraqi regime, as soon as Iraq invaded Kuwait in 1990 it seems they were no longer permitted to use any of the arms that had repeatedly been sold to them by the Western powers.

The largest arms deals in world history were conducted between the U.K. and Saudi Arabia in 1986 and 1988. These resulted in the sale of hundreds of military aircraft and naval vessels worth £40 billion. The deal became known as "Al Yamamah," which means "The Dove." This deal was only secured after Thatcher abandoned a holiday and entered the talks herself. It seems that this ensured an enormous and illegal "commission" for her son Mark who is estimated to have made £12 million during negotiations. Much of the deal was paid for in oil. Saudi Arabia agreed to supply the U. K. with 600,000 barrels of oil a day, a quantity which continues to account for about one third of all oil consumed in the U. K. at the present time. Shell and British Petroleum were given the rights to this much sought after substance. All profits, after deductions had been made by the oil companies, would then be given, via the government, to British Aerospace. It should not be forgotten that to trade with Saudi Arabia is to sanction a government which has no qualms about imprisoning or torturing its opponents.

All of these arguments and more took up the entire fourth floor of the museum. Whilst Maximilian felt it was a shame that the exhibition would not be seen by the public immediately, he still saw it as his own contribution of protest to a highly significant period in British political and social history. Even if it was to be some years before the museum had any visitors, he firmly believed that anyone seeing his exhibition in years to come would still note the importance of what he had to say.

Interview Performed by a Computer

(1995)

(The following "interview" took place after Maximilian formulated approximately one thousand potential questions to ask himself. Once he had completed this task, he fed them into a computer programme that would choose and present them to him at random. He waited six months before undergoing his self-interview, as he thought this would be the minimum span he would need in order to forget most of what he had wanted to ask.)

In what ways do you think that robots will influence the future?

For some time now I have been convinced that the future will be populated by many robots. This belief was shared by many other people during the 1950s, although I feel that the prevalent sense now is that such an idea is foolish and old-fashioned. Still, I persist in believing that robots will one day take over the majority of menial occupations, but only when humans well and truly lose their taste for enslaving one another.

Have you had any significant thoughts related to laundry in recent days?

I believe that the frequency with which bed sheets are cleaned, the style of ironing employed, the smell of steam and cleanliness which may or may not emanate from them, and the skill with which they have been deployed upon a bed . . . all of these things are reliable indications of the health of a given individual.

Are you a misanthrope?

I think, unfortunately, my answer must be given in the affirmative.

From a very early age I began to loathe much of what I saw of the world. Almost everyone I knew seemed quite incapable of looking beyond the confines of the social and economic class to which they'd been confined. There was no question of reformation. My contempt for those surrounding me grew into feelings of rage directed at almost everyone, at a society that refused to progress. This is still how I tend to feel about things. And yet, at the same time, there are undeniably feelings of pity lying within me. My desire to be a *philanthropist* is also a strong force that drives me. This is because I want to live in a different society. And because I want to help those who feel oppressed by the structures of this society.

Do you believe in what is popularly called madness?

Undoubtedly. There is a line that certain people cross. Once resident past that boundary, they exist beyond the perimeters of our culture. Very often there is no escaping this predicament.

What is your favourite form of transportation?

My time spent riding underground trains in the late 1950s was a source of great pleasure. I love the forms, the colours, the generous expansiveness of the London Underground map. I remain pleasingly overwhelmed by the number of neglected areas still to be found on it, and by the thought that all of these places are teeming with multitudes of lives. I love the fact that each train carriage contains an entirely different conjunction of people who have been thrown together at random. I love the dark smell of the machinery, the speed at which the trains hurtle through tunnels, the feeling of lurking beneath roads and buildings and pavements.

What frightens you?

Many things. The obvious disparity between different social groups. Ugliness of conduct. Observing the features of someone clearly enamoured with themselves and thus lacking all sensitivity towards others. Military atrocities. Any behaviour or thought, in fact, which is at all comparable with that of the military. The inability of human beings to leave aside their violent urges. The inevitability of death and its looming closeness with each passing moment of time. The arbitrary forms that nature takes, including, most prominently, as far as I am concerned, the shape of *Homo sapiens*.

Do you consider yourself to be an obsessive?

I don't think I could plausibly deny it. Nevertheless, I think it's easy to misuse the word . . . If we wanted to be kind we could use the word "dedicated." I think that would be the fairer thing.

Do you believe in the quality of "respectability"?

Usually this is a term which describes the façade that people throw over themselves in order to justify a series of behaviours which when scrutinized might seem considerably more dubious than at first sight. Those who seek respectability are often amongst the most contemptible people in a society. These are the people who tend to elect right-wing governments, who oppose individual liberties, who adhere to religious fictions. This does not mean that there are no people worthy of "respect." But that is surely a different quality altogether.

What bores you?

Whenever during the course of my life I've succumbed to watching television, I've become consumed almost instantaneously by a sense of monotony that I found quite astounding. Extended coach journeys, the pages of scientific textbooks, lengthy church sermons, and the experience of waiting in supermarket queues are also examples of things that have induced particularly debilitating attacks of tedium.

What embarrasses you?

Above all, my body.

What are your feelings about the suburbs?

I must admit, somewhat reluctantly, that the suburbs have always held rather an extraordinary fascination for me, despite the parochial attitudes held by those who live there (or the attitudes, in any case, popularly associated with such people). I don't really quite understand why anyone would want to live in a place that is basically a non-place, the absence of definitive location. A neighbour to nothingness, one is so easily tempted into joining the dance of absolute emptiness. Still, I have long believed that the atmosphere of these districts has a strangely calming, even blissful aspect, lulling one into a sense of security that I cannot help but find attractive. Peculiarly, I'm sure this is more or less the same view taken by the majority of the long-term residents.

How do you respond to allegories?

The allegory is one of my least favourite narrative or pedagogical forms. I am reminded of Latin lessons in badly heated rooms. Tight-fitting uniforms. Preachings about the nobility of masculine endeavour. That sort of thing.

What is triviality?

The absence of all significance. Perhaps the one thing that every last element of existence has in common.

If you knew that you were about to die, how would you respond?

With the terror of being conscious of the moment of its happening. I'm sure that all of my thoughts would be directed towards that end alone. Ideally, in such circumstances I would like to feel a certain levity, a Buddhist sense of calm, a state that I have been attempting to achieve through meditation for a number of decades now, but which nevertheless seems to evade me because I remain genuinely terrified of death. Many of my projects over the years were begun in order to attempt to transcend the fact of death, to obliterate its power through action, but whatever one does, death still insists on approaching and one cannot ultimately win when one attempts to challenge it. I've tried to do everything that I felt I had to do before dying.

What is sunlight?

Purity born of violence.

How would you describe yourself?

There is something to be said for the opinion that my life has been one long, sustained farce.

What do you feel the greatest advantages of invisibility would be?

I think my greatest fascination would simply be with watching people as they spent time alone. Individuals behind the closed doors of their rooms, resting with their own thoughts and engaging, doubtless, in all sorts of extraordinary behaviours.

How would you describe your relationship with money?

I never think about it anymore. I really have nothing to do with it. After a while, even being a counterfeiter—and the steps one must take to avoid being prosecuted for such—becomes second nature, like crossing the road safely or blowing out a match. Consequently, I think my relationship with money has been, uniquely, a very happy one—not because I have it in abundance, because all I've ever had was the faith that other people have put in my having it, but because I have managed to destroy its influence upon me.

Do you believe in ghosts?

I do think that I have felt their presence from time to time, mostly in ways impossible to adequately communicate.

How would you describe your relationship with the countryside?

I am forever attempting to negate the countryside, to behave in a way that denies its existence. For nearly the entire duration of my life I have been fascinated only by the things which exist almost exclusively within the metropolis: mechanisation, anonymity, abstraction . . .

What is the meaning of prosperity?

Perhaps there are as many kinds of prosperity as there have been people who've known it. One can be a millionaire of glances, a millionaire of footprints, a millionaire of sighs . . .

What is the purpose of hiding things?

To maintain the possibility of the sacred.

What conclusions can be drawn from the presence of linoleum?

Very few *definitive* conclusions can be drawn. Nevertheless, linoleum tends to signify one or another form of impoverishment. Sometimes this is noble, but often it is terribly sad.

How to Celebrate with Equanimity

(1996)

And so, all of a sudden, it seemed that the occasion of Maximilian's seventieth birthday had been reached. He believed that it was necessary to celebrate this particular anniversary with as much effort and enthusiasm as he could muster. Anxious to mark the passing of time, he vowed to leave no stone unturned, so that he could truly say he had lived without regrets, fighting nobly against the death that would one day inevitably claim him.

Awake before dawn, he commenced the day walking from Hackney to Mile End, observing the gradual shifts in light, the succession of empty double-decker buses, the early risers out and about walking their dogs. As soon as he found an off licence that was open he ventured inside and purchased a variety of bottles of ale—substances that he immediately began to consume.

Before noon arrived he had already obtained a consultation with a telephone psychic, played half a dozen low-scoring games of pinball, walked through a number of the rooms of the National Gallery backwards, given what he considered to be a fine performance on the kazoo to the figures emerging from Leicester Square underground station, and somehow found his way to the roof of the Langham Hotel where he commenced an episode of shouting, bellowing, and mumbling a tirade of obscenities into the bitter, raging winds of morning, somehow evading the attentions of all forces of authority.

After lunch at Simpsons-on-the-Strand, he began accosting pedestrians who happened to be walking down Charing Cross Road, partly in the hope of meeting "literary types," but mostly in the hope of finding a woman willing to fall in love with him and demand that this love find immediate physical expression. Mistaking him for one of the destitute, the individuals he approached were not about to supply the comforts that he longed for, but he did manage to engage one or two people in somewhat abrupt conversations that were generally cut short as a direct consequence of his reeking breath.

By two o'clock he was busy writing letters of complaint to a number of publications and institutions which had long irritated him, even daring to sign them all with his real name and address. For the most part these all got to the point extremely quickly, as he did not feel that he had a great deal of time to waste on that particular day. Irate in manner, they frequently dissolved into acts of swearing and it did not usually take long for these pieces to trail away into the sort of incoherence that might be conceivably referred to as "insolent," at least by those who did not support the terms on which such an approach was based.

After walking out halfway through a matinée screening of 3D short films held upon a barge in Little Venice, he scoured the streets for the nearest public house he could locate. Approaching the bar in the first establishment he had discovered, he decided to order three drinks simultaneously, an act which resulted in the bartender having to work out a set of conflicting arguments in his head about the morality of serving such a person. Nevertheless, Maximilian achieved his aim and so took his victory prizes over to what he would claim as his own table for the rest of the afternoon. Inspecting a pile of women's magazines stacked upon a shelf beside him, he was soon busy pondering over the value of Lycra.

Shortly after six o'clock, Maximilian found himself on his feet, spinning in circles, abruptly catching his fall by holding on to the bar, attempting but failing to achieve a coherent melody on his kazoo, then, stumbling a few steps rightwards, he was suddenly surrounded by human company. These unknown persons first led him towards a chair and then aimed a number of statements in his direction, words which managed to mingle a sense of amusement with a somewhat patronizing sarcasm. He was soon asked to leave.

On his way out to the street he encountered a whippet, doleful-eyed and panting, tied up to a pole. Pity welled up within

Maximilian's breast and he struck up a very short conversation with the creature, which lasted until he was rapidly ushered away, during which moment he caught sight of a bus out of the corner of his eye, a vehicle that he then rushed towards with gay abandon, managing to board it without tripping over his trailing shoelaces. Giving a conciliatory nod to the driver as he wandered past, he took his place at the front of the upper-deck.

Descending into heavy slumbers, he had a series of short, evidently interconnected dreams about taking a number of different hovercraft journeys. These were the first dreams that he had remembered upon waking for some years. Each dream possessed an atmosphere of disquiet, taking place within muted industrial shades of grey and dark-green. Somehow it was never clear just where the hovercraft might be venturing towards and why anyone might have embarked upon such a voyage in the first place, yet it was evident to Maximilian, although he could not say why exactly, that particularly sinister things were about to occur.

Waking up, doused in sweat, he discovered that night had descended. Leaving the bus he found himself staring with some fascination at an array of television screens which were arranged in the window of an electronics shop. A forgotten old black-and-white movie was playing and he looked on fascinated, attempting to identify its provenance. Blonde chorus girls wearing identical skimpy outfits, all spangled with silver sequins, were forming elaborate hand gestures, wiggling their hips in unison and singing lines that seemed to be about the joys of life after puberty. When the chorus came, half of the girls began drinking from long twirly plastic straws which descended in spirals towards an enormous vat of soda pop, alternating between sucking actions and singing, as the camera lunged in circular motions, dizzy with the spectacle it was so busy in creating.

He next travelled eastwards for half an hour with the sole intention of visiting the Woolwich Leisure Centre Café, a favourite haunt in recent years, probably for reasons mostly inexplicable, although if pushed on the subject Maximilian might well have mentioned the location beside the river and the pleasant view of the swimming pool below, with its looping anaconda water slide, fake tropical beach hut, and colourful octopus mural. For whatever reason, it was a place that he had come to enjoy relaxing in. That night he stayed there for a couple of hours, lost in meditative reveries. Later, in another public house, upon consumption of his third shot of tequila, he took to musing on the subject of the lack of children in his life. Scribbling outlines of the lives of imaginary offspring onto paper, he began to create some very partial pseudo-biographies of the various children that he was surely now never destined to have. Somehow he could only envisage failure taking place for them all, the initial hopes of late adolescence being followed by a debauched studenthood and then the sour disappointments of the workplace. Alcoholism, obscurity, death. Surely it was a good thing that he had never become a father.

Staring into his reflection in the bathroom mirrors, Maximilian felt as if he was truly seeing himself for the first time that day. Stripped now of joy, he was left only with the aching sadness he felt upon looking intently into the folds of his aging features. A lopsided fake ginger beard purchased in a joke shop hung disconsolately from his chin, wet at the fringes with liquor and dribble, and he could somehow not find the strength required to remove it. Children's badges lined the left lapel of his tweed jacket. A broken straw hat perched on top of his head somehow seemed to complete the picture of a broken, fallen man. He wondered, quite seriously, if things had gone too far that day.

Pirouetting and zigzagging through the streets after closing time, Maximilian eventually spotted a park. Gaining entry to it by crawling on his hands and knees and struggling through a hole that had been created in the bottom of the fence that surrounded its perimeter, he eventually reached the dark velvet of a lawn. Amidst the cool night-breezes he felt a sudden overwhelming desire to remove all of his clothes and commune with mystic forces. This he soon did.

Making a series of tiny jumps into the air he spread his arms out wide and ran across the spaces of the park pretending to be an aeroplane. Curious suddenly to inhale the odours of the trees surrounding him, he picked off a number of leaves, felt their shapes and textures, then crushed them with his fingers, rubbing the residue over his chest and belly, an act which caused him no little merriment.

Somehow he did manage to make it back home to the bungalow that evening, although in the morning he could not remember how. He fell asleep on the floor, in fact missing his bed by only a metre or so. At the moment of his collapse he had been busily biting into the succulent form of a cheese and piccalilli sandwich, but unfortunately this particular attempt at eating was to remain unfinished and the sandwich would lie upon the floor until morning, with tooth marks engraved upon its form and most of its contents spilt out onto the carpet.

Reflection in a Darkened Window

(1997)

the face of a man
      on the brink of old age
    catching himself in a mirror
      briefly formed
across the giant surface of a shop window

flurry of West End pedestrians unceasing

apprehension of the image
a moment of absolute clarity
that disappears almost at once

      an exact rendering of:

            age
            status
            situation

        greying lips
cheeks pitted with acne scars
      scratchy stubble bristles
   across haggard chin
        soft wisps of white hair
      sprouting outwards from ears
bloodshot eyes
      falling into blindness

the tyranny of the present
of naked reality

where all is lucid
and can be measured
in calm exactitude

noticing
behind his shoulder
another man
perhaps ten years older than himself
in solitude
hobbling

turning,
they share a brief look of grim recognition

a man who may as well possess the same history as him:
the same habits, obsessions, degenerations

but neither will ever see the other again

flurry of pedestrians unceasing

.

during its precocious lifetime
one particular fly
travelled all the way from Regent's Street to Blackfriar's Bridge
before dying without fame

meanwhile, the old ladies of Mayfair had mouths of false teeth and
neck's adorned with strings of real pearls
    and beggars with blackened fingers bent down desperately to pick
up greasy coins in the corners of doorways
    and steam rose from plates of food, placed with great ceremony
upon the fastidious tables of opulent restaurants
    and great flowing rivers of water and shit coursed through the spi-
ralling webs of pipes, towards the swollen mass of seas

.

declensions of time
        impossible to count
     disappear into hourglass void
            fragments of days dissolving
                    invisible

the mass of things exhausted and expended

(matchsticks, lightbulbs, pairs of socks, train tickets, wine glasses,
forgotten breaths . . .)

the irrational selections of memory

    the absolute glistening clarity
        of certain insignificant occasions

to remember:

the exact bone structure
and the particular imploring look
found resident in the eyes
of a shop assistant
long ago

to remember:

the warm smell
of the bread factory
permeating the air
of the dilapidated playground
by the dirty canal side

to remember:

the descent from the third floor of a building
undertaken solely to observe
the movements in the street below
resulting in the discovery
of nothing much—
the same rows of parked cars
the same unknown figures walking
midst scattered leaves
& flint-grey puddles
empty sweet wrappers
& overcast skies

.

tired limbs
  weary in pale dawn
constant shifting
  movements
to release tension

an exercise
which yields
few benefits

   so

   finally

the shifting ceases altogether

to instead enjoy
the pleasures of not moving
limiting the aches
to those that are known

     sciatica
    arthritic hands
  curvature of the spine
    harsh pains surging through
      soles of the feet
    the remaining teeth throbbing
  moderate deafness in left ear
      red rash forming across genitals

     the awful
   apprehension

of morning nudity
as the skeleton
becomes visible
pushing out
towards the surface

.

infinite layers of brickwork across the sea of rooftops
domes and statues and chimneys
smooth black *glissando* of taxicabs
through alleyways and city arteries
orange-red haloes thrown from streetlights
in the grey of the descending dusk
workers marching homewards in precise formation
boarding buses and trains in toil of daily exodus
huge looming empty churches with locked-up doors
frightening protrusions of the dark machineries of commerce
stray newspaper pages blown against the walls of mercantile
institutions
as illuminated windows provide momentary illusions of heavenly
prosperity

.

and yet the city can be anything

there are green paper dragons in Camden
quartz elephants in Harrow-on-the-Hill
tightrope walkers congregate in Poplar
a blind harmonium player practices in

The Currency of Paper

Walthamstow
giant aquariums fill small rooms in
Marylebone

a small girl in Brixton collects rainwater in old jam jars placed on a windowsill

an old man in Leytonstone has taught himself to speak Esperanto but has no one to practice with

there is a room in Soho that no one has entered in more than one hundred years

The Distribution of Resources

(1998)

After a lifetime spent hoarding funds and materials largely for his own means, it seemed appropriate to Maximilian that his final major artistic action should involve a mass donation of resources to a vast array of different individuals and organizations. He wished to reach anyone who he felt had been overlooked or neglected by society, and was particularly interested in helping artists whose work had not resulted in any great acclaim or financial reward. All of the many unsung creators and revolutionaries, whose works he had been pursuing for some time, would receive some form of recognition from the capacious depths of Maximilian's purse.

The plan to make these donations had been crucial to his thinking from the very beginning of his artistic schemings. His conviction that he would do this had somehow underpinned all else that he had done in his life, in a sense justifying all his other projects. All along, his relentless gathering together of examples of legitimate currency had largely been in order to make these donations. In performing this final act he believed that he was doing all that was in his power to behave in a benevolent way.

By this time in his life Maximilian had become remarkably knowledgeable about the financial and personal difficulties of many people whom he had never met, persons who often lived some miles away from him. Thumbing through his extensive filing systems, he perused the extraordinary number of documents that he had either copied or stolen from a vast range of businesses and organizations. Attempting to recall every last person whom he had ever considered as deserving of financial aid, he obsessively listed names until his handwriting had taken up many hundreds of reams of paper, straining towards a futile attempt to create a genuinely exhaustive, definitive list. Having long since intended to make such donations towards the end of his life, the numbers of potential recipients had built up into a ramshackle profusion of names and faces, a state of affairs that was by now desperate for some kind of formal articulation. To the names of the genuinely needy he added a certain number that he selected at random from the telephone directory.

In order to protect his anonymity, some years ago he had begun to create a steady succession of fake businesses and false identities. Pretending to deal in antiques, he had set up a number of bank accounts with a variety of addresses, an act which ensured that the sums of money passing through his hands would never seem too outlandish, and that the lack of any public premises could easily be explained. Forging documents of identification was an activity that he found he thoroughly enjoyed, a pleasant distraction that almost felt like a comforting pastime. After creating these identities there was no question of anyone thinking that all of the donations he made in 1998 could have emerged from a single source. The money simply disappeared into the vast mass of exchanges that took place each and every day.

Once he was ready, the donations were given out within the space of a few months. Sums that it had taken him an entire lifetime to build up would vanish during the course of a few seconds. Within a few weeks he was considerably poorer than he had been for many years. Each morning during this period, he would commence the day by authorizing a sizable number of donations, each to emerge from a separate bank account, to be sent to a variety of destinations, all of which he would proceed to cross out from one or another of his voluminous collection of lists. Once he had finished making all of the donations he felt an immense calm, a genuine sense of having relieved himself of a great burden. Grinning, whimsical, he took great pride in the fact that he had performed his civic duty.

The process was to lend him the experience of the joy of giving. Waves of tenderness and benevolence flowed through his body in undulating cycles. Suddenly, all that he encountered seemed brightened, magnified, as if he was seeing it all for the very first time. Because he had cast his net out so widely, it seemed to him that there was nothing and no one to escape the effect of his donations. Every last detail of the world seemed somehow related to his actions, which had left him feeling genuinely reborn.

If it was true that some persons received gifts that were of no use to them, others were given items that would prove to be absolutely invaluable to them in the years to come. Varying greatly in scale and quality it could be said that the only factor that really united the many gifts that he gave was their unexpectedness, their arcane randomness, extenuated by the anonymity with which the acts had been executed, a state of affairs that might make the donations look sinister in character to certain eyes. Some were gifts that were given in a heartfelt manner, whilst others had been selected using methods that might be accurately described as "flippant." Maximilian could only hope that some of his actions were destined to be wholly appreciated. Finally, when all of the donations were completed, there were hundreds of thousands of persons who received, between them, many millions of pounds worth of currency and materials.

The I.C.A. received hundreds of boxes of felt tip pens. The Horniman Museum a collection of rare ethnographies concerning Papua New Guinea. A Chinese Takeaway in Barking received a year's supply of noodles. A bureau de change in Westminster received several crates of banknotes taken from board games. A hair salon in Stepney received a delivery of shampoo.

Mr. B. Cookson, of Redbridge, received a model railway set. Mrs. P. Chandrasekaran, of Stockwell, received a helicopter. Mrs. M. Bevis, of Dulwich, received a purple telescope. Mr. R. Oyeniyi, of Tottenham, received a box of chocolates. Miss P. Dixon, of Peckham, received tickets to the Royal Opera House. Mr. A. Kyriakou, of Charlton, received a barrel of rum. Mr. D. Siewkiewicz, of Rotherhithe, received a replica of a diplodocus.

Switzerland received a singing telegram. Thailand received a cheetah. El Salvador received a piano. Egypt received a space station. Iceland received a silver hand mirror. Singapore received a wooden tower. Chile received a decorative tea set. Madagascar received a bouquet of artificial flowers.

Encyclopaedias were sent to schools. Microphones were sent to singers. Hats were sent to gentlemen. Violins were sent to dwarfs. Gadgets were sent to gardeners. Islands were sent to artists. Balloons were sent to melancholics. Gardenias were sent to nurses. Secrets were sent to poets.

The Alliance for Workers Liberty was given £1.2 million. The Communist Party of Great Britain was given £2.3 million. The Revolutionary Communist Party of Britain was given £2.4 million. The Socialist Party was given £3.6 million. The Socialist Equality Party was given £4.2 million. The Socialist Party of Great Britain was given £5.1 million. The Socialist Workers Party was given £6.2 million. The International Socialist Group was given £6.3 million.

No one was disappointed by their gifts.

Millions and Millions and Millions

(1999)

roseate faces at the concert hall   scattered light thrown from a ker-
osene lamp   a bundle of clothes tied with brown string   clear
glass of water radiant in sunlight   a row of empty flagpoles   lost
umbrellas collected in the train station depot   shaving lather
smeared over sink basin   red fairy lights throwing hue across
low sloping ceiling   black cat curled into a ball on top of wicker
chair   teenagers laughing as they circle the ice rink   an octopus specialist consults his library   broken glass glinting from
the dark of the gutter   sodium-orange light falling onto tarmac
floor of car park   sunflower emerging from clay pot on windowsill   softly biting into the green flesh of a ripe pear   purity of
soprano voice ascending   boxes of jigsaw puzzles tied together
with thick rubber bands   smoke curling towards the timber raf-
ters of the attic   a hall filled with handicraft stalls   torchlight
thrown out from the doors of a tent erected in a back garden   silver glitter coating feminine eyelids   black ink scrawled across
address book pages   a green-and-white stripy shoelace tied into
a curly knot   photograph of a sand castle built on a beach in
Mexico   pastel drawing of a smiling mermaid   a man holding a watermelon walks along the platform   a conveyor belt
carrying plates of sushi   diagrams of matchstick men taped to
a wall   apron spattered with stains of wet clay   faces of children peeping out from a window on the second floor   brass cyl-
inders placed across a blue table   pink worm wriggling through
air   a green hilltop covered with ruins   tuning a zither to the
sound of a piano   cutting out a paper snowflake with a pair of
scissors   cucumber slices on a paper plate   catching a sentence of a stranger's conversation   green apples beside silver
candelabra   words underlined in pencil   consulting the face

of a sundial   a green velvet jacket hanging in a bamboo ward-
robe   Tibetan prayer flags dangling from a second floor window   boogie-woogie tunes available on the jukebox   an oak
leaf floats across the surface of a pond   aloe plant wet with the
steam of the shower   giant reflections in the dressing room mirrors   words scrawled in red chalk   viewing newsprint through
a magnifying glass   smoothing the edges of a moustache   floorboards creaking underneath the weight of yellow shoes   a collection
of wooden masks   froth plashing from the head of a brass fountain   shreds of ginger frying in olive oil   baskets heaped with
oyster shells   attempted cultivation of pumpkin seeds   waving
sparklers in the air in circular motions   licking at a ball of candy-
floss   polished marble floors of echoing corridors   an ancient
parrot resplendent in a living room   tarot cards laid out across the
floor   pinching a ball of soil between thumb and forefinger   a
yo-yo travels downwards   faces coated in flour   static from
the pocket radio   ink drawings of tiny faces   using a rolled
up newspaper as a telescope   long chains of numbers flashing across a screen   the giraffe tentatively moves a few inches
westward   cascading artificial waterfall at the entrance to an
office   silence within the descending elevator   tying a silk
cravat around a neck   odour of fresh-cut lawns   a budgerigar
sings inside a wire cage   aeroplane fuselage glinting silver in heat
haze   yellow droplets falling from a glass pipette   fingers feeling along the surface of a pebble   surge of electricity through an
amplifier   twirling a ball of spaghetti against a spoon   lingering taste of camomile on the tongue   arms raised up skywards
and joyful   following the rotations of wooden cogs   the
downwards stroke of a hairbrush   remembered pictures from old
calendars   applying lipstick in a round pocket mirror   hair
falling on to the floor of a barber shop   coloured plastic
straws bunched together in a glass   boiling a pan of milk and
brandy   listening as a key enters the lock of a front door   a

samba dancing class in an old church hall   dandelion seeds scattered over the lid of a drain   a child pointing at the moon with her index finger   reciting tales of female aviators   warming wet feet against a radiator   a thermometer fixed to the wall of the greenhouse   sketching the shoulder of a woman reclining   splitting open a ripe pomegranate   a secret drawer of thimbles   observing the movements of an iguana   soap lather falling over arms   amber light wavering in drowsy heat   blackcurrant cordial poured into a tall glass   delicately painting slender fingernails   a broach crafted in the shape of a whale   a tray filled with tiny plastic beads   whirring judders of a ceiling fan   sugar dissolving into a cup of warm liquid   cutting into stalks of celery   a bunch of feathers protruding from a cracked jug   a face hidden amidst white collonades   mahogany caskets holding stacks of maps   upward thrust of vibrating organ pipes   buttoning up a waistcoat adorned with branches of fruit trees   linen gloves draped over the back of an armchair   expanses of shade thrown from a canvas awning   tangled green vines cascading down a concrete wall   an ammonite used as a paperweight   the scent of sun lotion drifts across the veranda   a small heap of apricots on a circular table   puzzle diagrams given due consideration   gesturing in the air with a comb   pushing down onto typewriter keys   a stack of laundered hand towels   rapid revolutions of a whirligig   a battered attaché case holding a collection of antique spoons   glistening strands of seaweed entwined   trickling of rubber sap into a burnished copper bowl   arrangements of dominos across a coffee table   performing pelicans resting in the shade   coloured streamers emerging from the mouth of a bronze statuette

ALEX KOVACS was born in 1982. *The Currency of Paper* is his first novel. He has studied at the University of Edinburgh and at Goldsmiths, University of London.

SELECTED DALKEY ARCHIVE TITLES

MICHAL AJVAZ, *The Golden Age.*
The Other City.
PIERRE ALBERT-BIROT, *Grabinoulor.*
YUZ ALESHKOVSKY, *Kangaroo.*
FELIPE ALFAU, *Chromos.*
Locos.
IVAN ÂNGELO, *The Celebration.*
The Tower of Glass.
ANTÓNIO LOBO ANTUNES, *Knowledge of Hell.*
The Splendor of Portugal.
ALAIN ARIAS-MISSON, *Theatre of Incest.*
JOHN ASHBERY AND JAMES SCHUYLER,
A Nest of Ninnies.
ROBERT ASHLEY, *Perfect Lives.*
GABRIELA AVIGUR-ROTEM, *Heatwave
and Crazy Birds.*
DJUNA BARNES, *Ladies Almanack.*
Ryder.
JOHN BARTH, *LETTERS.*
Sabbatical.
DONALD BARTHELME, *The King.*
Paradise.
SVETISLAV BASARA, *Chinese Letter.*
MIQUEL BAUÇÀ, *The Siege in the Room.*
RENÉ BELLETTO, *Dying.*
MAREK BIEŃCZYK, *Transparency.*
ANDREI BITOV, *Pushkin House.*
ANDREJ BLATNIK, *You Do Understand.*
LOUIS PAUL BOON, *Chapel Road.*
My Little War.
Summer in Termuren.
ROGER BOYLAN, *Killoyle.*
IGNÁCIO DE LOYOLA BRANDÃO,
Anonymous Celebrity.
Zero.
BONNIE BREMSER, *Troia: Mexican Memoirs.*
CHRISTINE BROOKE-ROSE, *Amalgamemnon.*
BRIGID BROPHY, *In Transit.*
GERALD L. BRUNS, *Modern Poetry and
the Idea of Language.*
GABRIELLE BURTON, *Heartbreak Hotel.*
MICHEL BUTOR, *Degrees.*
Mobile.
G. CABRERA INFANTE, *Infante's Inferno.*
Three Trapped Tigers.
JULIETA CAMPOS,
The Fear of Losing Eurydice.
ANNE CARSON, *Eros the Bittersweet.*
ORLY CASTEL-BLOOM, *Dolly City.*
LOUIS-FERDINAND CÉLINE, *Castle to Castle.*
Conversations with Professor Y.
London Bridge.
Normance.
North.
Rigadoon.
MARIE CHAIX, *The Laurels of Lake Constance.*
HUGO CHARTERIS, *The Tide Is Right.*
ERIC CHEVILLARD, *Demolishing Nisard.*
MARC CHOLODENKO, *Mordechai Schamz.*
JOSHUA COHEN, *Witz.*
EMILY HOLMES COLEMAN, *The Shutter
of Snow.*
ROBERT COOVER, *A Night at the Movies.*
STANLEY CRAWFORD, *Log of the S.S. The
Mrs Unguentine.*
Some Instructions to My Wife.
RENÉ CREVEL, *Putting My Foot in It.*
RALPH CUSACK, *Cadenza.*
NICHOLAS DELBANCO, *The Count of Concord.*
Sherbrookes.
NIGEL DENNIS, *Cards of Identity.*

PETER DIMOCK, *A Short Rhetoric for
Leaving the Family.*
ARIEL DORFMAN, *Konfidenz.*
COLEMAN DOWELL,
Island People.
Too Much Flesh and Jabez.
ARKADII DRAGOMOSHCHENKO, *Dust.*
RIKKI DUCORNET, *The Complete
Butcher's Tales.*
The Fountains of Neptune.
The Jade Cabinet.
Phosphor in Dreamland.
WILLIAM EASTLAKE, *The Bamboo Bed.*
Castle Keep.
Lyric of the Circle Heart.
JEAN ECHENOZ, *Chopin's Move.*
STANLEY ELKIN, *A Bad Man.*
*Criers and Kibitzers, Kibitzers
and Criers.*
The Dick Gibson Show.
The Franchiser.
The Living End.
Mrs. Ted Bliss.
FRANÇOIS EMMANUEL, *Invitation to a
Voyage.*
SALVADOR ESPRIU, *Ariadne in the
Grotesque Labyrinth.*
LESLIE A. FIEDLER, *Love and Death in
the American Novel.*
JUAN FILLOY, *Op Oloop.*
ANDY FITCH, *Pop Poetics.*
GUSTAVE FLAUBERT, *Bouvard and Pécuchet.*
KASS FLEISHER, *Talking out of School.*
FORD MADOX FORD,
The March of Literature.
JON FOSSE, *Aliss at the Fire.*
Melancholy.
MAX FRISCH, *I'm Not Stiller.*
Man in the Holocene.
CARLOS FUENTES, *Christopher Unborn.*
Distant Relations.
Terra Nostra.
Where the Air Is Clear.
TAKEHIKO FUKUNAGA, *Flowers of Grass.*
WILLIAM GADDIS, *J R.*
The Recognitions.
JANICE GALLOWAY, *Foreign Parts.*
The Trick Is to Keep Breathing.
WILLIAM H. GASS, *Cartesian Sonata
and Other Novellas.*
Finding a Form.
A Temple of Texts.
The Tunnel.
Willie Masters' Lonesome Wife.
GÉRARD GAVARRY, *Hoppla! 1 2 3.*
ETIENNE GILSON,
The Arts of the Beautiful.
Forms and Substances in the Arts.
C. S. GISCOMBE, *Giscome Road.*
Here.
DOUGLAS GLOVER, *Bad News of the Heart.*
WITOLD GOMBROWICZ,
A Kind of Testament.
PAULO EMÍLIO SALES GOMES, *P's Three
Women.*
GEORGI GOSPODINOV, *Natural Novel.*
JUAN GOYTISOLO, *Count Julian.*
Juan the Landless.
Makbara.
Marks of Identity.

FOR A FULL LIST OF PUBLICATIONS, VISIT:
www.dalkeyarchive.com

SELECTED DALKEY ARCHIVE TITLES

HENRY GREEN, *Back.*
Blindness.
Concluding.
Doting.
Nothing.
JACK GREEN, *Fire the Bastards!*
JIŘÍ GRUŠA, *The Questionnaire.*
MELA HARTWIG, *Am I a Redundant Human Being?*
JOHN HAWKES, *The Passion Artist.*
Whistlejacket.
ELIZABETH HEIGHWAY, ED., *Contemporary Georgian Fiction.*
ALEKSANDAR HEMON, ED., *Best European Fiction.*
AIDAN HIGGINS, *Balcony of Europe.*
Blind Man's Bluff
Bornholm Night-Ferry.
Flotsam and Jetsam.
Langrishe, Go Down.
Scenes from a Receding Past.
KEIZO HINO, *Isle of Dreams.*
KAZUSHI HOSAKA, *Plainsong.*
ALDOUS HUXLEY, *Antic Hay.*
Crome Yellow.
Point Counter Point.
Those Barren Leaves.
Time Must Have a Stop.
NAOYUKI II, *The Shadow of a Blue Cat.*
GERT JONKE, *The Distant Sound.*
Geometric Regional Novel.
Homage to Czerny.
The System of Vienna.
JACQUES JOUET, *Mountain R.*
Savage.
Upstaged.
MIEKO KANAI, *The Word Book.*
YORAM KANIUK, *Life on Sandpaper.*
HUGH KENNER, *Flaubert.*
Joyce and Beckett: The Stoic Comedians.
Joyce's Voices.
DANILO KIŠ, *The Attic.*
Garden, Ashes.
The Lute and the Scars
Psalm 44.
A Tomb for Boris Davidovich.
ANITA KONKKA, *A Fool's Paradise.*
GEORGE KONRÁD, *The City Builder.*
TADEUSZ KONWICKI, *A Minor Apocalypse.*
The Polish Complex.
MENIS KOUMANDAREAS, *Koula.*
ELAINE KRAF, *The Princess of 72nd Street.*
JIM KRUSOE, *Iceland.*
AYŞE KULIN, *Farewell: A Mansion in Occupied Istanbul.*
EMILIO LASCANO TEGUI, *On Elegance While Sleeping.*
ERIC LAURRENT, *Do Not Touch.*
VIOLETTE LEDUC, *La Bâtarde.*
EDOUARD LEVÉ, *Autoportrait.*
Suicide.
MARIO LEVI, *Istanbul Was a Fairy Tale.*
DEBORAH LEVY, *Billy and Girl.*
JOSÉ LEZAMA LIMA, *Paradiso.*
ROSA LIKSOM, *Dark Paradise.*
OSMAN LINS, *Avalovara.*
The Queen of the Prisons of Greece.
ALF MAC LOCHLAINN, *The Corpus in the Library.*
Out of Focus.
RON LOEWINSOHN, *Magnetic Field(s).*
MINA LOY, *Stories and Essays of Mina Loy.*

D. KEITH MANO, *Take Five.*
MICHELINE AHARONIAN MARCOM, *The Mirror in the Well.*
BEN MARCUS, *The Age of Wire and String.*
WALLACE MARKFIELD, *Teitlebaum's Window.*
To an Early Grave.
DAVID MARKSON, *Reader's Block.*
Wittgenstein's Mistress.
CAROLE MASO, *AVA.*
LADISLAV MATEJKA AND KRYSTYNA POMORSKA, EDS., *Readings in Russian Poetics: Formalist and Structuralist Views.*
HARRY MATHEWS, *Cigarettes.*
The Conversions.
The Human Country: New and Collected Stories.
The Journalist.
My Life in CIA.
Singular Pleasures.
The Sinking of the Odradek Stadium.
Tlooth.
JOSEPH MCELROY, *Night Soul and Other Stories.*
ABDELWAHAB MEDDEB, *Talismano.*
GERHARD MEIER, *Isle of the Dead.*
HERMAN MELVILLE, *The Confidence-Man.*
AMANDA MICHALOPOULOU, *I'd Like.*
STEVEN MILLHAUSER, *The Barnum Museum.*
In the Penny Arcade.
RALPH J. MILLS, JR., *Essays on Poetry.*
MOMUS, *The Book of Jokes.*
CHRISTINE MONTALBETTI, *The Origin of Man.*
Western.
OLIVE MOORE, *Spleen.*
NICHOLAS MOSLEY, *Accident.*
Assassins.
Catastrophe Practice.
Experience and Religion.
A Garden of Trees.
Hopeful Monsters.
Imago Bird.
Impossible Object.
Inventing God.
Judith.
Look at the Dark.
Natalie Natalia.
Serpent.
Time at War.
WARREN MOTTE, *Fables of the Novel: French Fiction since 1990.*
Fiction Now: The French Novel in the 21st Century.
Oulipo: A Primer of Potential Literature.
GERALD MURNANE, *Barley Patch.*
Inland.
YVES NAVARRE, *Our Share of Time.*
Sweet Tooth.
DOROTHY NELSON, *In Night's City.*
Tar and Feathers.
ESHKOL NEVO, *Homesick.*
WILFRIDO D. NOLLEDO, *But for the Lovers.*
FLANN O'BRIEN, *At Swim-Two-Birds.*
The Best of Myles.
The Dalkey Archive.
The Hard Life.
The Poor Mouth.

FOR A FULL LIST OF PUBLICATIONS, VISIT:
www.dalkeyarchive.com